It is the tradition of the dustjacket "blurb" to exaggerate the excellences of a book in hopes of enticing readers between its covers. But I do not follow that custom when I say that *Stranger Things Happen* is one of the very best books I have ever read. These stories will amaze, provoke, and intrigue. Best of all, they will delight. Kelly Link is terrific!
This is not blurbese. It is the living truth.
—Fred Chappell, author of *Family Gathering*

Finally, Kelly Link's wonderful stories have been collected. My only complaint is the brevity of her oeuvre to date; as an avid reader of her work, I want her to continue to create more gems for me to read. I predict that "The Specialist's Hat," winner of the World Fantasy Award, will become part of the canon of classic supernatural tales.
—Ellen Datlow, fiction editor for SCIFI.COM

I've been impatiently awaiting a collection of Kelly Link's stories. Now that it's here, it will sit in my library on that very short shelf of books I read again and again. For those who think Fantasy tired, *Stranger Things Happen* is a wake-up call.
—Jeffrey Ford, author of *The Beyond*

Link's writing is gorgeous, mischievous, sexy and unsettling. Unexpected images burst on your brain like soap bubbles on a dog's tongue. I've been trying to imitate her since I first read one of her stories. It's impossible. Instead I find myself curling up with a satisfied sigh and enjoying once more.
—Nalo Hopkinson, author of *Midnight Robber*

Kelly Link is a brilliant writer. Her stories seem to come right out of your own dreams, the nice ones and the nightmares both. These stories will burrow right into your subconscious and stay with you forever.
—Tim Powers, author of *Declare*

Of all the books you'll read this year, this is the one you'll remember. Kelly Link's stories are like gorgeous tattoos; they get under your skin and stay forever and change your life. Buy this book, read it, read it again, congratulate yourself, and then start buying *Stranger Things Happen* for your friends.
—Sarah Smith, author of *A Citizen of the Country*

Kelly Link makes spells, not stories. She is the carrier of an eerie, tender sorcery; each enchantment takes you like a curse, leaving you dizzy, wounded, and elated at once. Her vision is always compassionate, and frequently very funny—but don't let that fool you. This book, like all real magic, is terribly dangerous. You open it at your peril.
—Sean Stewart, author of *Galveston*

If Kelly Link is not the "future of horror," a ridiculous phrase, she ought to be. To have a future at all, horror in general, by which I might as well mean fiction in general, requires precisely her freshness, courage, intelligence, and resistance to received forms and values. Kelly Link seems always to speak from a deep, deeply personal, and unexpected standpoint. Story by story, she is creating new worlds, new frameworks for perception, right in front of our eyes. I think she is the most impressive writer of her generation.
—Peter Straub, author of *Magic Terror*

STRANGER
THINGS
HAPPEN

STRANGER
THINGS
HAPPEN

KELLY LINK

Small Beer Press
Brooklyn, NY

Small Beer Press
360 Atlantic Ave., PMB #132
Brooklyn, NY 11217
www.lcrw.net
info@lcrw.net

www.kellylink.net

Cataloging-in-Publication Data
(*Provided by Quality Books, Inc.*)

Link, Kelly.
      Stranger things happen / Kelly Link. -- 1st ed.
      p.cm.
      LCCN 2001087879
      ISBN 1-931520-00-3

      1. Fantastic fiction. I. Title.

PS3562.I5177S77 2001   813'.6
                          QBI01-700342

First edition 1 2 3 4 5 6 7 8 9 0

A Jelly Ink book. Jelly Ink is an imprint of Small Beer Press.
Printed with soy inks on 60# Glatfelder recycled paper by Thomson-Shore of Dexter, MI.
Text set in Centaur 12/24.
Cover painting by Shelley Jackson.

CONTENTS

For

Susie Link

and

Jenna A. Felice

CARNATION, LILY,
LILY, ROSE

Dear Mary (if that is your name),
I bet you'll be pretty surprised to hear from me. It really is
me, by the way, although I have to confess at the moment
that not only can I not seem to keep your name straight in my head,
Laura? Susie? Odile? but I seem to have forgotten my own name. I
plan to keep trying different combinations: Joe loves Lola, Willy loves
Suki, Henry loves you, sweetie, Georgia?, honeypie, darling. Do any
of these seem right to you?

All last week I felt like something was going to happen, a sort of bees
and ants feeling. Something was going to happen. I taught my classes
and came home and went to bed, all week waiting for the thing that
was going to happen, and then on Friday I died.

One of the things I seem to have misplaced is how, or maybe I mean
why. It's like the names. I know that we lived together in a house on

a hill in a small comfortable city for nine years, that we didn't have kids—except once, almost—and that you're a terrible cook, oh my darling, Coraline? Coralee? and so was I, and we ate out whenever we could afford to. I taught at a good university, Princeton? Berkeley? Notre Dame? I was a good teacher, and my students liked me. But I can't remember the name of the street we lived on, or the author of the last book I read, or your last name which was also my name, or how I died. It's funny, Sarah? but the only two names I know for sure are real are Looly Bellows, the girl who beat me up in fourth grade, and your cat's name. I'm not going to put your cat's name down on paper just yet.

We were going to name the baby Beatrice. I just remembered that. We were going to name her after your aunt, the one that doesn't like me. Didn't like me. Did she come to the funeral?

I've been here for three days, and I'm trying to pretend that it's just a vacation, like when we went to that island in that country. Santorini? Great Britain? The one with all the cliffs. The one with the hotel with the bunkbeds, and little squares of pink toilet paper, like handkerchiefs. It had seashells in the window too, didn't it, that were transparent like bottle glass? They smelled like bleach? It was a very nice island. No trees. You said that when you died, you hoped heaven would be an island like that. And now I'm dead, and here I am.

This is an island too, I think. There is a beach, and down on the beach is a mailbox where I am going to post this letter. Other than the beach, the mailbox, there is the building in which I sit and write this letter. It seems to be a perfectly pleasant resort hotel with no other guests, no receptionist, no host, no events coordinator, no bellboy. Just me. There is a television set, very old-fashioned, in the hotel lobby. I fiddled the antenna for a long time, but never got a picture. Just static. I tried to make images, people out of the static. It looked like they were waving at me.

My room is on the second floor. It has a sea view. All the rooms here have views of the sea. There is a desk in my room, and a good supply of plain, waxy white paper and envelopes in one of the drawers. Laurel? Maria? Gertrude?

I haven't gone out of sight of the hotel yet, Lucille? because I am afraid that it might not be there when I get back.

Yours truly,
You know who.

The dead man lies on his back on the hotel bed, his hands busy and curious, stroking his body up and down as if it didn't really belong to him at all. One hand cups his testicles, the other tugs hard at his erect penis. His heels push against the mattress and his eyes are open, and his mouth. He is trying to say someone's name.

Outside, the sky seems much too close, made out of some grey stuff that only grudgingly allows light through. The dead man has noticed that it never gets any lighter or darker, but sometimes the air begins to feel heavier, and then stuff falls out of the sky, fist-sized lumps of whitish-grey doughy matter. It falls until the beach is covered, and immediately begins to dissolve. The dead man was outside, the first time the sky fell. Now he waits inside until the beach is clear again. Sometimes he watches television, although the reception is poor.

The sea goes up and back the beach, sucking and curling around the mailbox at high tide. There is something about it that the dead man doesn't like much. It doesn't smell like salt the way a sea should. Cara? Jasmine? It smells like wet upholstery, burnt fur.

Dear May? April? Ianthe?

My room has a bed with thin, limp sheets and an amateurish painting of a woman sitting under a tree. She has nice breasts, but a peculiar expression on her face, for a woman in a painting in a hotel room, even in a hotel like this. She looks disgruntled.

I have a bathroom with hot and cold running water, towels, and a mirror. I looked in the mirror for a long time, but I didn't look familiar. It's the first time I've ever had a good look at a dead person. I have brown hair, receding at the temples, brown eyes, and good teeth, white, even, and not too large. I have a small mark on my shoulder, Celeste? where you bit me when we were making love that last time. Did you somehow realize it would be the last time we made love? Your expression was sad; also, I seem to recall, angry. I remember your expression now, Eliza? You glared up at me without blinking and when you came, you said my name, and although I can't remember my name, I remember you said it as if you hated me. We hadn't made love for a long time.

I estimate my height to be about five feet, eleven inches, and although I am not unhandsome, I have an anxious, somewhat fixed expression. This may be due to circumstances.

I was wondering if my name was by any chance Roger or Timothy or Charles. When we went on vacation, I remember there was a similar confusion about names, although not ours. We were trying to think of one for her, I mean, for Beatrice. Petrucchia, Solange? We wrote them all with long pieces of stick on the beach, to see how they looked. We started with the plain names, like Jane and Susan and Laura. We tried practical names like Polly and Meredith and Hope, and then we became extravagant. We dragged our sticks through the sand and produced entire families of scowling little girls named Gudrun, Jezebel, Jerusalem, Zedeenya, Zerilla. How about Looly, I said. I knew a girl named Looly Bellows once. Your hair was all snarled around your face, stiff with salt. You had about a zillion freckles. You were laughing so hard you had to prop yourself up with your stick. You said that sounded like a made-up name.

Love,
You know who.

The dead man is trying to act as if he is really here, in this place. He is trying to act in a normal and appropriate fashion. As much as is possible. He is trying to be a good tourist.

He hasn't been able to fall asleep in the bed, although he has turned the painting to the wall. He is not sure that the bed is a bed. When his eyes are closed, it doesn't seem to be a bed. He sleeps on the floor, which seems more floorlike than the bed seems bedlike. He lies on the floor with nothing over him and pretends that he isn't dead. He pretends that he is in bed with his wife and dreaming. He makes up a nice dream about a party where he has forgotten everyone's name. He touches himself. Then he gets up and sees that the white stuff that has fallen out of the sky is dissolving on the beach, little clumps of it heaped around the mailbox like foam.

Dear Elspeth? Deborah? Frederica?
Things are getting worse. I know that if I could just get your name straight, things would get better.

I told you that I'm on an island, but I'm not sure that I am. I'm having doubts about my bed and the hotel. I'm not happy about the sea or the sky, either. The things that have names that I'm sure of, I'm not sure they're those things, if you understand what I'm saying, Mallory? I'm not sure I'm still breathing, either. When I think about it, I do. I

13

only think about it because it's too quiet when I'm not. Did you know, Alison? that up in those mountains, the Berkshires? the altitude gets too high, and then real people, live people forget to breathe also? There's a name for when they forget. I forget what the name is.

But if the bed isn't a bed, and the beach isn't a beach, then what are they? When I look at the horizon, there almost seem to be corners. When I lay down, the corners on the bed receded like the horizon.

Then there is the problem about the mail. Yesterday I simply slipped the letter into a plain envelope, and slipped the envelope, unaddressed, into the mailbox. This morning the letter was gone and when I stuck my hand inside, and then my arm, the sides of the box were damp and sticky. I inspected the back side and discovered an open panel. When the tide rises, the mail goes out to sea. So I really have no idea if you, Pamela? or, for that matter, if anyone is reading this letter.

I tried dragging the mailbox further up the beach. The waves hissed and spit at me, a wave ran across my foot, cold and furry and black, and I gave up. So I will simply have to trust to the local mail system.

Hoping you get this soon,
You know who.

The dead man goes for a walk along the beach. The sea keeps its distance, but the hotel stays close behind him. He notices that the tide retreats when he walks towards it, which is good. He doesn't want to get his shoes wet. If he walked out to sea, would it part for him like that guy in the bible? Onan?

He is wearing his second-best suit, the one he wore for interviews and weddings. He figures it's either the suit that he died in, or else the one that his wife buried him in. He has been wearing it ever since he woke up and found himself on the island, disheveled and sweating, his clothing wrinkled as if he had been wearing it for a long time. He takes his suit and his shoes off only when he is in his hotel room. He puts them back on to go outside. He goes for a walk along the beach. His fly is undone.

The little waves slap at the dead man. He can see teeth under that water, in the glassy black walls of the larger waves, the waves farther out to sea. He walks a fair distance, stopping frequently to rest. He tires easily. He keeps to the dunes. His shoulders are hunched, his head down. When the sky begins to change, he turns around. The hotel is right behind him. He doesn't seem at all surprised to see it there. All the time he has been walking, he has had the feeling that just over the next dune someone is waiting for him. He hopes that maybe it is his wife, but on the other hand if it were his wife, she'd be dead too, and if she were dead, he could remember her name.

Dear Matilda? Ivy? Alicia?

I picture my letters sailing out to you, over those waves with the teeth, little white boats. Dear reader, Beryl? Fern? you would like to know how I am so sure these letters are getting to you? I remember that it always used to annoy you, the way I took things for granted. But I'm sure you're reading this in the same way that even though I'm still walking around and breathing (when I remember to) I'm sure I'm dead. I think that these letters are getting to you, mangled, sodden but still legible. If they arrived the regular way, you probably wouldn't believe they were from me, anyway.

I remembered a name today, Elvis Presley. He was the singer, right? Blue shoes, kissy fat lips, slickery voice? Dead, right? Like me. Marilyn Monroe too, white dress blowing up like a sail, Gandhi, Abraham Lincoln, Looly Bellows (remember?) who lived next door to me when we were both eleven. She had migraine headaches all through the school year, which made her mean. Nobody liked her, before, when we didn't know she was sick. We didn't like her after. She broke my nose because I pulled her wig off one day on a dare. They took a tumor out of her head that was the size of a chicken egg but she died anyway.

When I pulled her wig off, she didn't cry. She had brittle bits of hair tufting out of her scalp and her face was swollen with fluid like she'd been stung by bees. She looked so old. She told me that when she was dead she'd come back and haunt me, and after she died, I pretended that I could see not just her—but whole clusters of fat, pale, hairless ghosts lingering behind trees, swollen and humming like hives. It was a scary fun game I played with my friends. We called the ghosts loolies, and we made up rules that kept us safe from them. A certain kind of walk, a diet of white food—marshmallows, white bread rolled into pellets, and plain white rice. When we got tired of the loolies, we killed them off by decorating her grave with the remains of the powdered donuts and Wonderbread our suspicious mothers at last refused to buy for us.

Are you decorating my grave, Felicity? Gay? Have you forgotten me yet? Have you gotten another cat yet, another lover? or are you still in mourning for me? God, I want you so much, Carnation, Lily? Lily? Rose? It's the reverse of necrophilia, I suppose—the dead man who wants one last fuck with his wife. But you're not here, and if you were here, would you go to bed with me?

I write you letters with my right hand, and I do the other thing with my left hand that I used to do with my left hand, ever since I was fourteen, when I didn't have anything better to do. I seem to recall that when I was fourteen there wasn't anything better to do. I think about you, I think about touching you, think that you're touching me, and I see you naked, and you're glaring at me, and I'm about to shout out your name, and then I come and the name on my lips is the name of some dead person, or some totally made-up name.

Does it bother you, Linda? Donna? Penthesilia? Do you want to know the worst thing? Just a minute ago I was grinding into the pillow, bucking and pushing and pretending it was you, Stacy? under me, oh fuck it felt good, just like when I was alive and when I came I said, "Beatrice." And I remembered coming to get you in the hospital after the miscarriage.

There were a lot of things I wanted to say. I mean, neither of us was really sure that we wanted a baby and part of me, sure, was relieved that I wasn't going to have to learn how to be a father just yet, but there were still things that I wish I'd said to you. There were a lot of things I wish I'd said to you.

You know who.

The dead man sets out across the interior of the island. At some point after his first expedition, the hotel moved quietly back to its original location, the dead man in his room, looking into the mirror, expression intent, hips tilted against the cool tile. This flesh is dead. It should not rise. It rises. Now the hotel is back beside the mailbox, which is empty when he walks down to check it.

The middle of the island is rocky, barren. There are no trees here, the dead man realizes, feeling relieved. He walks for a short distance—less than two miles, he calculates, before he stands on the opposite shore. In front of him is a flat expanse of water, sky folded down over the horizon. When the dead man turns around, he can see his hotel, looking forlorn and abandoned. But when he squints, the shadows on the back veranda waver, becoming a crowd of people, all looking back at him. He has his hands inside his pants, he is touching himself. He takes his hands out of his pants. He turns his back on the shadowy porch.

He walks along the shore. He ducks down behind a sand dune, and then down a long hill. He is going to circle back. He is going to sneak up on the hotel if he can, although it is hard to sneak up on something that always seems to be trying to sneak up on you. He walks for a while, and what he finds is a ring of glassy stones, far up on the beach, driftwood piled inside the ring, charred and black. The ground is trampled all around the fire, as if people have stood there, waiting and pacing. There is something left in tatters and skin on a spit in the center of the campfire, about the size of a cat. The dead man doesn't look too closely at it.

He walks around the fire. He sees tracks indicating where the people who stood here, watching a cat roast, went away again. It would be hard to miss the direction they are taking. The people leave together, rushing untidily up the dune, barefoot and heavy, the imprints of the balls of the foot deep, heels hardly touching the sand at all. They are headed back towards the hotel. He follows the footprints, sees the single track of his own footprints, coming down to the fire. Above, in a line parallel to his expedition and to the sea, the crowd has walked this way, although he did not see them. They are walking more carefully now, he pictures them walking more quietly.

His footprints end. There is the mailbox, and this is where he left the hotel. The hotel itself has left no mark. The other footprints continue towards the hotel, where it stands now, small in the distance. When the dead man gets back to the hotel, the lobby floor is dusted with sand, and the television is on. The reception is slightly improved. But no one is there, although he searches every room. When he stands on the back veranda, staring out over the interior of the island, he imagines he sees a group of people, down beside the far shore, waving at him. The sky begins to fall.

Dear Araminta? Kiki?
Lolita? Still doesn't have the right ring to it, does it? Sukie? Ludmilla? Winifred?

I had that same not-dream about the faculty party again. She was there, only this time you were the one who recognized her, and I was trying to guess her name, who she was. Was she the tall blonde with the nice ass, or the short blonde with the short hair who kept her mouth a little open, like she was smiling all the time? That one looked like she knew something I wanted to know, but so did you. Isn't that funny? I never told you who she was, and now I can't remember. You probably knew the whole time anyway, even if you didn't think you did. I'm pretty sure you asked me about that little blond girl, when you were asking.

I keep thinking about the way you looked, that first night we slept together. I'd kissed you properly on the doorstep of your mother's house, and then, before you went inside, you turned around and looked at me. No one had ever looked at me like that. You didn't need to say anything at all. I waited until your mother turned off all the lights downstairs, and then I climbed over the fence, and up the tree in your backyard, and into your window. You were leaning out of the window, watching me climb, and you took off your shirt so that I could see your breasts, I almost fell out of the tree, and then you took off your jeans and your underwear had a day of the week embroidered on it, Holiday? and then you took off your underwear too. You'd bleached the hair on your head yellow, and then streaked it with red, but the hair on your pubis was black and soft when I touched it.

We lay down on your bed, and when I was inside you, you gave me that look again. It wasn't a frown, but it was almost a frown, as if you had expected something different, or else you were trying to get something just right. And then you smiled and sighed and twisted under me. You lifted up smoothly and strongly as if you were going to levitate right off the bed, and I lifted with you as if you were carrying me and I almost got you pregnant for the first time. We never were good about birth control, were we, Eliane? Rosemary? And then I heard your mother out in the backyard, right under the elm I'd just climbed, yelling "Tree? Tree?"

I thought she must have seen me climb it. I looked out the window and saw her directly beneath me, and she had her hands on her hips, and the first thing I noticed were her breasts, moonlit and plump, pushed up under her dressing gown, fuller than yours and almost as nice. That was pretty strange, realizing that I was the kind of guy who could have fallen in love with someone after not so much time, really, truly, deeply in love, the forever kind, I already knew, and still notice this middle-aged woman's tits. Your mother's tits. That was the second thing I learned. The third thing was that she wasn't looking back at me. "Tree?" she yelled one last time, sounding pretty pissed.

So, okay, I thought she was crazy. The last thing, the thing I didn't learn, was about names. It's taken me a while to figure that out. I'm still not sure what I didn't learn, Aina? Jewel? Kathleen? but at least I'm willing. I mean, I'm here still, aren't I?

Wish you were here,
You know who.

At some point, later, the dead man goes down to the mailbox. The water is particularly unwaterlike today. It has a velvety nap to it, like hair. It raises up in almost discernable shapes. It is still afraid of him, but it hates him, hates him, hates him. It never liked him, never. "Fraidy cat, fraidy cat," the dead man taunts the water.

When he goes back to the hotel, the loolies are there. They are watching television in the lobby. They are a lot bigger than he remembers.

Dear Cindy, Cynthia, Cenfenilla,
There are some people here with me now. I'm not sure if I'm in their

place—if this place is theirs, or if I brought them here, like luggage. Maybe it's some of one, some of the other. They're people, or maybe I should say a person I used to know when I was little. I think they've been watching me for a while, but they're shy. They don't talk much.

Hard to introduce yourself, when you have forgotten your name. When I saw them, I was astounded. I sat down on the floor of the lobby. My legs were like water. A wave of emotion came over me, so strong I didn't recognize it. It might have been grief. It might have been relief. I think it was recognition. They came and stood around me, looking down. "I know you," I said. "You're loolies."

They nodded. Some of them smiled. They are so pale, so fat! When they smile, their eyes disappear in folds of flesh. But they have tiny soft bare feet, like children's feet. "You're the dead man," one said. It had tiny soft voice. Then we talked. Half of what they said made no sense at all. They don't know how I got here. They don't remember Looly Bellows. They don't remember dying. They were afraid of me at first, but also curious.

They wanted to know my name. Since I didn't have one, they tried to find a name that fit me. Walter was put forward, then rejected. I was un-Walter-like. Samuel, also Milo, also Rupert. Quite a few of them liked Alphonse, but I felt no particular leaning towards Alphonse. "Tree," one of the loolies said.

Tree never liked me very much. I remember your mother standing under the green leaves that leaned down on bowed branches, dragging the ground like skirts. Oh, it was such a tree! the most beautiful tree I'd ever seen. Halfway up the tree, glaring up at me, was a fat black cat with long white whiskers, and an elegant sheeny bib. You pulled me away. You'd put a T-shirt on. You stood in the window. "I'll get him," you said to the woman beneath the tree. "You go back to bed, mom. Come here, Tree."

Tree walked the branch to the window, the same broad branch that had lifted me up to you. You, Ariadne? Thomasina? plucked him off the sill and then closed the window. When you put him down on the bed, he curled up at the foot, purring. But when I woke up, later, dreaming that I was drowning, he was crouched on my face, his belly heavy as silk against my mouth.

I always thought Tree was a silly name for a cat. When he got old and slept out in the garden, he still didn't look like a tree. He looked like a cat. He ran out in front of my car, I saw him, you saw me see him, I realized that it would be the last straw—a miscarriage, your husband sleeps with a graduate student, then he runs over your cat—I was trying to swerve, to not hit him. Something tells me I hit him.
I didn't mean to, sweetheart, love, Pearl? Patsy? Portia?

You know who.

The dead man watches television with the loolies. Soap operas. The loolies know how to get the antenna crooked so that the reception is decent, although the sound does not come in. One of them stands beside the TV to hold it just so. The soap opera is strangely dated, the clothes old-fashioned, the sort the dead man imagines his grandparents wore. The women wear cloche hats, their eyes are heavily made up.

There is a wedding. There is a funeral, also, although it is not clear to the dead man watching, who the dead man is. Then the characters are walking along a beach. The woman wears a black-and-white striped bathing costume that covers her modestly, from neck to mid-thigh. The man's fly is undone. They do not hold hands. There is a buzz of comment from the loolies. "Too dark," one says, about the woman. *"Still alive,"* another says.

"Too thin," one says, indicating the man. *"Should eat more. Might blow away in a wind."*

"Out to sea."

"Out to Tree." The loolies look at the dead man. The dead man goes to his room. He locks the door. His penis sticks up, hard as a tree. It is pulling him across the room, towards the bed. The man is dead, but his body doesn't know it yet. His body still thinks that it is alive. He begins to say out loud the names he knows, beautiful names, silly names, improbable names. The loolies creep down the hall. They stand outside his door and listen to the list of names.

Dear Bobbie? Billie?
I wish you would write back.

You know who.

When the sky changes, the loolies go outside. The dead man watches them pick the stuff off the beach. They eat it methodically, chewing it down to a paste. They swallow, and pick up more. The dead man goes outside. He picks up some of the stuff. Angel food cake? Manna? He smells it. It smells like flowers: like carnations, lilies, like lilies, like roses. He puts some in his mouth. It tastes like nothing at all. The dead man kicks at the mailbox.

Dear Daphne? Proserpine? Rapunzel?
Isn't there a fairy tale where a little man tries to do this? Guess a woman's name? I have been making stories up about my death. One death I've imagined is when I am walking down to the subway, and then there is a strong wind, and the mobile sculpture by the subway, the one that spins in the wind, lifts up and falls on me. Another death is you and I, we are flying to some other country, Canada? The flight is crowded, and you sit one row ahead of me. There is a crack! and the plane splits

in half, like a cracked straw. Your half rises up and my half falls down. You turn and look back at me, I throw out my arms. Wineglasses and newspapers and ribbons of clothes fall up in the air. The sky catches fire. I think maybe I stepped in front of a train. I was riding a bike, and someone opened a car door. I was on a boat and it sank.

This is what I know. I was going somewhere. This is the story that seems the best to me. We made love, you and I, and afterwards you got out of bed and stood there looking at me. I thought that you had forgiven me, that now we were going to go on with our lives the way they had been before. Bernice? you said. Gloria? Patricia? Jane? Rosemary? Laura? Laura? Harriet? Jocelyn? Nora? Rowena? Anthea?

I got out of bed. I put on clothes and left the room. You followed me. Marly? Genevieve? Karla? Kitty? Soibhan? Marnie? Lynley? Theresa? You said the names staccato, one after the other, like stabs. I didn't look at you, I grabbed up my car keys, and left the house. You stood in the door, watched me get in the car. Your lips were still moving, but I couldn't hear.

Tree was in front of the car and when I saw him, I swerved. I was already going too fast, halfway out of the driveway. I pinned him up against the mailbox, and then the car hit the lilac tree. White petals were raining down. You screamed. I can't remember what happened next.

I don't know if this is how I died. Maybe I died more than once, but it finally took. Here I am. I don't think this is an island. I think that I am a dead man, stuffed inside a box. When I'm quiet, I can almost hear the other dead men scratching at the walls of their boxes.

Or maybe I'm a ghost. Maybe the waves, which look like fur, are fur, and maybe the water which hisses and spits at me is really a cat, and the cat is a ghost, too.

Maybe I'm here to learn something, to do penance. The loolies have forgiven me. Maybe you will, too. When the sea comes to my hand, when it purrs at me, I'll know that you've forgiven me for what I did. For leaving you after I did it.

Or maybe I'm a tourist, and I'm stuck on this island with the loolies until it's time to go home, or until you come here to get me, Poppy? Irene? Delores? which is why I hope you get this letter.

You know who.

WATER OFF A BLACK
DOG'S BACK

T*ell me which you could sooner do without, love or water."*
"*What do you mean?"*
"*I mean, could you live without love, or could you live without water?"*
"*Why can't I have both?"*

Rachel Rook took Carroll home to meet her parents two months
after she first slept with him. For a generous girl, a girl who took off
her clothes with abandon, she was remarkably close-mouthed about
some things. In two months Carroll had learned that her parents lived
on a farm several miles outside of town; that they sold strawberries
in summer, and Christmas trees in the winter. He knew that they
never left the farm; instead, the world came to them in the shape of
weekend picnickers and driveby tourists.

"Do you think your parents will like me?" he said. He had spent
the afternoon preparing for this visit as carefully as if he were preparing for an exam. He had gotten his hair cut, trimmed his nails,

washed his neck and behind his ears. The outfit he had chosen, khaki pants and a blue button-down shirt—no tie—lay neatly folded on the bed. He stood before Rachel in his plain white underwear and white socks, gazing at her as if she were a mirror.

"No," she said. It was the first time she had been to his apartment, and she stood square in the center of his bedroom, her arms folded against her body as if she was afraid to sit down, to touch something.

"Why?"

"My father will like you," she said. "But he likes everyone. My mother's more particular—she thinks that you lack a serious nature."

Carroll put on his pants, admiring the crease. "So you've talked to her about me."

"Yes."

"But you haven't talked about her to me."

"No."

"Are you ashamed of her?"

Rachel snorted. Then she sighed in a way that seemed to suggest she was regretting her decision to take him home. "You're ashamed of me," he guessed, and Rachel kissed him and smiled and didn't say anything.

Rachel still lived on her parents' farm, which made it all the more remarkable that she had kept Carroll and her parents apart for so long. It suggested a talent for daily organization that filled Carroll's heart with admiration and lust. She was nineteen, two years younger than Carroll; she was a student at Jellicoh College and every weekday she rose at seven and biked four miles into town, and then back again on her bike, four miles uphill to the farm.

Carroll met Rachel in the Jellicoh College library, where he had a part-time job. He sat at the checkout desk, stamping books and reading *Tristram Shandy* for a graduate class; he was almost asleep when someone said, "Excuse me."

He looked up. The girl who stood before the tall desk was red-headed. Sunlight streaming in through a high window opposite her lit up the fine hairs on her arm, the embroidered flowers on the collar of her white shirt. The sunlight turned her hair to fire and Carroll found it difficult to look directly at her. "Can I help you?" he said.

She placed a shredded rectangle on the desk, and Carroll picked it up between his thumb and forefinger. Pages hung in tatters from the sodden blue spine. Title, binding, and covers had been gnawed away. "I need to pay for a damaged book," she said.

"What happened? Did your dog eat it?" he said, making a joke.

"Yes," she said, and smiled.

"What's your name?" Carroll said. Already, he thought he might be in love.

The farmhouse where Rachel lived had a wrap-around porch like an apron. It had been built on a hill, and looked down a long green slope of Christmas trees towards the town and Jellicoh College. It looked old-fashioned and a little forlorn.

On one side of the house was a small barn, and behind the barn was an oval pond, dark and fringed with pine trees. It winked in the twilight like a glossy lidless eye. The sun was rolling down the grassy rim of the hill towards the pond, and the exaggerated shadows of Christmas trees, long and pointed as witches' hats, stitched black triangles across the purple-grey lawn. House, barn, and hill were luminous in the fleet purple light.

Carroll parked the car in front of the barn and went around to Rachel's side to hand her out. A muffled, ferocious breathing emanated from the barn, and the doors shuddered as if something inside was hurling itself repeatedly towards them, through the dark and airless space. There was a sour animal smell. "What's in there?" Carroll asked.

"The dogs," Rachel said. "They aren't allowed in the house and they don't like to be separated from my mother."

"I like dogs," Carroll said.

There was a man sitting on the porch. He stood up as they approached the house and came forward to meet them. He was of medium build, and had pink-brown hair like his daughter. Rachel said, "Daddy, this is Carroll Murtaugh. Carroll, this is my daddy."

Mr. Rook had no nose. He shook hands with Carroll. His hand was warm and dry, flesh and blood. Carroll tried not to stare at Mr. Rook's face.

In actual fact, Rachel's father did have a nose, which was carved out of what appeared to be pine. The nostrils of the nose were flared slightly, as if Mr. Rook were smelling something pleasant. Copper wire ran through the bridge of the nose, attaching it to the frame of a pair of glasses; it nestled, delicate as a sleeping mouse, between the two lenses.

"Nice to meet you, Carroll," he said. "I understand that you're a librarian down at the college. You like books, do you?" His voice was deep and sonorous, as if he were speaking out of a well: Carroll was later to discover that Mr. Rook's voice changed slightly, depending on which nose he wore.

"Yes, sir," Carroll said. Just to be sure, he looked back at Rachel. As he had thought, her nose was unmistakably the genuine article. He shot her a second accusatory glance. *Why didn't you tell me?* She shrugged.

Mr. Rook said, "I don't have anything against books myself. But my wife can't stand 'em. Nearly broke her heart when Rachel decided to go to college." Rachel stuck out her lower lip. "Why don't you give your mother a hand, Rachel, setting the table, while Carroll and I get to know each other?"

"All right," Rachel said, and went into the house.

Mr. Rook sat down on the porch steps and Carroll sat down with him. "She's a beautiful girl," Mr. Rook said. "Just like her mother."

"Yes sir," Carroll said. "Beautiful." He stared straight ahead and spoke forcefully, as if he had not noticed that he was talking to a man with a wooden nose.

"You probably think it's odd, don't you, a girl her age, still living at home."

Carroll shrugged. "She seems attached to both of you. You grow Christmas trees, sir?"

"Strawberries too," Mr. Rook said. "It's a funny thing about strawberries and pine trees. People will pay you to let them dig up their own. They do all the work and then they pay you for it. They say the strawberries taste better that way, and they may be right. Myself, I can't taste much anyway."

Carroll leaned back against the porch rail and listened to Mr. Rook speak. He sneaked sideways looks at Mr. Rook's profile. From a few feet away, in the dim cast of the porch light, the nose had a homely, thoughtful bump to it: it was a philosopher's nose, a questing nose. White moths large as Carroll's hand pinwheeled around the porch light. They threw out tiny halos of dark and stirred up breaths of air with their wings, coming to rest on the porch screen, folding themselves into stillness like fans. Moths have no noses either, Carroll thought.

"I can't smell the pine trees either," Mr. Rook said. "I have to appreciate the irony in that. You'll have to forgive my wife, if she seems a bit awkward at first. She's not used to strangers."

Rachel danced out onto the porch. "Dinner's almost ready," she said. "Has Daddy been keeping you entertained?"

"He's been telling me all about your farm," Carroll said.

Rachel and her father looked at each other thoughtfully. "That's great," Rachel said. "You know what he's really dying to ask, Daddy.

Tell him about your collection of noses."

"Oh no," Carroll protested. "I wasn't wondering at all—"

But Mr. Rook stood up, dusting off the seat of his pants. "I'll go get them down. I almost wore a fancier one tonight, but it's so windy tonight, and rather damp. I didn't trust it not to rain." He hurried off into the house.

Carroll leaned over to Rachel. "Why didn't you tell me?" he said, looking up at her from the porch rail.

"What?"

"That your father has a wooden nose."

"He has several noses, but you heard him. It might rain. Some of them," she said, "are liable to rust."

"Why does he have a wooden nose?" Carroll said He was whispering.

"A boy named Biederbecke bit it off, in a fight." The alliteration evidently pleased her, because she said a little louder, "Biederbecke bit it off, when you were a boy. Isn't that right, Daddy?"

The porch door swung open again, and Mr. Rook said, "Yes, but I don't blame him, really I don't. We were little boys and I called him a stinking Kraut. That was during the war, and afterwards he was very sorry. You have to look on the bright side of things—your mother would never have noticed me if it hadn't had been for my nose. That was a fine nose. I modeled it on Abraham Lincoln's nose, and carved it out of black walnut." He set a dented black tackle box down next to Carroll, squatting beside it. "Look here."

The inside of the tackle box was lined with red velvet and the mild light of the October moon illuminated the noses, glowing as if a jeweler's lamp had been turned upon them: noses made of wood, and beaten copper, tin and brass. One seemed to be silver, veined with beads of turquoise. There were aquiline noses; noses pointed like gothic spires; noses with nostrils curled up like tiny bird claws. "Who made these?" Carroll said.

Mr. Rook coughed modestly. "It's my hobby," he said. "Pick one up if you like."

"Go ahead," Rachel said to Carroll.

Carroll chose a nose that had been painted over with blue and pink flowers. It was glassy-smooth and light in his hand, like a blown eggshell. "It's beautiful," he said. "What's it made out of?"

"Papier-mâché. There's one for every day of the week." Mr. Rook said.

"What did the . . . original look like?" Carroll asked.

"Hard to remember, really. It wasn't much of a nose," Mr. Rook said. "Before."

"Back to the question, please. Which do you choose, water or love?"

"What happens if I choose wrong?"

"You'll find out, won't you."

"Which would you choose?"

"That's my question, Carroll. You already asked yours."

"You still haven't answered me, either. All right, all right, let me think for a bit."

Rachel had straight reddish-brown hair that fell precisely to her shoulders and then stopped. Her eyes were fox-colored, and she had more small, even teeth than seemed absolutely necessary to Carroll. She smiled at him, and when she bent over the tacklebox full of noses, Carroll could see the two wings of her shoulderblades beneath the thin cotton T-shirt, her vertebrae outlined like a knobby strand of coral. As they went in to dinner she whispered in his ear, "My mother has a wooden leg."

She led him into the kitchen to meet her mother. The air in the kitchen was hot and moist and little beads of sweat stood out on Mrs. Rook's face. Rachel's mother resembled Rachel in the way that Mr. Rook's wooden nose resembled a real nose, as if someone had hacked Mrs. Rook out of wood or granite. She had large hands with long, yellowed fingernails, and all over her black dress were short black dog hairs. "So you're a librarian," she said to Carroll.

"Part-time," Carroll said. "Yes, ma'am."

"What do you do the rest of the time?" she said.

"I take classes."

Mrs. Rook stared at him without blinking. "Are your parents still alive?"

"My mother is, "Carroll said. "She lives in Florida. She plays bridge."

Rachel grabbed Carroll's arm. "Come on," she said. "The food's getting cold."

She pulled him into a dining room with dark wood paneling and a long table set for four people. The long black hem of Mrs. Rook's dress hissed along the floor as she pulled her chair into the table. Carroll sat down next to her. Was it the right or the left? He tucked his feet under his chair. Both women were silent and Carroll was silent between them. Mr. Rook talked instead, filling in the awkward empty pause so that Carroll was glad that it was his nose and not his tongue that the Biederbecke boy had bitten off.

How had she lost her leg? Mrs. Rook watched Carroll with a cold and methodical eye as he ate, and he held Rachel's hand under the table for comfort. He was convinced that her mother knew this and disapproved. He ate his pork and peas, balancing the peas on the blade of his knife. He hated peas. In between mouthfuls, he gulped down the pink wine in his glass. It was sweet and strong and tasted of burnt sugar. "Is this apple wine?" he asked. "It's delicious."

"It's strawberry wine," Mr. Rook said, pleased. "Have more. We make up a batch every year. I can't taste it myself but it's strong stuff."

Rachel filled Carroll's empty glass and watched him drain it instantly. "If you've finished, why don't you let my mother take you to meet the dogs? You look like you could use some fresh air. I'll stay here and help Daddy do the dishes. Go on," she said. "Go."

Mrs. Rook pushed her chair back from the table, pushed herself out of the chair. "Well, come on," she said. "I don't bite."

Outside, the moths beat at his face, and he reeled beside Rachel's mother on the moony-white gravel, light as a thread spun out on its spool. She walked quickly, leaning forward a little as her right foot came down, dragging the left foot through the small stones.

"What kind of dogs are they?" he said.

"Black ones," she said.

"What are their names?"

"Flower and Acorn," she said, and flung open the barn door. Two labradors, slippery as black trout in the moonlight, surged up at Carroll. They thrust their velvet muzzles at him, uttering angry staccato coughs, their rough breath steaming at his face. They were the size of small ponies and their paws left muddy prints on his shirt. Carroll pushed them back down, and they snapped at his hands.

"Heel," Mrs. Rook said, and instantly the two dogs went to her, arranging themselves on either side like bookends. Against the folds of her skirt, they were nearly invisible, only their saucer-like eyes flashing wickedly at Carroll.

"Flower's pregnant," Mrs. Rook said. "We've tried to breed them before, but it never took. Go for a run, girl. Go with her, Acorn."

The dogs loped off, moonlight spilling off their coats like water. Carroll watched them run; the stale air of the barn washed over him, and under the bell of Mrs. Rook's skirt he pictured the dark wood of the left leg, the white flesh of the right leg, like a pair of mismatched dice. Mrs. Rook drew in her breath. She said, "I don't mind you sleeping with my daughter but you had better not get her pregnant."

Carroll said, "No, ma'am."

35

KELLY LINK

"If you give her a bastard, I'll set the dogs on you," she said, and went back towards the house. Carroll scrambled after her.

On Friday, Carroll was shelving new books on the third floor. He stood, both arms lifted up to steady a wavering row of psychology periodicals. Someone paused in the narrow row, directly behind him, and a small cold hand insinuated itself into his trousers, slipping under the waistband of his underwear.

"Rachel?" he said, and the hand squeezed, slowly. He jumped and the row of books toppled off their shelf, like dominoes. He bent to pick them up, not looking at her. "I forgive you," he said.

"That's nice," she said. "For what?"

"For not telling me about your father's—" he hesitated, looking for the word, "—wound."

"I thought you handled that very well," she said. "And I did tell you about my mother's leg."

"I wasn't sure whether or not to believe you. How did she lose it?"

"She swims down in the pond. She was walking back up to the house. She was barefoot. She sliced her foot open on something. By the time she went to see a doctor, she had septicemia and her leg had to be amputated just below the knee. Daddy made her a replacement out of walnut; he said the prosthesis that the hospital wanted to give her looked nothing like the leg she'd lost. It has a name carved on it. She used to tell me that a ghost lived inside it and helped her walk. I was four years old." She didn't look at him as she spoke, flicking the dust off the spine of a tented book with her long fingers.

"What was its name?" Carroll asked.

"Ellen," Rachel said.

Two days after they had first met, Carroll was in the basement stacks. It was dark in the aisles, the tall shelves curving towards each other.

The lights were controlled by timers, and went on and off untouched by human hand: there was the ominous sound of ticking as the timers clicked off row by row. Puddles of dirty yellow light wavered under his feet, the floor as slick as water. There was one other student on this floor, a boy who trod at Carroll's heels, breathing heavily.

Rachel was in a back corner, partly hidden by a shelving cart. "Goddammit, goddammit to hell," she was saying, as she flung a book down. "Stupid book, stupid, useless, stupid, know-nothing books." She kicked at the book several more times, and stomped on it for good measure. Then she looked up and saw Carroll and the boy behind him. "Oh," she said. "You again."

Carroll turned and glared at the boy. "What's the matter," he said. "Haven't you ever seen a librarian at work?"

The boy fled. "What's the matter?" Carroll said again.

"Nothing," Rachel said. "I'm just tired of reading stupid books about books about books. It's ten times worse then my mother ever said." She looked at him, weighing him up. She said, "Have you ever made love in a library?"

"Um," Carroll said. "No."

Rachel stripped off her woolly sweater, her blue undershirt. Underneath, her bare flesh burned. The lights clicked off two rows down, then the row beside Carroll, and he moved forward to find Rachel before she vanished. Her body was hot and dry, like a newly extinguished bulb.

Rachel seemed to enjoy making love in the library. The library officially closed at midnight, and on Tuesdays and Thursdays when he was the last of the staff to leave, Carroll left the East Entrance unlocked for Rachel while he made up a pallet of jackets and sweaters from the Lost and Found.

The first night, he had arranged a makeshift bed in the aisle between PR878W6B37, *Relative Creatures*, and PR878W6B35,

Corrupt Relations. In the summer, the stacks had been much cooler than his un-air-conditioned room. He had hoped to woo her into his bed by the time the weather turned, but it was October already. Rachel pulled PR878W6A9 out to use as a pillow. "I thought you didn't like books," he said, trying to make a joke.

"My mother doesn't like books," she said. "Or libraries. Which is a good thing. You don't ever have to worry about her looking for me here."

When they made love, Rachel kept her eyes closed. Carroll watched her face, her body rocking beneath him like water. He closed his eyes, opening them quickly again, hoping to catch her looking back at him. Did he please her? He pleased himself, and her breath quickened upon his neck. Her hands smoothed his body, moving restlessly back and forth, until he gathered them to himself, biting at her knuckles.

Later he lay prone as she moved over him, her knees clasping his waist, her narrow feet cupped under the stirrups of his knees. They lay hinged together and Carroll squinted his eyes shut to make the Exit sign fuzzy in the darkness. He imagined that they had just made love in a forest, and the red glow was a campfire. He imagined they were not on the third floor of a library, but on the shore of a deep, black lake in the middle of a stand of tall trees.

"When you were a teenager," Rachel said, "what was the worst thing you ever did?"

Carroll thought for a moment. "When I was a teenager," he said, "I used to go into my room every day after school and masturbate. And my dog Sunny used to stand outside the door and whine. I'd come in a handful of Kleenex, and afterward I never knew what to do with them. If I threw them in the wastebasket, my mother might notice them piling up. If I dropped them under the bed, then Sunny would sneak in later and eat them. It was a revolting dilemma, and every day I swore I wouldn't ever do it again."

"That's disgusting, Carroll."

Carroll was constantly amazed at the things he told Rachel, as if love was some sort of hook she used to drag secrets out of him, things that he had forgotten until she asked for them. "Your turn," he said.

Rachel curled herself against him. "Well, when I was little, and I did something bad, my mother used to take off her wooden leg and spank me with it. When I got older, and started being asked out on dates, she would forbid me. She actually said *I forbid you to go*, just like a Victorian novel. I would wait until she took her bath after dinner, and steal her leg and hide it. And I would stay out as late as I wanted. When I got home, she was always sitting at the kitchen table, with the leg strapped back on. She always found it before I got home, but I always stayed away as long as I could. I never came home before I had to.

"When I was little I hated her leg. It was like her other child, the obedient daughter. I was the one she had to spank. I thought the leg told her when I was bad, and I could feel it gloating whenever she punished me. I hid it from her in closets, or in the belly of the grandfather clock. Once I buried it out in the strawberry field because I knew it hated the dark: it was scared of the dark, like me."

Carroll eased away from her, rolling over on his stomach. The whole time she had been talking, her voice had been calm, her breath tickling his throat. Telling her about Sunny, the semen-eating dog, he had sprouted a cheerful little erection. Listening to her, it had melted away, and his balls had crept up his goose-pimpled thighs.

Somewhere a timer clicked and a light turned off. "Let's make love again," she said, and seized him in her hand. He nearly screamed.

In late November, Carroll went to the farm again for dinner. He parked just outside the barn, where, malignant and black as tar, Flower lolled on her side in the cold dirty straw. She was swollen and too lazy to do more than show him her teeth; he admired them. "How pregnant is she?" Carroll asked Mr. Rook, who had emerged from the barn.

"She's due any day," Mr. Rook said. "The vet says there might be six puppies in there." Today he wore a tin nose, and his words had a distinct echo, whistling out double shrill, like a teakettle on the boil. "Would you like to see my workshop?" he said.

"Okay," Carroll said. The barn smelled of gasoline and straw, old things congealing in darkness; it smelled of winter. Along the right inside wall, there were a series of long hooks, and depending from them were various pointed and hooked tools. Below was a table strewn with objects that seemed to have come from the city dump: bits of metal; cigar boxes full of broken glass sorted according to color; a carved wooden hand, jointed and with a dime-store ring over the next-to-last finger.

Carroll picked it up, surprised at its weight. The joints of the wooden fingers clicked as he manipulated them, the fingers long and heavy and perfectly smooth. He put it down again. "It's very nice," he said and turned around. Through the thin veil of sunlight and dust that wavered in the open doors, Carroll could see a black glitter of water. "Where's Rachel?"

"She went to find her mother, I'll bet. They'll be down by the pond. Go and tell them it's dinner time." Mr. Rook looked down at the black and rancorous Flower. "Six puppies!" he remarked, in a sad little whistle.

Carroll went down through the slanted grove of Christmas trees. At the base of the hill was a circle of twelve oaks, their leaves making a thick carpet of gold. The twelve trees were spaced evenly around the perimeter of the pond, like the numbers on a clock face. Carroll paused under the eleven o'clock oak, looking at the water. He saw Rachel in the pond, her white arm cutting through the gaudy leaves that clung like skin, bringing up black droplets of water. Carroll stood in his corduroy jacket and watched her swim laps across the pond. He wondered how cold the water was. Then he realized that it wasn't Rachel in the pond.

Rachel sat on a quilt on the far side of the pond, under the six o'clock oak. Acorn sat beside her, looking now at the swimmer, now at Carroll. Rachel and her mother were both oblivious to his presence, Mrs. Rook intent on her exercise, Rachel rubbing linseed oil into her mother's wooden leg. The wind carried the scent of it across the pond. The dog stood, stiff-legged, fixing Carroll in its dense liquid gaze. It shook itself, sending up a spray of water like diamonds.

"Cut it out, Acorn!" Rachel said without looking up. All the way across the pond, Carroll felt the drops of water fall on him, cold and greasy.

He felt himself turning to stone with fear. He was afraid of the leg that Rachel held in her lap. He was afraid that Mrs. Rook would emerge from her pond, and he would see the space where her knee hung above the ground. He backed up the hill slowly, almost falling over a small stone marker at the top. As he looked at it, the dog came running up the path, passing him without a glance, and after that, Rachel, and her mother, wearing the familiar black dress. The ground was slippery with leaves and Mrs. Rook leaned on her daughter. Her hair was wet and her cheeks were as red as leaves.

"I can't read the name," Carroll said.

"It's Ellen," Mrs. Rook said. "My husband carved it."

Carroll looked at Rachel. *Your mother has a tombstone for her leg?* Rachel looked away.

"You can't live without water."

"So that's your choice?"

"I'm just thinking out loud. I know what you want me to say."

No answer.

41

"*Rachel, look. I choose water, okay?*"

No answer.

"*Let me explain. You can lie to water—you can say no, I'm not in love, I don't need love, and you can be lying—how is the water supposed to know that you're lying? It can't tell if you're in love or not, right? Water's not that smart. So you fool the water into thinking you'd never dream of falling in love, and when you're thirsty, you drink it.*"

"*You're pretty sneaky.*"

"*I love you, Rachel. Will you please marry me? Otherwise your mother is going to kill me.*"

No answer.

After dinner, Carroll's car refused to start. No one answered when they rang a garage, and Rachel said, "He can take my bike, then."

"Don't be silly," Mr. Rook said. "He can stay here and we'll get someone in the morning. Besides, it's going to rain soon."

"I don't want to put you to any trouble," Carroll said.

Rachel said, "It's getting dark. He can call a taxi." Carroll looked at her, hurt, and she frowned at him.

"He'll stay in the back room," Mrs. Rook said. "Come and have another glass of wine before you go to bed, Carroll." She grinned at him in what might have been a friendly fashion, except that at some point after dinner, she had removed her dentures.

Rachel brought him a pair of her father's pajamas and led him off to the room where he was to sleep. The room was small and plain and the only beautiful thing in it was Rachel, sitting on a blue and scarlet quilt. "Who made this?" he said.

"My mother did," Rachel said. "She's made whole closetsful of quilts. It's what she used to do while she waited for me to get home from a date. Now get in bed."

"Why didn't you want me to spend the night?" he asked.

She stuck a long piece of hair in her mouth, and sucked on it, staring at him without blinking. He tried again. "How come you never spend the night at my apartment?"

She shrugged. "Are you tired?"

Carroll yawned, and gave up. "Yes," he said and Rachel kissed him goodnight. It was a long, thoughtful kiss. She turned out the light and went down the hall to her own bedroom. Carroll rolled on his side and fell asleep and dreamed that Rachel came back in the room and stood naked in the moonlight. Then she climbed in bed with him and they made love and then Mrs. Rook came into the room. She beat at them with her leg as they hid under the quilt. She struck Rachel and turned her into wood.

As Carroll left the next morning, it was discovered that Flower had given birth to seven puppies in the night. "Well, it's too late now," Rachel said.

"Too late for what?" Carroll asked. His car started on the first try.

"Never mind," Rachel said gloomily. She didn't wave as he drove away.

Carroll discovered that if he said "I love you," to Rachel, she would say "I love you too," in an absent-minded way. But she still refused to come to his apartment, and because it was colder now, they made love during the day, in the storage closet on the third floor. Sometimes he caught her watching him now, when they made love. The look in her eyes was not quite what he had hoped it would be, more shrewd than passionate. But perhaps this was a trick of the cold winter light.

Sometimes, now that it was cold, Rachel let Carroll drive her home from school. The sign beside the Rooks' driveway now said, "Get your Christmas Trees early." Beneath that it said, "Adorable black Lab Puppies free to a Good home."

But no one wanted a puppy. This was understandable; already the puppies had the gaunt, evil look of their parents. They spent their days catching rats in the barn, and their evenings trailing like sullen shadows around the black skirts of Mrs. Rook. They tolerated Mr. Rook and Rachel; Carroll they eyed hungrily.

"You have to look on the bright side," Mr. Rook said. "They make excellent watchdogs."

Carroll gave Rachel a wooden bird on a gold chain for Christmas, and the complete works of Jane Austen. She gave him a bottle of strawberry wine and a wooden box, with six black dogs painted on the lid. They had fiery red eyes and red licorice tongues. "My father carved it, but I painted it," she said.

Carroll opened the box. "What will I put in it?" he said.

Rachel shrugged. The library was closed for the weekend, and they sat on the dingy green carpet in the deserted lounge. The rest of the staff was on break, and Mr. Cassatti, Carroll's supervisor, had asked Carroll to keep an eye on things.

There had been some complaints, he said, of vandalism in the past few weeks. Books had been knocked off their shelves, or disarranged, and even more curious, a female student claimed to have seen a dog up on the third floor. It had growled at her, she said, and then slunk off into the stacks. Mr. Cassatti, when he had gone up to check, had seen nothing. Not so much as a single hair. He wasn't worried about the dog, Mr. Cassatti had said, but some books had been discovered, the pages ripped out. *Maimed,* Mr. Cassatti had said.

Rachel handed Carroll one last parcel. It was wrapped in a brown paper bag, and when he opened it, a blaze of scarlet and cornflower blue spilled out onto his lap. "My mother made you a quilt just like the one in the spare bedroom," Rachel said. "I told her you thought it was pretty."

"It's beautiful," Carroll said. He snapped the quilt out, so that it spread across the library floor, as if they were having a picnic. He tried to imagine making love to Rachel beneath a quilt her mother had made. "Does this mean that you'll make love with me in a bed?"

"I'm pregnant," Rachel said.

He looked around to see if anyone else had heard her, but of course they were alone. "That's impossible," he said. "You're on the pill."

"Yes, well." Rachel said. "I'm pregnant anyway. It happens sometimes."

"How pregnant?" he asked.

"Three months."

"Does your mother know?"

"Yes," Rachel said.

"Oh God, she's going to put the dogs on me. What are we going to do?"

"What am I going to do," Rachel said, looking down at her cupped hands so that Carroll could not see her expression. "What am *I* going to do," she said again.

There was a long pause and Carroll took one of her hands in his. "Then we'll get married?" he said, a quaver in his voice turning the statement into a question.

"No," she said, looking straight at him, the way she looked at him when they made love. He had never noticed what a sad hopeless look this was.

Carroll dropped his own eyes, ashamed of himself and not quite sure why. He took a deep breath. "What I meant to say, Rachel, is I love you very much and would you please marry me?"

Rachel pulled her hand away from him. She said in a low angry voice, "What do you think this is, Carroll? Do you think this is a book? Is this supposed to be the happy ending—we get married and live happily ever after?"

She got up, and he stood up too. He opened his mouth, and nothing came out, so he just followed her as she walked away. She stopped so abruptly that he almost fell against her. "Let me ask you a question first," she said, and turned to face him. "What would you choose, love or water?"

The question was so ridiculous that he found he was able to speak again. "What kind of a question is that?" he said.

"Never mind. I think you better take me home in your car," Rachel said. "It's starting to snow."

Carroll thought about it during the car ride. He came to the conclusion that it was a silly question, and that if he didn't answer it correctly, Rachel wasn't going to marry him. He wasn't entirely sure that he wanted to give the correct answer, even if he knew what it was.

He said, "I love you, Rachel." He swallowed and he could hear the snow coming down, soft as feathers on the roof and windshield of the car. In the two beams of the headlights the road was dense and white as an iced cake, and in the reflected snow-light Rachel's face was a beautiful greenish color. "Will you marry me anyway? I don't know how you want me to choose."

"No."

"Why not?" They had reached the farm; he turned the car into driveway, and stopped.

"You've had a pretty good life so far, haven't you?" she said.

"Not too bad," he said sullenly.

"When you walk down the street," Rachel said, "do you ever find pennies?"

"Yes," he said.

"Are they heads or tails?"

"Heads, usually," he said.

"Do you get good grades?"

"As and Bs," he said.

"Do you have to study hard? Have you ever broken a mirror? When you lose things," she said, "do you find them again?"

"What is this, an interview?"

Rachel looked at him. It was hard to read her expression, but she sounded resigned. "Have you ever even broken a bone? Do you ever have to stop for red lights?"

"Okay, okay," he snapped. "My life is pretty easy. I've gotten everything I ever wanted for Christmas, too. And I want you to marry me, so of course you're going to say yes."

He reached out, put his arms around her. She sat brittle and stiff in the circle of his embrace, her face turned into his jacket. "Rachel—"

"My mother says I shouldn't marry you," she said. "She says I don't really know you, that you're feckless, that you've never lost anything that you cared about, that you're the wrong sort to be marrying into a family like ours."

"Is your mother some kind of oracle, because she has a wooden leg?"

"My mother knows about losing things," Rachel said, pushing at him. "She says it'll hurt, but I'll get over you."

"So tell me, how hard has your life been?" Carroll said. "You've got your nose, and both your legs. What do you know about losing things?"

"I haven't told you everything," Rachel said and slipped out of the car. "You don't know everything about me." Then she slammed the car door. He watched her cross the driveway and go up the hill into the snow.

Carroll called in sick all the next week. The heating unit in his apartment wasn't working, and the cold made him sluggish. He thought about going in to the library, just to be warm, but instead he spent most of his time under the quilt that Mrs. Rook had made, hoping to dream about Rachel. He dreamed instead about being devoured by dogs, about drowning in icy black water.

He lay in his dark room, under the weight of the scarlet quilt, when he wasn't asleep, and held long conversations in his head with Rachel, about love and water. He told her stories about his childhood; she almost seemed to be listening. He asked her about the baby and she told him she was going to name it Ellen if it was a girl. When he took his own temperature on Wednesday, the thermometer said he had a fever of 103, so he climbed back into bed.

When he woke up on Thursday morning, he found short black hairs covering the quilt, which he knew must mean that he was hallucinating. He fell asleep again and dreamed that Mr. Rook came to see him. Mr. Rook was a Black Lab. He was wearing a plastic Groucho Marx nose. He and Carroll stood beside the black lake that was on the third floor of the library.

The dog said, "You and I are a lot alike, Carroll."

"I suppose," Carroll said.

"No, really," the dog insisted. It leaned its head on Carroll's knee, still looking up at him. "We like to look on the bright side of things. You have to do that, you know."

"Rachel doesn't love me anymore," Carroll said. "Nobody likes me." He scratched behind Mr. Rook's silky ear.

"Now, is that looking on the bright side of things?" said the dog. "Scratch a little to the right. Rachel has a hard time, like her mother. Be patient with her."

"So which would you choose," Carroll said. "Love or water?"

"Who says anyone gets to choose anything? You said you picked water, but there's good water and there's bad water. Did you ever think about that?" the dog said. "I have a much better question for you. Are you a good dog or a bad dog?"

"Good dog!" Carroll yelled, and woke himself up.

He called the farmhouse in the morning, and when Rachel answered, he said, "This is Carroll. I'm coming to talk to you."

But when he got there, no one was there. The sight of the leftover Christmas trees, tall and gawky as green geese, made him feel homesick. Little clumps of snow like white flowers were melting in the gravel driveway. The dogs were not in the barn and he hoped that Mrs. Rook had taken them down to the pond.

He walked up to the house, and knocked on the door. If either of Rachel's parents came to the door, he would stand his ground and demand to see their daughter. He knocked again, but no one came. The house, shuttered against the snow, had an expectant air, as if it were waiting for him to say something. So he whispered, "Rachel? Where are you?" The house was silent. "Rachel, I love you. Please come out and talk to me. Let's get married—we'll elope. You steal your mother's leg, and by the time your father carves her a new one, we'll be in Canada. We could go to Niagara Falls for our honeymoon—we could take your mother's leg with us, if you want—Ellen, I mean— we'll take Ellen with us!"

Carroll heard a delicate cough behind him as if someone were clearing their throat. He turned and saw Flower and Acorn and their six enormous children sitting on the gravel by the barn, next to his car. Their fur was spiky and wet, and they curled their black lips at him. Someone in the house laughed. Or perhaps it was the echo of a splash, down at the pond.

One of the dogs lifted its head and bayed at him. "Hey," he said. "Good dog! Good Flower, good Acorn! Rachel, help!"

She had been hiding behind the front door. She slammed it open and came out onto the porch. "My mother said I should just let the dogs eat you," she said. "If you came."

She looked tired; she wore a shapeless woolen dress that looked like one of her mother's. If she really was pregnant, Carroll couldn't see any evidence yet. "Do you always listen to your mother?" he said. "Don't you love me?"

"When I was born," she said. "I was a twin. My sister's name was Ellen. When we were seven years old, she drowned in the pond—I lost her. Don't you see? People start out losing small things, like noses. Pretty soon you start losing other things too. It's sort of an accidental leprosy. If we got married, you'd find out."

Carroll heard someone coming up the path from the pond, up through the thin ranks of Christmas trees. The dogs pricked up their ears, but their black eyes stayed fastened to Carroll. "You'd better hurry," Rachel said. She escorted him past the dogs to his car.

"I'm going to come back."

"That's not a good idea," she said. The dogs watched him leave, crowding close around her, their black tails whipping excitedly. He went home and in a very bad temper, he picked up the quilt to inspect it. He was looking for the black hairs he had seen that morning. But of course there weren't any.

The next day he went back to the library. He was lifting books out of the overnight collection box, when he felt something that was neither rectangular nor flat. It was covered in velvety fur, and damp. He felt warm breath steaming on his hand. It twisted away when he tried to pick it up, and when he reached out for it again, it snarled at him.

He backed away from the collection box, and a long black dog wriggled out of the box after him. Two students stopped to watch what was happening. "Go get Mr. Cassatti, please," Carroll said to one of them. "His office is around the corner."

The dog approached him. Its ears were laid back flat against its skull and its neck moved like a snake.

"Good dog?" Carroll said, and held out his hand. "Flower?" The dog lunged forward and, snapping its jaws shut, bit off his pinky just below the fingernail.

The student screamed. Carroll stood still and looked down at his right hand, which was slowly leaking blood. The sound that the dog's jaw had made as it severed his finger had been crisp and businesslike. The dog stared at Carroll in a way that reminded him of Rachel's stare. "Give me back my finger," Carroll said.

The dog growled and backed away. "We have to catch it," the student said. "So they can reattach your finger. Shit, what if it has rabies?"

Mr. Cassatti appeared, carrying a large flat atlas, extended like a shield. "Someone said that there was a dog in the library," he said.

"In the corner over there," Carroll said. "It bit off my finger." He held up his hand for Mr. Cassatti to see, but Mr. Cassatti was looking towards the corner and shaking his head.

He said, "I don't see a dog."

The two students hovered, loudly insisting that they had both seen the dog a moment ago, while Mr. Cassatti tended to Carroll. The floor in the corner was sticky and wet, as if someone had spilled a Coke. There was no sign of the dog.

Mr. Cassatti took Carroll to the hospital, where the doctor at the hospital gave him a shot of codeine, and tried to convince him that it would be a simple matter to reattach the fingertip. "How?" Mr. Cassatti said. "He says the dog ran away with it."

"What dog?" the doctor asked.

"It was bitten off by a dog," Carroll told the doctor.

The doctor raised his eyebrows. "A dog in a library? This looks like he stuck his finger under a paper cutter. The cut is too tidy—a dog bite would be a mess. Didn't anyone bring the finger?"

"The dog ate it," Carroll said. "Mrs. Rook said the dog would eat me, but it stopped. I don't think it liked the way I tasted."

Mr. Cassatti and the doctor went out into the hall to discuss something. Carroll stood at the door and waited until they had turned towards the nurses' station. He opened the door and snuck down the hallway in the opposite direction and out of the hospital. It was a little hard, walking on the ground—the codeine seemed to affect gravity. When he walked, he bounced. When walking got too difficult, he climbed in a taxi and gave the driver the address of the Rook farm.

His hand didn't hurt at all; he tried to remember this, so he could tell Rachel. They had bound up his hand in white gauze bandages, and it looked like someone else's hand entirely. Under the white bandages, his hand was pleasantly warm. His skin felt stretched, tight and thin as a rubber glove. He felt much lighter: it might take a while, but he thought he could get the hang of losing things; it seemed to come as easily to him as everything else did.

Carroll thought maybe Rachel and he would get married down by the pond, beneath the new leaves of the six o'clock oak tree. Mr. Rook could wear his most festive nose, the one with rose-velvet lining, or perhaps the one painted with flowers. Carroll remembered the little grave at the top of the path that led to the pond—not the pond, he decided—they should be married in a church. Maybe in a library.

"Just drop me off here," he told the taxi driver at the top of the driveway.

"Are you sure you'll be okay?" the driver said. Carroll shook his head, yes, he was sure. He watched the taxi drive away, waving the hand with the abbreviated finger.

Mrs. Rook could make her daughter a high-waisted wedding dress, satin and silk and lace, moth-pale, and there would be a cake with eight laughing dogs made out of white frosting, white as snow. For some reason he had a hard time making the church come out right. It kept changing, church into library, library into black pond. The windows were high and narrow and the walls were wet like the inside of a well. The aisle kept changing, the walls getting closer, becoming stacks of books, dark, velvety waves. He imagined standing at the altar with Rachel—black water came up to their ankles as if their feet had been severed. He thought of the white cake again: if he sliced into it, darkness would gush out like ink.

He shook his head, listening. There was a heavy dragging noise, coming up the side of the hill through the Christmas trees. It would be a beautiful wedding and he considered it a lucky thing that he had lost his pinky and not his ring finger. You had to look on the bright side after all. He went down towards the pond, to tell Rachel this.

THE SPECIALIST'S HAT

W hen you're Dead," Samantha says, "you don't have to brush your teeth . . ."

"When you're Dead," Claire says, "you live in a box, and it's always dark, but you're not ever afraid."

Claire and Samantha are identical twins. Their combined age is twenty years, four months, and six days. Claire is better at being Dead than Samantha.

The babysitter yawns, covering up her mouth with a long white hand. "I said to brush your teeth and that it's time for bed," she says. She sits crosslegged on the flowered bedspread between them. She has been teaching them a card game called Pounce, which involves three decks of cards, one for each of them. Samantha's deck is missing the Jack of Spades and the Two of Hearts, and Claire keeps on cheating. The babysitter wins anyway. There are still flecks of dried shaving cream and toilet paper on her arms. It is hard to tell how old she is— at first they thought she must be a grownup, but now she hardly looks older than them. Samantha has forgotten the babysitter's name.

Claire's face is stubborn. "When you're Dead," she says, "you stay up all night long."

"When you're dead," the babysitter snaps, "it's always very cold and damp, and you have to be very, very quiet or else the Specialist will get you."

"This house is haunted," Claire says.

"I know it is," the babysitter says. "I used to live here."

Something is creeping up the stairs,
Something is standing outside the door,
Something is sobbing, sobbing in the dark;
Something is sighing across the floor.

Claire and Samantha are spending the summer with their father, in the house called Eight Chimneys. Their mother is dead. She has been dead for exactly 282 days.

Their father is writing a history of Eight Chimneys and of the poet Charles Cheatham Rash, who lived here at the turn of the century, and who ran away to sea when he was thirteen, and returned when he was thirty-eight. He married, fathered a child, wrote three volumes of bad, obscure poetry, and an even worse and more obscure novel, *The One Who is Watching Me Through the Window*, before disappearing again in 1907, this time for good. Samantha and Claire's father says that some of the poetry is actually quite readable and at least the novel isn't very long.

When Samantha asked him why he was writing about Rash, he replied that no one else had and why didn't she and Samantha go play outside. When she pointed out that she was Samantha, he just scowled and said how could he be expected to tell them apart when they both wore blue jeans and flannel shirts, and why couldn't one of them dress all in green and the other in pink?

Claire and Samantha prefer to play inside. Eight Chimneys is as big as a castle, but dustier and darker than Samantha imagines a castle would be. There are more sofas, more china shepherdesses with chipped fingers, fewer suits of armor. No moat.

The house is open to the public, and, during the day, people—families—driving along the Blue Ridge Parkway will stop to tour the grounds and the first story; the third story belongs to Claire and Samantha. Sometimes they play explorers, and sometimes they follow the caretaker as he gives tours to visitors. After a few weeks, they have memorized his lecture, and they mouth it along with him. They help him sell postcards and copies of Rash's poetry to the tourist families who come into the little gift shop.

When the mothers smile at them and say how sweet they are, they stare back and don't say anything at all. The dim light in the house makes the mothers look pale and flickery and tired. They leave Eight Chimneys, mothers and families, looking not quite as real as they did before they paid their admissions, and of course Claire and Samantha will never see them again, so maybe they aren't real. Better to stay inside the house, they want to tell the families, and if you must leave, then go straight to your cars.

The caretaker says the woods aren't safe.

Their father stays in the library on the second story all morning, typing, and in the afternoon he takes long walks. He takes his pocket recorder along with him and a hip flask of Gentleman Jack, but not Samantha and Claire.

The caretaker of Eight Chimneys is Mr. Coeslak. His left leg is noticeably shorter than his right. He wears one stacked heel. Short black hairs grow out of his ears and his nostrils and there is no hair at all on top of his head, but he's given Samantha and Claire permission to explore the whole of the house. It was Mr. Coeslak who told them that there are copperheads in the woods, and that the house is haunted. He says they are all, ghosts and snakes, a pretty badtempered lot, and Samantha and Claire should stick to the marked trails, and stay out of the attic.

Mr. Coeslak can tell the twins apart, even if their father can't; Claire's eyes are grey, like a cat's fur, he says, but Samantha's are *gray*, like the ocean when it has been raining.

Samantha and Claire went walking in the woods on the second day that they were at Eight Chimneys. They saw something. Samantha thought it was a woman, but Claire said it was a snake. The staircase that goes up to the attic has been locked. They peeked through the keyhole, but it was too dark to see anything.

> *And so he had a wife, and they say she was real pretty. There was another man who wanted to go with her, and first she wouldn't, because she was afraid of her husband, and then she did. Her husband found out, and they say he killed a snake and got some of this snake's blood and put it in some whiskey and gave it to her. He had learned this from an island man who had been on a ship with him. And in about six months snakes created in her and they got between her meat and the skin. And they say you could just see them running up and down her legs. They say she was just hollow to the top of her body, and it kept on like that till she died. Now my daddy said he saw it.*
>
> —An Oral History of Eight Chimneys

Eight Chimneys is over two hundred years old. It is named for the eight chimneys that are each big enough that Samantha and Claire can both fit in one fireplace. The chimneys are red brick, and on each floor there are eight fireplaces, making a total of twenty-four. Samantha imagines the chimney stacks stretching like stout red tree trunks, all the way up through the slate roof of the house. Beside each fireplace is a heavy black firedog, and a set of wrought iron pokers shaped like snakes. Claire and Samantha pretend to duel with the snake-pokers before the fireplace in their bedroom on the third floor. Wind rises up the back of the chimney. When they stick their faces in, they can feel the air rushing damply upwards, like a river. The flue smells old and sooty and wet, like stones from a river.

Their bedroom was once the nursery. They sleep together in a poster bed which resembles a ship with four masts. It smells of mothballs, and Claire kicks in her sleep. Charles Cheatham Rash slept here when he was a little boy, and also his daughter. She disappeared when her father did. It might have been gambling debts. They may have moved to New Orleans. She was fourteen years old, Mr. Coeslak said. What was her name, Claire asked. What happened to her mother, Samantha wanted to know. Mr. Coeslak closed his eyes in an almost wink. Mrs. Rash had died the year before her husband and daughter disappeared, he said, of a mysterious wasting disease. He can't remember the name of the poor little girl, he said.

Eight Chimneys has exactly one hundred windows, all still with the original wavery panes of handblown glass. With so many windows, Samantha thinks, Eight Chimneys should always be full of light, but instead the trees press close against the house, so that the rooms on the first and second story—even the third-story rooms—are green and dim, as if Samantha and Claire are living deep under the sea. This is the light that makes the tourists into ghosts. In the morning, and again towards evening, a fog settles in around the house. Sometimes it is grey like Claire's eyes, and sometimes it is gray, like Samantha's eyes.

> *I met a woman in the wood,*
> *Her lips were two red snakes.*
> *She smiled at me, her eyes were lewd*
> *And burning like a fire.*

59

A few nights ago, the wind was sighing in the nursery chimney. Their father had already tucked them in and turned off the light. Claire dared Samantha to stick her head into the fireplace, in the dark, and so she did. The cold wet air licked at her face and it almost sounded like voices talking low, muttering. She couldn't quite make out what they were saying.

Their father has mostly ignored Claire and Samantha since they arrived at Eight Chimneys. He never mentions their mother. One evening they heard him shouting in the library, and when they came downstairs, there was a large sticky stain on the desk, where a glass of whiskey had been knocked over. It was looking at me, he said, through the window. It had orange eyes.

Samantha and Claire refrained from pointing out that the library is on the second story.

At night, their father's breath has been sweet from drinking, and he is spending more and more time in the woods, and less in the library. At dinner, usually hot dogs and baked beans from a can, which they eat off of paper plates in the first floor dining room, beneath the Austrian chandelier (which has exactly 632 leaded crystals shaped like teardrops) their father recites the poetry of Charles Cheatham Rash, which neither Samantha nor Claire cares for.

He has been reading the ship diaries that Rash kept, and he says that he has discovered proof in them that Rash's most famous poem, "The Specialist's Hat," is not a poem at all, and in any case, Rash didn't write it. It is something that the one of the men on the whaler used to say, to conjure up a whale. Rash simply copied it down and stuck an end on it and said it was his.

The man was from Mulatuppu, which is a place neither Samantha nor Claire has ever heard of. Their father says that the man was supposed to be some sort of magician, but he drowned shortly before

Rash came back to Eight Chimneys. Their father says that the other sailors wanted to throw the magician's chest overboard, but Rash persuaded them to let him keep it until he could be put ashore, with the chest, off the coast of North Carolina.

> *The specialist's hat makes a noise like an agouti;*
> *The specialist's hat makes a noise like a collared peccary;*
> *The specialist's hat makes a noise like a white-lipped peccary;*
> *The specialist's hat makes a noise like a tapir;*
> *The specialist's hat makes a noise like a rabbit;*
> *The specialist's hat makes a noise like a squirrel;*
> *The specialist's hat makes a noise like a curassow;*
> *The specialist's hat moans like a whale in the water;*
> *The specialist's hat moans like the wind in my wife's hair;*
> *The specialist's hat makes a noise like a snake;*
> *I have hung the hat of the specialist upon my wall.*

The reason that Claire and Samantha have a babysitter is that their father met a woman in the woods. He is going to see her tonight, and they are going to have a picnic supper and look at the stars. This is the time of year when the Perseids can be seen, falling across the sky on clear nights. Their father said that he has been walking with the woman every afternoon. She is a distant relation of Rash and besides, he said, he needs a night off and some grownup conversation.

Mr. Coeslak won't stay in the house after dark, but he agreed to find someone to look after Samantha and Claire. Then their father couldn't find Mr. Coeslak, but the babysitter showed up precisely at seven o'clock. The babysitter, whose name neither twin quite caught, wears a blue cotton dress with short floaty sleeves. Both Samantha and Claire think she is pretty in an old-fashioned sort of way.

They were in the library with their father, looking up Mulatuppu in the red leather atlas, when she arrived. She didn't knock on the front door, she simply walked in and then up the stairs, as if she knew where to find them.

Their father kissed them goodbye, a hasty smack, told them to be good and he would take them into town on the weekend to see the Disney film. They went to the window to watch as he walked into the woods. Already it was getting dark and there were fireflies, tiny yellow-hot sparks in the air. When their father had entirely disappeared into the trees, they turned around and stared at the babysitter instead. She raised one eyebrow. "Well," she said. "What sort of games do you like to play?"

> *Widdershins around the chimneys,*
> *Once, twice, again.*
> *The spokes click like a clock on the bicycle;*
> *They tick down the days of the life of a man.*

First they played Go Fish, and then they played Crazy Eights, and then they made the babysitter into a mummy by putting shaving cream from their father's bathroom on her arms and legs, and wrapping her in toilet paper. She is the best babysitter they have ever had.

At nine-thirty, she tried to put them to bed. Neither Claire nor Samantha wanted to go to bed, so they began to play the Dead game. The Dead game is a let's pretend that they have been playing every day for 274 days now, but never in front of their father or any other adult. When they are Dead, they are allowed to do anything they want to. They can even fly by jumping off the nursery bed, and just waving their arms. Someday this will work, if they practice hard enough.

The Dead game has three rules.

One. Numbers are significant. The twins keep a list of important numbers in a green address book that belonged to their mother. Mr.

Coeslak's tour has been a good source of significant amounts and tallies: they are writing a tragical history of numbers.

Two. The twins don't play the Dead game in front of grownups. They have been summing up the babysitter, and have decided that she doesn't count. They tell her the rules.

Three is the best and most important rule. When you are Dead, you don't have to be afraid of anything. Samantha and Claire aren't sure who the Specialist is, but they aren't afraid of him.

To become Dead, they hold their breath while counting to thirty-five, which is as high as their mother got, not counting a few days.

"You never lived here," Claire says. "Mr. Coeslak lives here."

"Not at night," says the babysitter. "This was my bedroom when I was little."

"Really?" Samantha says. Claire says, "Prove it."

The babysitter gives Samantha and Claire a look, as if she is measuring them: how old, how smart, how brave, how tall. Then she nods. The wind is in the flue, and in the dim nursery light they can see the milky strands of fog seeping out of the fireplace. "Go stand in the chimney," she instructs them. "Stick your hand as far up as you can, and there is a little hole on the left side, with a key in it."

Samantha looks at Claire, who says, "Go ahead." Claire is fifteen minutes and some few uncounted seconds older than Samantha, and therefore gets to tell Samantha what to do. Samantha remembers the muttering voices and then reminds herself that she is Dead. She goes over to the fireplace and ducks inside.

When Samantha stands up in the chimney, she can only see the very edge of the room. She can see the fringe of the mothy blue rug, and one bed leg, and beside it, Claire's foot, swinging back and forth like a metronome. Claire's shoelace has come undone and there is a Band-Aid on her ankle. It all looks very pleasant and peaceful from inside the chimney, like a dream, and for a moment she almost wishes she didn't have to be Dead. But it's safer, really.

She sticks her left hand up as far as she can reach, trailing it along the crumbly wall, until she feels an indentation. She thinks about spiders and severed fingers, and rusty razorblades, and then she reaches inside. She keeps her eyes lowered, focused on the corner of the room and Claire's twitchy foot.

Inside the hole, there is a tiny cold key, its teeth facing outward. She pulls it out, and ducks back into the room. "She wasn't lying," she tells Claire.

"Of course I wasn't lying," the babysitter says. "When you're Dead, you're not allowed to tell lies."

"Unless you want to," Claire says.

> *Dreary and dreadful beats the sea at the shore.*
> *Ghastly and dripping is the mist at the door.*
> *The clock in the hall is chiming one, two, three, four.*
> *The morning comes not, no, never, no more.*

Samantha and Claire have gone to camp for three weeks every summer since they were seven. This year their father didn't ask them if they wanted to go back and, after discussing it, they decided that it was just as well. They didn't want to have to explain to all their friends how they were half-orphans now. They are used to being envied, because they are identical twins. They don't want to be pitiful.

It has not even been a year, but Samantha realizes that she is forgetting what her mother looked like. Not her mother's face so much as the way she smelled, which was something like dry hay and something like Chanel No. 5, and like something else too. She can't remember whether her mother had gray eyes, like her, or grey eyes, like Claire. She doesn't dream about her mother anymore, but she does dream about Prince Charming, a bay whom she once rode in the horse show at her camp. In the dream, Prince Charming did not smell like a horse at all. He smelled like Chanel No. 5. When she is Dead, she can have all the horses she wants, and they all smell like Chanel No. 5.

"Where does the key go to?" Samantha says.

The babysitter holds out her hand. "To the attic. You don't really need it, but taking the stairs is easier than the chimney. At least the first time."

"Aren't you going to make us go to bed?" Claire says.

The babysitter ignores Claire. "My father used to lock me in the attic when I was little, but I didn't mind. There was a bicycle up there and I used to ride it around and around the chimneys until my mother let me out again. Do you know how to ride a bicycle?"

"Of course," Claire says.

"If you ride fast enough, the Specialist can't catch you."

"What's the Specialist?" Samantha says. Bicycles are okay, but horses can go faster.

"The Specialist wears a hat," says the babysitter. "The hat makes noises."

She doesn't say anything else.

> When you're dead, the grass is greener
> Over your grave. The wind is keener.
> Your eyes sink in, your flesh decays. You
> Grow accustomed to slowness; expect delays.

The attic is somehow bigger and lonelier than Samantha and Claire thought it would be. The babysitter's key opens the locked door at the end of the hallway, revealing a narrow set of stairs. She waves them ahead and upwards.

It isn't as dark in the attic as they had imagined. The oaks that block the light and make the first three stories so dim and green and mysterious during the day, don't reach all the way up. Extravagant moonlight, dusty and pale, streams in the angled dormer windows. It lights the length of the attic, which is wide enough to hold a softball game in, and lined with trunks where Samantha imagines people could sit, could be hiding and watching. The ceiling slopes down, impaled upon the eight thickwaisted chimney stacks. The chimneys seem too alive, somehow, to be contained in this empty, neglected place; they thrust almost angrily through the roof and attic floor. In the moonlight they look like they are breathing. "They're so beautiful," she says.

"Which chimney is the nursery chimney?" Claire says.

The babysitter points to the nearest righthand stack. "That one," she says. "It runs up through the ballroom on the first floor, the library, the nursery."

Hanging from a nail on the nursery chimney is a long black object. It looks lumpy and heavy, as if it were full of things. The babysitter takes it down, twirls it on her finger. There are holes in the black thing and it whistles mournfully as she spins it. "The Specialist's hat," she says.

"That doesn't look like a hat," says Claire. "It doesn't look like anything at all." She goes to look through the boxes and trunks that are stacked against the far wall.

"It's a special hat," the babysitter says. "It's not supposed to look like anything. But it can sound like anything you can imagine. My father made it."

"Our father writes books," Samantha says.

"My father did too." The babysitter hangs the hat back on the nail. It curls blackly against the chimney. Samantha stares at it. It nickers at her. "He was a bad poet, but he was worse at magic."

Last summer, Samantha wished more than anything that she could have a horse. She thought she would have given up anything for one—even being a twin was not as good as having a horse. She still doesn't have a horse, but she doesn't have a mother either, and she can't help wondering if it's her fault. The hat nickers again, or maybe it is the wind in the chimney.

"What happened to him?" Claire asks.

"After he made the hat, the Specialist came and took him away. I hid in the nursery chimney while it was looking for him, and it didn't find me."

"Weren't you scared?"

There is a clattering, shivering, clicking noise. Claire has found the babysitter's bike and is dragging it towards them by the handlebars. The babysitter shrugs. "Rule number three," she says.

Claire snatches the hat off the nail. "I'm the Specialist!" she says, putting the hat on her head. It falls over her eyes, the floppy shapeless brim sewn with little asymmetrical buttons that flash and catch at the moonlight like teeth. Samantha looks again and sees that they are teeth. Without counting, she suddenly knows that there are exactly fifty-two teeth on the hat, and that they are the teeth of agoutis, of curassows, of white-lipped peccaries, and of the wife of Charles Cheatham Rash. The chimneys are moaning, and Claire's voice booms hollowly beneath the hat. "Run away, or I'll catch you. I'll eat you!"

Samantha and the babysitter run away, laughing as Claire mounts the rusty, noisy bicycle and pedals madly after them. She rings the bicycle bell as she rides, and the Specialist's hat bobs up and down on her head. It spits like a cat. The bell is shrill and thin, and the bike wails and shrieks. It leans first towards the right and then to the left. Claire's knobby knees stick out on either side like makeshift counterweights.

Claire weaves in and out between the chimneys, chasing Samantha and the babysitter. Samantha is slow, turning to look behind. As Claire approaches, she keeps one hand on the handlebars and stretches the other hand out towards Samantha. Just as she is about to grab Samantha, the babysitter turns back and plucks the hat off Claire's head.

"Shit!" the babysitter says, and drops it. There is a drop of blood forming on the fleshy part of the babysitter's hand, black in the moonlight, where the Specialist's hat has bitten her.

Claire dismounts, giggling. Samantha watches as the Specialist's hat rolls away. It picks up speed, veering across the attic floor, and disappears, thumping down the stairs. "Go get it," Claire says. "You can be the Specialist this time."

"No," the babysitter says, sucking at her palm. "It's time for bed."

When they go down the stairs, there is no sign of the Specialist's hat. They brush their teeth, climb into the ship-bed, and pull the covers up to their necks. The babysitter sits between their feet. "When you're Dead," Samantha says, "do you still get tired and have to go to sleep? Do you have dreams?"

"When you're Dead," the babysitter says, "everything's a lot easier. You don't have to do anything that you don't want to. You don't have to have a name, you don't have to remember. You don't even have to breathe."

She shows them exactly what she means.

When she has time to think about it, (and now she has all the time in the world to think) Samantha realizes with a small pang that she is now stuck indefinitely between ten and eleven years old, stuck with Claire and the babysitter. She considers this. The number 10 is pleasing and round, like a beach ball, but all in all, it hasn't been an easy year. She wonders what 11 would have been like. Sharper, like needles maybe. She has chosen to be Dead, instead. She hopes that she's made the right decision. She wonders if her mother would have decided to be Dead, instead of dead, if she could have.

Last year they were learning fractions in school, when her mother died. Fractions remind Samantha of herds of wild horses, piebalds and pintos and palominos. There are so many of them, and they are, well, fractious and unruly. Just when you think you have one under control, it throws up its head and tosses you off. Claire's favorite number is 4, which she says is a tall, skinny boy. Samantha doesn't care for boys that much. She likes numbers. Take the number 8 for instance, which can be more than one thing at once. Looked at one way, 8 looks like a bent woman with curvy hair. But if you lay it down on its side, it looks like a snake curled with its tail in its mouth. This is sort of like the difference between being Dead, and being dead. Maybe when Samantha is tired of one, she will try the other.

On the lawn, under the oak trees, she hears someone calling her name. Samantha climbs out of bed and goes to the nursery window. She looks out through the wavy glass. It's Mr. Coeslak. "Samantha, Claire!" he calls up to her. "Are you all right? Is your father there?" Samantha can almost see the moonlight shining through him. "They're always locking me in the tool room. Goddamn spooky things," he says. "Are you there, Samantha? Claire? Girls?"

The babysitter comes and stands beside Samantha. The babysitter puts her finger to her lip. Claire's eyes glitter at them from the dark bed. Samantha doesn't say anything, but she waves at Mr. Coeslak. The babysitter waves too. Maybe he can see them waving, because after a little while he stops shouting and goes away. "Be careful," the babysitter says. "*He'll* be coming soon. It will be coming soon."

She takes Samantha's hand, and leads her back to the bed, where Claire is waiting. They sit and wait. Time passes, but they don't get tired, they don't get any older.

Who's there?
Just air.

The front door opens on the first floor, and Samantha, Claire, and the babysitter can hear someone creeping, creeping up the stairs. "Be quiet," the babysitter says. "It's the Specialist."

Samantha and Claire are quiet. The nursery is dark and the wind crackles like a fire in the fireplace.

"Claire, Samantha, Samantha, Claire?" The Specialist's voice is blurry and wet. It sounds like their father's voice, but that's because the hat can imitate any noise, any voice. "Are you still awake?"

"Quick," the babysitter says. "It's time to go up to the attic and hide."

Claire and Samantha slip out from under the covers and dress quickly and silently. They follow her. Without speech, without breathing, she pulls them into the safety of the chimney. It is too dark to see, but they understand the babysitter perfectly when she mouths the word, *Up*. She goes first, so they can see where the finger-holds are, the bricks that jut out for their feet. Then Claire. Samantha watches her sister's foot ascend like smoke, the shoelace still untied.

"Claire? Samantha? Goddammit, you're scaring me. Where are you?" The Specialist is standing just outside the half-open door. "Samantha? I think I've been bitten by something. I think I've been bitten by a goddamn snake." Samantha hesitates for only a second. Then she is climbing up, up, up the nursery chimney.

FLYING LESSONS

I. Going to hell. Instructions and advice.

Listen, because I'm only going to do this once. You'll have to get there by way of London. Take the overnight train from Waverly. Sit in the last car. Speak to no one. Don't fall asleep.

When you arrive at Kings Cross, go down into the Underground. Get on the Northern line. Sit in the last car. Speak to no one. Don't fall asleep.

The Northern line stops at Angel, at London Bridge, at Elephant and Castle, Tooting Broadway. The last marked station is Morden: stay in your seat. Other passengers will remain with you in the car. Speak to no one.

These are some of the unlisted stations you will pass: Howling Green. Duke's Pit. Sparrowkill. Stay in your seat. Don't fall asleep. If you look around the car, you may notice that the other passengers have started to glow. The bulbs on the car dim as the passengers give off more and more light. If you look down you may find that you yourself are casting light into the dark car.

The final stop is Bonehouse.

2. June in Edinburgh in June.

June stole £7 from Rooms Two and Three. That would be trainfare, with some left over for a birthday present for Lily. Room Three was American again, and Americans never knew how much currency they had in the first place. They left pound coins lying upon the dresser. It made her fingers itchy.

She ticked off the morning jobs on her right hand. The washroom at the end of the hall was clean. Beds were made up, and all the ashtrays were cleared out. Rooms One through Four were done, and Room Five at the top of the house was honeymooners from Dallas. They hadn't been at breakfast for three days, living on love, she supposed. Why travel from Dallas to Edinburgh merely to have sex? She imagined a great host of Texans, rising on white wings and fanning out across the Atlantic, buoyed up by love. Falling into bed at journey's end, exhausted by such travel. Nonsense.

She emptied the wastebasket in Room Three, and went thumping down the stairs with the cleaning box in one hand, and the room keys swinging in the other. "Here, ma," she said, handing the keys and the box over to Lily.

"Right," Lily said sourly. "Finished up, have you?" Her face was flushed, and her black hair snaked down the back of her neck. Walter was in the kitchen, his elbows plunged into soapy water, singing along with Radio Three as he worked, an opera program.

"Where are you off to?" Lily said, raising her voice.

June ducked past her. "Dunno exactly," she said. "I'll be back in time for tea tomorrow. Goodbye, Walter!" she shouted. "Bake Lily a lovely cake."

3. *Arrows of Beauty*.

June went to St. Andrews. She thought it would be pleasant to spend a day by the sea. The train was full and she sat next to a fat, freckled woman eating sandwiches, one after the other. June watched her mouth open and close, measuring out the swish and click of the train on the tracks like a metronome.

When the sandwiches were gone, the woman took out a hardcover book. There was a man and a woman on the cover, embracing, his face turned into her shoulder, her hair falling across her face. As if they were ashamed to be caught like this, half-naked before the eyes of strangers. Lily liked that sort of book.

The name of the author was Rose Read. It sounded like a conjuring name, an ingredient in a love spell, a made-up, let's pretend name. Leaning over the woman's speckled-egg arm, June looked at the photo on the back. Mile-long curlicued eyelashes, and a plump, secretive smile. Probably the author's real name was Agnes Frumple; probably those eyelashes weren't real, either. The woman saw June staring. "It's called *Arrows of Beauty*. Quite good," she said. "All about Helen of Troy, and it's very well researched."

"Really," June said. She spent the next half an hour looking across the aisle, out of the opposite window. There were several Americans on the train, dressed in tourist plaids, their voices flat and bright and bored. June wondered if her honeymooners would come to this someday, traveling not out of love but boredom, shifting restlessly in their narrow seats. *Are we there yet? Where are we?*

Shortly before the train pulled into Leuchars station, the woman fell asleep. *Arrows of Beauty* dropped from her slack fingers, and slid down the incline of her lap. June caught it before it hit the floor. She got onto the station platform, the book tucked under her arm.

4. Fine Scents.

The wind tipped and rattled at the tin sides of the St. Andrews bus. It whipped at June's hair, until she scraped the loose tendrils back to her scalp with a barrette. The golf course came into view, the clipped lawns like squares of green velvet. Behind the golf course was the North Sea, and somewhere over the sea, June supposed, was Norway or Finland. She'd never even been to England. It might be nice to travel: she pictured her mother waving goodbye with a white handkerchief, *so long, kid! Just like her father, you know.* Goodbye, good riddance.

St. Andrews was three streets wide, marching down to the curved mouth of the harbor. A sea wall ran along the cliffs at the edge of the town, from the broken-backed cathedral to a castle, hollowed out like an old tooth, and green in the middle. Castle and cathedral leaned towards each other, pinching the sea between them.

June got off the bus on Market Street. She bought a box of Black Magic chocolates in the Woolworth's and then went down an alley cobbled with old stones from the cathedral, worn down to glassy smoothness. Iron railings ran along storefronts, the rails snapped off near the base, and she remembered a school chaperone saying it had been done for the war effort. Taken to be made into cannons and shrapnel and belt buckles, just as the town had harvested stone from the cathedral. Ancient history, scrapped and put to economical uses.

An old-fashioned sign swinging above an open shop door caught her eye. It read "Fine Scents. I.M. Kew, Prop." Through the window she could see a man behind the counter, smiling anxiously at a well-dressed woman. She was saying something to him that June couldn't make out, but it was her velvety-rough voice that pulled June into the store.

". . . don't know if the rest of the aunties can keep her off him. It's her hobby, you know, pulling wings off flies. You know how fond of him Minnie and I are, but Di and Prune are absolutely no help, she'll do the poor boy just like his mother . . ."

The marvelous voice trailed off, and the woman lifted a stopper out of a bottle. "Really, darling, I don't like it. Sweet and wet as two virgins kissing. It's not up to your usual standards."

The man shrugged, still smiling. His fingers drummed on the counter. "I thought you might like a change, is all," he said. "So my Rose-By-Any-Other-Name, I'll make you up a standard batch. May I help you, dearie?"

"I was just looking," June said.

"We don't have anything here for your sort," he said, not unkindly. "All custom scents, see."

"Oh." She looked at the woman, who was examining her makeup, her long smudgy eyelashes, in a compact. Rhinestones on the compact lid spelled out RR, and June remembered where she had seen the woman's face. "Excuse me, but don't you write books?"

The compact snapped shut in the white hand. A wing of yellow, helmeted hair swung forward as the woman turned to June. "Yes," she said, pink pointed tongue slipping between the small teeth. "Are you the sort that buys my books?"

No, June thought. I'm the sort that steals them. She delved into her sack. "This is for my mother," she said. "Would you sign it for her?"

"How lovely," Rose Read said. She signed the book with a fountain pen proffered by the man behind the counter, in a child's careful looped cursive. "There. Have you got a lover, my dear?"

"That's none of your business," June said, grabbing the book back.

"Is it my business, Mr. Kew?" Rose Read said to the shopkeeper. He snickered. She had said his name the way two spies meeting at a party might use made-up names.

"She doesn't have a lover," he said. "I'd smell him on her if she did."

June took a step back, then another, hesitating. The man and woman stared at her blandly. She found the store and the pair of them unnerving. She wanted to flee the store, to get away from them. She wanted to take something from them, to steal something. At that moment, a large family, noisy, redheaded, mother and father, how extravagant! June thought, poured into the shop. They pressed up to the counter, shaking a battered copy of *Fodors* at Mr. Kew, all speaking at once. June pocketed the unwanted perfume and quickly left the store.

5. Going to hell. Instructions and advice.

It is late morning when you arrive at Bonehouse, but the sky is dark. As you walk, you must push aside the air, like heavy cloth. Your foot stumbles on the mute ground.

You are in a flat place where the sky presses down, and the buildings creep close along the streets, and all the doors stand open. Grass grows on the roofs of the houses; the roofs are packed sod, and the grass raises up tall like hair on a scalp. Follow the others. They are dead and know the way better than you. Speak to no one.

At last you will arrive at a door in an alley, with a dog asleep on the threshold. He has many heads and each head has many teeth, and his teeth are sharp and eager as knives.

6. What was in the bottle.

June sat happy and quiet in the grassy bowl of the castle. Students in their red gowns and tourists in various plaids clambered over the worn and tumbled steps that went over the drawbridge between the squat towers. Outside the castle wall, there were more steps winding down to the rocky beach. She could hear people complaining loudly as they came back up, the wind pushing them backwards. Inside the wall the air was still, the sky arched like a glass lid, shot through with light.

Ravens sleek and round as kettles patrolled the grass. They lifted in lazy circles when the tourists came too close, settling down near June, hissing and croaking. She took the perfume out of her knapsack and turned it in her hands. The bottle was tall and slim and plainly made. The stopper was carved out of a rosy stone and where it plunged into the mouth of the decanter the glass was faceted like the rhinestones on Rose Read's compact. June took out the stopper.

She touched it to her wrist, then held her wrist up to her nose and sniffed. It smelled sweet and greeny-ripe as an apple. It made her head spin. She closed her eyes, and when she opened them again there was someone watching her.

Up in the tilted crown of the lefthand tower, Mr. Kew, Prop. was looking straight down at her. He smiled and winked one eye shut. He cocked his index finger, sighted, and squeezed his fist closed. *Pow*, he said silently, pulling his lips tight in exaggeration around the word. Then he turned to make his way down the stairs.

June jumped up. If she went out over the drawbridge they would meet at the foot of the stairs. She grabbed up her pack and went in the opposite direction. She stopped at the wall and looked over. A cement bulwark, about five feet below, girdled up the cliffs that the castle sat on; she tossed the pack over and followed it, heels first, holding hard to the crumbling wall.

7. She hears a story about birds.

Down on June's right was the beach, invisible past the curve of the castle's bulk, cliffs and marshy land to her left. Waves slapped against the concrete barriers below her. She sat on the ledge, wondering how long she would have to wait before climbing back up to the castle or down to the beach. The wind cut straight through her jersey.

She turned her head, and saw there was a man standing next to her. Her heart slammed into her chest before she saw that it was a boy her own age, seventeen or eighteen, with a white face and blue eyes. His eyebrows met, knitted together above the bridge of his nose.

"Before you climbed down," he said, "did you happen to notice if there were a lot of birds up there?"

"You mean girls?" June said, sneering at him. His eyes were very blue.

"No, birds. You know, with wings." He flapped his arms.

"Ravens," June said. "And maybe some smaller ones, like sparrows."

He sat down beside her, folding his arms around his knees. "Damn," he said. "I thought maybe if I waited for a while, they might get bored and leave. They have a very short attention span."

"You're hiding from birds?"

"I have a phobia," he said, and turned bright red. "Like claustrophobia, you know."

"That's unfortunate," June said. "I mean, birds are everywhere."

"It's not all birds," he said. "Or it's not all the time. Sometimes they bother me, sometimes they don't. They look at me funny."

"I'm afraid of mice," June said. "Once when I was little I put my foot into a shoe and there was a dead mouse inside. I still shake out my shoes before I put them on."

"When I was five, my mother was killed by a flock of peacocks." he said, as if it had happened to someone else's mother, and he had read about it in a newspaper.

"What?" June said.

He sounded embarrassed. "Okay. Um, my mother took me to see the castle at Inverness. She said that my father was a king who lived in a castle. She was always making stories up like that. I don't remember the castle very well, but afterwards we went for a walk in the garden. There was a flock of peacocks and they were stalking us. They were so big—they seemed really big—as big as I was. My mother stuck me in a cherry tree and told me to yell for help as loudly as I could."

He took a deep breath. "The tailfeathers sounded like silk dresses brushing against the ground. I remember that. They sounded like women in long silk dresses. I didn't make a sound. If I made a sound, they might notice me. They crowded my mother up against the curb of a stone fountain, and she was pushing at them with her hands, shooing them, and then she just fell backwards. The fountain only had two inches of water in it. I heard her head crack against the bottom when she fell. It knocked her unconscious and she drowned before anyone came."

His face was serious and beseeching. She could see the small flutter of pulse against the white flesh—thin as paper—of his jaw.

"That's horrible," June said. "Who took care of you?"

"My mother and father weren't married," he said. "He already had a wife. My mother didn't have any family, so my father gave me to his sisters. Aunt Minnie, Aunt Prune, Aunt Di, and Aunt Rose."

"My father emigrated to Australia when I was two," June said. "I don't remember him much. My mother remarried about a year ago."

"I've never seen my father," the boy said. "Aunt Rose says it would be too dangerous. His wife, Vera, hates me even though she's never seen me, because I'm her husband's bastard. She's a little insane."

"What's your name?"

"Humphrey Bogart Stoneking," he said. "My mother was a big fan. What's your name?"

"June," said June.

They were silent for a moment. June rubbed her hands together for comfort. "Are you cold?" asked Humphrey. She nodded and he moved closer and put his arm around her.

"You smell nice," he said after a moment. He sniffed thoughtfully. "Familiar, sort of."

"Yeah?" She turned her head and their mouths bumped together, soft and cold.

8. Rose Read on young lovers.

It's all the fault of that damned perfume, and that mooning, meddling, milky-faced perfumer. He could have had it back and no harm done, if he didn't love mischief more than his mother. So it might have been my idea—it might have been an accident. Or maybe it was Fate. If I'm still around, so is that tired old hag. Do you think that I have the time to see to every love affair in the world personally?

Those hesitating kisses, the tender fumbles and stumbles and awkward meetings of body parts give me indigestion. Heartburn. Give me two knowledgeable parties who know what is up and what fits where; give me Helen of Troy, fornicating her way across the ancient world, Achilles and Patroclos amusing themselves in a sweaty tent.

A swan, a bull, a shower of gold, something new, something old, something borrowed, something blue. He seduced Sarah Stoneking in an empty movie house, stepped right off of the screen during the matinee and lisped "Shweetheart" at her. She fell into the old goat's arms. I know, I was there.

9. In which a discovery is made.

The sky stayed clear and pale all night long. When they were cold again, they wrapped themselves in Humphrey's coat, and leaned back against the wall. June took out the box of chocolates and ate them as Humphrey explored her pack. He pulled out the perfume. "Where'd you get this?"

"I nicked it from a perfume shop off Market Street."

"I should have known." He pulled out the book. "Aunt Rose," he said.

"She's your aunt?" June said. "I guess I should give it to you to give back."

He shook his head. "If she didn't mean for you to have it, you wouldn't even have thought of taking it. Might as well keep it now. She probably set this whole thing up."

"How?" June said. "Is she psychic or something?"

"This must be how they're planning to stop me," Humphrey said. "They think if I have a girlfriend, I'll give up on the flying lessons, take up fucking as a new hobby."

"Right." June said, affronted. "It was nice to meet you too. I don't usually go around doing this."

"Wait," he said, catching at her pack as she stood up. "I didn't mean it that way. You're right. This is a complete coincidence. And I didn't think that you did."

He smiled up at her. June sat back down, mollified, stretching her legs out in front of her. "Why are you taking flying lessons?"

"I've been saving up for it," he said. "I went to see a psychologist about a year ago, and he suggested that flying lessons might make me less afraid of birds. Besides, I've always wanted to. I used to dream about it. The aunts say it's a bad idea, but they're just superstitious. I have my first lesson tomorrow. Today, actually."

"I think flying would be wonderful," June said. She was shivering. It was because she was cold. It wasn't because she was cold. She slipped her hands up inside his shirt. "But I know something just as nice."

"What?" he said. So she showed him. His mouth was so sweet.

10. Going to hell. Instructions and advice.

As the others step over the dog he doesn't wake. If you step over him, he will smell live flesh and he will tear you to pieces.

Take this perfume with you and when you come to Bonehouse, dab it behind your ears, at your wrists and elbows, at the back of your knees. Stroke it into the vee of your sex, as you would for a lover. The scent is heavy and rich, like the first cold handful of dirt tossed into the dug grave. It will trick the dog's nose.

Inside the door, there is no light but the foxfire glow of your own body. The dead flicker like candles around you. They are burning their memories for warmth. They may brush up against you, drawn to what is stronger and hotter and brighter in you. Don't speak to them.

There are no walls, no roof above you except darkness. There are no doors, only the luminous windows that the dead have become. Unravel the left arm of his sweater and let it fall to the ground.

11. In the All-Night Bakery at dawn.

June and Humphrey went around the corner of the bulwark, down over an outcropping of rocks, slick with gray light, down to the beach. A seagull, perched like a lantern upon the castle wall, watched them go.

They walked down Market Street, the heavy, wet air clinging like ghosts to their hair and skin. The sound of their feet, hollow and sharp, rang like bells on the cobblestones. They came to the All-Night Bakery and June could hear someone singing inside.

Behind the counter there were long rows of white ovens and cooling racks, as tall as June. A woman stood with her strong back to them, sliding trays stacked with half-moon loaves into an oven, like a mother tucking her children into warm sheets.

She was singing to herself, low and deep, and as June watched and listened, the fat loaves, the ovens, the woman and her lullaby threw out light, warmth. The ovens, the loaves, the woman grew brighter and larger and crowded the bakery and June's senses so that she began to doubt there was room for herself, for the houses and street, the dawn outside to exist. The woman shut the oven door, and June was afraid that presently she would turn around and show June her face, flickering pale and enormous as the moon.

She stumbled back outside. Humphrey followed her, his pockets stuffed with doughnuts and meat pies.

"My Aunt Di," he said. He handed June a pastry. "Some nights I work here with her."

He went with her to the station, and wrapped up two greasy bacon pies and gave them to her. She wrote her address and telephone on a corner of the napkin, and then reached into her pocket. She took out the crumpled banknotes, the small, heavy coins. "Here," she said. "For your flying lesson."

She dumped them into his cupped hands, and then before she could decide if the blush on his face was one of pleasure or embarrassment, the train was coming into the station. She got on and didn't look back.

She slept on the train and dreamed about birds.

Home again, and Lily and Walter were finishing the breakfast cleanup. June handed the book and the perfume to her mother. "Happy birthday, Lily."

"Where were you last night?" Lily said. She held the perfume bottle between her thumb and middle finger as if it were a dead rat.

"With a friend," June said vaguely, and pretended not to see Lily's frown. She went up the stairs to the top of the house, to her room in the attic. The honeymooner's door was shut, but she could hear them as she went past in the hall. It sounded just like pigeons, soft little noises and gasps. She slammed her door shut and went straight to sleep. What did she dream about? More birds? When she woke up, she couldn't remember, but her hands hurt as if she had been holding on to something.

When she came down again—hands and face washed, hair

combed back neat—the cake that Walter had made, square and plain, with a dozen pink candles spelling out Lily's name, was on the table. Lily was looking at it as if it might explode. June said, "How do you like the perfume?"

"I don't," Lily said. She clattered the knives and forks down. "It smells cheap and too sweet. Not subtle at all."

Walter came up behind Lily and squeezed her around the middle. She pushed at him, but not hard. "I quite liked it," he said. "Your mother's been sitting with her feet up in the parlor all day, reading the rubbishy romance you got her. Very subtle, that."

"Rubbish is right," Lily said. She blew out the candles with one efficient breath, a tiny smile on her face.

12. The occupant in Room Five.

Two days later the honeymooners left. When June went into the room, she could smell sex, reeky and insistent. She flung open the windows and stripped the ravaged bed, but the smell lingered in the walls and in the carpet.

In the afternoon, a woman dressed in expensive dark clothing came looking for a room. "It would be for some time," the woman said. She spoke very carefully, as if she was used to being misunderstood. June, sitting in the parlor, idly leafing through sex advice columns in American magazines left behind by the honeymooners, looked up for a second. She thought the woman in black had an antique look about her, precise and hard, like a face on a cameo.

"We do have a room," said Lily. "But I don't know that you'll want it. We try to be nice here, but you look like you might be accustomed to better."

The woman sighed. "I am getting a divorce from my husband," she said. "He has been unfaithful. I don't want him to find me, so I will stay here where he would not think to look. You were recommended to me."

"Really?" said Lily, looking pleased. "By who?"

But the woman couldn't remember. She signed her name, Mrs. Vera Ambrosia, in a thick slant of ink, and produced £40, and another £40 as a deposit. When June showed her up to Room Five, her nostrils flared, but she said nothing. She had with her one small suitcase, and a covered box. Out of the box she took a birdcage on a collapsible stand. There was nothing in the birdcage but dust.

When June left, she was standing at the window looking out. She was smiling at something.

13. A game of golf.

June tried not to think about Humphrey. It was a silly name anyway. She went out with her friends and she never mentioned his name. They would have laughed at his name. It was probably made up.

She thought of describing how his eyebrows met, in a straight bar across his face. She decided that it should repulse her. It did. And he was a liar too. Not even a good liar.

All the same, she rented old movies, *Key Largo* and *Casablanca*, and watched them with Walter and Lily. And sometimes she wondered if he had been telling the truth. Her period came and so she didn't have to worry about that; she worried anyway, and she began to notice the way that birds watched from telephone lines as she walked past them. She counted them, trying to remember how they added up for joy, how for sorrow.

She asked Walter who said, "Sweetheart, for you they mean joy. You're a good girl and you deserve to be happy." He was touching up the red trim around the front door. June sat hunched on the step beside him, swirling the paint around in the canister.

"Didn't my mother deserve to be happy?" she said sharply.

"Well, she's got me, hasn't she?" Walter said, his eyebrows shooting up. He pretended to be wounded. "Oh, I see. Sweetheart, you've got to be patient. Plenty of time to fall in love when you're a bit older."

"She was my age when she had me!" June said. "And where were you then? And where is *he* now?" She got up awkwardly and ran inside, past a pair of startled guests, past Lily who stood in the narrow hall and watched her pass, no expression at all on her mother's face.

That night June had a dream. She stood in her nightgown, an old one that had belonged to her mother, her bare feet resting on cold silky grass. The wind went through the holes in the flannel, curled around her body and fluttered the hem of the nightgown. She tasted salt in her mouth, and saw the white moth-eaten glow of the waves below her, stitching water to the shore. The moon was sharp and thin as if someone had eaten the juicy bit and left the rind.

"Fore!" someone called. She realized she was standing barefoot and nearly naked on the St. Andrews golf course. "Why hello, little thief," someone said.

June pinched herself, and it hurt just a little, and she didn't wake up. Rose Read still stood in front of her, dressed all in white: white cashmere sweater; white wool trousers; spotless white leather shoes and gloves. "You look positively frost-bitten, darling child," Rose Read said.

She leaned towards June and pressed her soft, warm mouth against June's mouth. June opened her mouth to protest, and Rose Read breathed down her throat. It was delicious, like drinking fire. She felt Rose Read's kiss rushing out towards her ten fingers, her icy feet, pooling somewhere down below her stomach. She felt like a June-shaped bowl brimming over with warmth and radiance.

Rose Read removed her mouth. "There," she said.

"I want to kiss her too," said a querulous voice. "It's my turn, Rosy."

There were two other women standing on the green. The one who had spoken was tall and gaunt and brittle as sticks, her dark, staring eyes fixing June like two straight pins.

"June, you remember Di, don't you, Humphrey's other aunt?" Rose said.

"She was different," June said, remembering the giantess in the bakery, whose voice had reflected off the walls like light.

"Want a kiss," Humphrey's aunt Di said again.

"Don't mind her," Rose Read said. "It's that time of the month. Humphrey's minding the bakery: it helps her to be outside. Let her kiss your cheek, she won't hurt you."

June closed her eyes, lightly brushed her cheek against the old woman's lips. It was like being kissed by a faint and hungry ghost. Humphrey's aunt stepped back sighing.

"That's a good girl," Rose said. "And this is another aunt, Minnie. Minnie Mousy. You don't have to kiss her, she's not much for the things of the flesh, is Mousy Minnie."

"Hello, June," the woman said, inclining her head. She looked like the headmistress of June's comprehensive—so old that Lily had once been her student—who had called June into her office two years ago, when June's O-level results had come back.

It's a pity, the headmistress had said, *because you seem to have a brain in your head. But if you are determined to make yourself into nothing at all, then I can't stop you. Your mother was the same sort, smart enough but willful—oh yes, I remember her quite well. It was a pity. It's always a pity.*

"I'm dreaming," June said.

"It would be a mistake to believe that," said Rose Read. "An utter failure of the imagination. In any case, while you're here, you might as well solve a little argument for us. As you can see, here are two golf balls sitting nice and pretty on the green at your feet. And here is the third"—she pointed at the cup—"only we can't agree which of us it was that put it there."

The moon went behind a wisp of cloud, but the two golf balls still shone like two white stones. Light spilled out of the cup and beaded on the short blades of grayish grass. "How do I know whose ball that is?" June said. "I didn't see anything, I wasn't here until now—I mean—"

Rose Read cut her off. "It doesn't really matter whose ball it is, little thief, just whose ball you *say* it is."

"But I don't know!" June protested.

"You people are always so greedy," Rose Read said. "Very well: say it belongs to Minnie, she'll can pull a few strings, get you into the university of your choice; Di, well, you saw how much she likes you. Tell me what you want, June."

June took a deep breath. Suddenly she was afraid that she would wake up before she had a chance to answer. "I want Humphrey," she said.

"My game, ladies," Rose Read said, and the moon came out again.

June woke up. The moon was bright and small in the dormer window above her, and she could hear the pigeons' feet chiming against the leaded glass.

14. The view from the window.

Before Humphrey came to see June, the woman in Room Five had paid for her third week in advance, and June found the perfume she had given her mother in the rubbish bin. She took it up to her room, put a dab on her wrist.

He was sitting on the front steps when she swept the dust out of the door. "I lost your address," he said.

"Oh?" she said coolly, folding her arms the way Lily did.

"I did," he said. "But I found it again yesterday."

His eyebrows didn't repulse her as much as she had hoped they would. His sweater was blue like his eyes. "You're lying," she said.

"Yes," he said. "I didn't come to see you because I thought maybe Aunt Rose tricked you into liking me. I thought maybe you wouldn't like me anymore. Do you?"

She looked at him. "Maybe," she said. "How was your flying lesson?"

"I've been up in the plane twice. It's a Piper Cub, just one engine and you can feel the whole sky rushing around you when you're up there. The last time we went up, Tiny—he's the instructor—let me take the controls. It was like nothing I've ever done before—that is," he said warily, "it was quite nice. You look lovely, June. Have you missed me too?"

"I suppose," she said.

"Aunt Di gave me the night off. Will you come for a walk with me?" he said.

They went for a walk. They went to the movies. He bought her popcorn. They came home again when the sky above the streetlights was plush and yellow as the fur of a tiger. "Would you like to come in?" she asked him.

"Yes, please." But they didn't go inside yet. They stood on the steps, smiling at each other. June heard a sound, a fluttering and cooing. She looked up and saw a flock of pigeons, crowding on the window ledge two stories above them. Two hands, white and pressed flat with the weight of many rings, lay nestled like doves among the pigeons. Humphrey cried out, crouching and raising his own hands to cover his head.

June pulled him into the cover of the door. She fumbled the key into the lock, and they stumbled inside. "It was just the woman in Room Five," she said. "She's a little strange about birds. She puts crumbs on the sill for them. She says they're her babies." She rubbed

Humphrey's back. The sweater felt good beneath her hands, furry and warm like a live animal.

"I'm okay now," he said. "I think the lessons are helping." He laughed, shuddering in a great breath. "I think you're helping."

They kissed and then she took him up the stairs to her room. As they passed the door of Room Five, they could hear the woman crooning and the pigeons answering back.

15. Rose Read on motherhood.

I never had a mother. I remember being born, the salt of that old god's dying upon my lips, the water bearing me up as I took my first steps. Minnie never had a mother either. Lacking example, we did the best we could with Humphrey. I like to think he grew up a credit to us both.

Prune runs Bonne Hause half the year, and we used to send Humphrey to her in the autumn. It wasn't the best place for a lively boy. He tried to be good, but he always ended up shattering the nerves of Prune's wispy convalescents, driving her alcoholics back to the drink, stealing the sweets her spa patients hoard. Raising the dead, in fact, and driving poor, anemic Prune into pale hysterics.

Di's never had much use for men, but she's fond of him in her own way.

We read to him a lot. Di's bakery came out of his favorite book, the one he read to pieces when he was little. All about the boy in the night kitchen, and the airplane . . . it was to be expected that he'd want to learn to fly. They always do. We moved around to keep him safe and far away from Vera, but you can't keep him away from the sky. If he comes to a bad end, then we kept his feet safely planted on the ground as long as we could.

We tried to teach him to take precautions. Minnie knitted him a beautiful blue sweater and he needn't be afraid of birds nor goddesses while he keeps that on. We did the best we could.

16. The Skater.

In the morning, it was raining. Humphrey helped June with her chores. Lily said nothing when she met him, only nodded and gave him a mop.

Walter said, "So you're the boy she's been pining after," and laughed when June made a face. They tidied the first four rooms on the second floor, and when June came out of the washroom with the wastebasket, she saw Humphrey standing in front of Room Five, his hand on the doorknob. Watery light from the window at the end of the hall fell sharply on his neck, his head bent towards the door.

"Stop," June hissed. He turned to her, his face white and strained. "She doesn't like us to come into her room, she does everything herself."

"I thought I could hear someone in there," Humphrey said. "They were saying something."

June shook her head violently. "She's gone. She goes to Charlotte Square every day, and sits and feeds the pigeons."

"But it's raining," Humphrey said.

She grabbed his hand. "Come on, let's go somewhere."

They went to the National Gallery on the Royal Mile. Inside everything was red and gold and marble, kings and queens on the walls frowning down from ornate frames at Humphrey and June, like people peering through windows. Their varied expressions were so lively, so ferocious and joyful and serene by turn, that June felt all the more wet and bedraggled. She felt like a thief sneaking into an abandoned house, only to discover the owners at home, awake, drinking and talking and dancing and laughing.

Humphrey tugged at her hand. They sat down on a bench in front of Raeburn's *The Reverend Robert Walker Skating on Duddiston Loch.* "This is my favorite painting," he said.

June looked at the Reverend Walker, all in black like a crow, floating above the gray ice, his cheeks rosy with the cold. "I know why you like it," she said. "He looks like he's flying."

"He looks like he's happy," Humphrey said. "Do you remember your father?"

"No," June said. "I suppose when I look in the mirror. I never knew him. But my mother says—how about you?"

Humphrey said, "I used to make up stories about him. Because of my name—I thought he was American, maybe even a gangster. I used to pretend that he was part of the Mafia, like Capone. Aunt Minnie says I'm not too far off."

"I know," June said. "Let's pick out fathers here. Can I have the Reverend Robert Walker? He looks like Walter. Who do you want?"

They walked through the gallery, June making suggestions, Humphrey vetoing prospective parents. "Definitely not. I do not want Sir Walter Scott," he said as June paused in front of a portrait. "An aunt who writes historical romances is enough. Besides, we look nothing alike."

June peered into the next room. "Well," she said. "You'll have to go without, then. All this gallery is old gloomy stuff. There's not one decent dad in the lot of them."

She turned around. Humphrey stood in front of an enormous painting of a woman and a swan. The swan arched, his wings spread over the supine woman, as large as the boy who stood in front of him.

"Oh," she said tentatively. "Do birds bother you in paintings too?"

He said "No," his eyes still fixed on the painting. "It's all rubbish, anyway. Let's go."

17. Bonne Hause.

The summer wore on and the nights were longer and darker. Humphrey came on the train from Leuchars every weekend, and at the beginning of August, they climbed to the top of Arthur's Seat for a picnic supper. Edinburgh was crouched far below them, heaped up like a giant's bones, the green cloak of grass his bed, the castle his crown.

Ravens stalked the hill, pecking at the grass, but Humphrey ignored them. "Next weekend Tiny says I can make my solo flight," he said. "If the weather's good."

"I wish I could see you," June said. "but Lily will kill me if I'm not here to help. Things get loopy right before the Festival." Already, the bed and breakfast was full. Lily had even put a couple from Strasburg into June's attic room. June was sleeping on a cot in the kitchen.

"S'all right," Humphrey said. "I'd probably be even more nervous with you there. I'll come on the eight o'clock train and meet you in Waverly Station. We'll celebrate. Go out and see something."

June nodded and shivered, leaning against him. He said, "Are you cold? Take my sweater. I've got something else for you, too." He pulled a flat oblong package from his pack and gave it to her along with the sweater.

"It's a book," June said. "Is it something by your aunt?" She tore off the paper, the wind snatching it from her hands. It was a children's book, with a picture on the cover of a man with flaming hair, a golden sun behind him. "*D'Aulaire's Greek Mythology?*"

He didn't look at her. "Read it and tell me what you think."

June flipped through it. "Well, at least it's got pictures," she said. It was getting too dark to look at the book properly. The city, the path leading back down the hill, were purpley-dark; the hill they sat on seemed to be about to float away on a black sea. The ravens were moveable blots of inky stain, and the wind lifted and beat with murmurous breath at blades of grass and pinion feathers. She pulled the blue sweater tight around her shoulders.

"What will we do at the end of the summer?" Humphrey asked. He picked up one of her hands, and looked into it, as if he might see the future in the cup of her palm. "Normally I go to Aunt Prune's for a few weeks. She runs a clinic outside of London called Bonne Hause. For alcoholics and depressed rich people. I help the groundskeepers."

"Oh," June said.

"I don't want to go," Humphrey said. "That's the thing. I want to be with you, maybe go to Greece. My father lives there, sometimes. I want to see him, just once I'd like to see him. Would you go with me?"

"Is that why you gave me this?" she said, frowning and holding up the book of mythology. "It's not exactly a guide book."

"More like family history," he said. The ravens muttered and cackled. "Have you ever dreamed you could fly, I mean with wings?"

"I've never even been in a plane," June said.

He told her something wonderful.

18. Why I write.

You may very well ask what the goddess of love is doing in St. Andrews, writing trashy romances. Adapting. Some of us have managed better than others, of course. Prune with her clinic and her patented Pomegranate Weight Loss System, good for the health and the spirits. Di has her bakery. Minnie is more or less a recluse—she makes up crossword puzzles and designs knitting patterns, and feuds with prominent Classics scholars via the mail. No one has seen Paul in ages. He can't stand modern music, he says. He's living somewhere in Kensington with a nice deaf man.

Zeus and that malevolent birdbrained bitch are still married, can you believe it? As if the world would stop spinning if she admitted that the whole thing was a mistake. It infuriates her to see anyone else having fun, especially her husband. We've never gotten on well—she fights with everyone sooner or later, which is why most of us are exiled to this corner of the world. I miss the sun, but never the company.

19. An unkindness of ravens.

June waited at Waverly Station for three and a half hours. The Fringe was in full swing, and performers in beads and feather masks dashed past her, chasing a windblown kite shaped like a wing. They smelled of dust and sweat and beer. They looked at her oddly, she thought, as they ran by. The kite blew towards her again, low on the ground, and she stuck out her foot. The kite lifted over her in a sudden gust of wind.

She rested her head in her hands. Someone nearby laughed, insinuating and hoarse, and she looked up to see one of the kite-chasers standing next to her. He was winding string in his hand, bringing the kite down. Bright eyes gleamed at her like jet buttons, above a yellow papier-mâché beak. "What's the matter, little thief?" the peacock said. "Lose something?"

Another man, in crow-black, sat down on the bench beside her. He said nothing, and his pupils were not round, but elongated and flat like those of an owl. June jumped up and ran. She dodged raucous strangers with glittering eyes, whose clothing had the feel of soft spiky down, whose feet were scaly and knobbed and struck sparks from the pavement. They put out arms to stop her, and their arms were wings, their fingers feathers. She swung wildly at them and ran on. On Queen Street, she lost them in a crowd, but she kept on running anyway.

Lily was sitting in the parlor when she got home. "Humphrey's

Aunt Rose called," she said without preamble. "There's been an accident."

"What?" June said. Her chest heaved up and down. She thought she felt the tickle of feathers in her lungs. She thought she might throw up.

"His plane crashed. A flock of birds flew into the propeller. He died almost instantly."

"He's not dead," June said.

Lily didn't say anything. Her arms were folded against her body as if she were afraid they might extend, unwanted, towards her daughter. "He was a nice boy," she said finally.

"I need to go up to my room," June said. Of course he wasn't dead: she'd read the book. He'd explained the whole thing to her. When you're immortal, you don't die. *Half*-immortal, she corrected herself. So maybe *half*-dead, she could live with that.

Lily said, "The woman in Room Five left this afternoon. I haven't cleaned it yet, but I thought we might move the guests in your room. I'll help you."

"No!" June said. "I'll do it." She hesitated. "Thanks, Lily."

"I'll make up a pot of tea, then," Lily said, and went into the kitchen. June took the ring of keys from the wall and went up to her room. She took the blue sweater out of the cupboard and put it on. She picked up the bottle of perfume, and then she paused. She bent and thumbed open the suitcase of the Strasburg honeymooners, reaching down through the folded clothes until her hand closed around a wad of notes. She took them all without counting.

The last two things she took were the two books: *D'Aulaire's Greek Myths* and *Arrows of Beauty*.

She went out of her room without locking it, down the stairs to Room Five. The light didn't come on when she lowered the switch and things brushed against her, soft and damp. She ran to the drapes and flung them back.

The window swung open and suddenly the room was full of whiteness. At first, blinking hard, she thought that it was snowing inside. Then she saw that the snowflakes were goosedown. Both pillows had been torn open and the duvet was rent down the middle. Feathers dusted the floor, sliding across June's palm and her cheek. She choked on a feather, spat it out.

As she moved across the room, the feathers clung to her. She felt them attaching themselves to her back, growing into two great wings. "Stop it!" she cried.

She opened the *D'Aulaire*, flipping past Hera's mad, triumphant face, to a picture of rosy-cheeked Venus. She pulled the stopper from the perfume bottle and tipped it over on the drawing. She poured out half the bottle on the book and behind her someone sneezed. She turned around.

It was Humphrey's aunt, Rose Read. She looked almost dowdy—travel-stained and worn, as if she had come a long way. She didn't look anything like the woman in the picture book. June said, "Where is he?"

Aunt Rose shrugged, brushing feathers off her wrinkled coat. "He's gone to see his Aunt Prune, I suppose."

"I want to go to him," June said. "I know that's possible."

"I suppose you had Classics at your comprehensive," said Aunt Rose, and sneezed delicately, like a cat. "Really, these feathers—"

"I want you to send me to him."

"If I sent you there," Rose said, "you might not come back. Or he might not want to come back. It isn't my specialty either. If you're so clever, you've figured that out, too."

"I know you've sent people there before, so stop playing games with me!" June said.

"Your mother could tell you what to do when a lover leaves," Rose Read said in a voice like cream. "So why are you asking my advice?"

"She didn't go after him!" June shouted. "She had to stay here and look after me, didn't she?"

Rose Read drew herself up very tall, smoothing her hands down her sides. She looked almost pleased. "Very well," she said. "Fortunately Hell is a much cheaper trip, much nearer to hand than Australia. Are you ready? Good. So listen, because I'm only going to tell you this once."

20. Going to hell. Instructions and advice.

"If you don't let the sweater fall from your hands, if you follow the sleeve until it is only yarn, it will lead you to him. He won't be as you remember him, he's been eating his memories to keep warm. He is not asleep, but if you kiss him he'll wake up. Just like the fairy tales. His lips will be cold at first.

"Say to him, *Follow me*, and unravel the right arm of the sweater. It will take you to a better place, little thief. If you do it right and don't look back, then you can steal him out of the Bonehouse."

June stared instead at the birdcage, gilt and forlorn upon its single hinged leg. Down was caught like smoke in a sieve in the grill of the cage. "What now?" she said. "Do you disappear in a puff of smoke, or wave a wand? Can I just leave?"

"Not through the door," Rose said. "It's time you had your flying lessons." She stepped upon the windowsill, crouching in her coat like a great black wing beneath the weight of the moon. She held out her hand to June. "Come on. Are you afraid?"

June took her hand. "I won't be afraid," she said. She climbed up on the sill beside Rose, and pointed her shoes toward the moon, away from the scratch of quills against the walls and ceiling. She didn't look back, but stepped off the edge of the known world.

TRAVELS WITH THE
SNOW QUEEN

Part of you is always traveling faster, always traveling ahead. Even when you are moving, it is never fast enough to satisfy that part of you. You enter the walls of the city early in the evening, when the cobblestones are a mottled pink with reflected light, and cold beneath the slap of your bare, bloody feet. You ask the man who is guarding the gate to recommend a place to stay the night, and even as you are falling into the bed at the inn, the bed, which is piled high with quilts and scented with lavender, perhaps alone, perhaps with another traveler, perhaps with the guardsman who had such brown eyes, and a mustache that curled up on either side of his nose like two waxed black laces, even as this guardsman, whose name you didn't ask calls out a name in his sleep that is not your name, you are dreaming about the road again. When you sleep, you dream about the long white distances that still lie before you. When you wake up, the guardsman is back at his post, and the place between your legs aches pleasantly, your legs sore as if you had continued walking all night in your sleep. While you were sleeping, your feet have healed again. You were careful not to kiss the guardsman on the lips, so it doesn't really count, does it.

Your destination is North. The map that you are using is a mirror. You are always pulling the bits out of your bare feet, the pieces of the map that broke off and fell on the ground as the Snow Queen flew overhead in her sleigh. Where you are, where you are coming from, it is impossible to read a map made of paper. If it were that easy then everyone would be a traveler. You have heard of other travelers whose maps are breadcrumbs, whose maps are stones, whose maps are the four winds, whose maps are yellow bricks laid one after the other. You read your map with your foot, and behind you somewhere there must be another traveler whose map is the bloody footprints that you are leaving behind you.

There is a map of fine white scars on the soles of your feet that tells you where you have been. When you are pulling the shards of the Snow Queen's looking-glass out of your feet, you remind yourself, you tell yourself to imagine how it felt when Kay's eyes, Kay's heart were pierced by shards of the same mirror. Sometimes it is safer to read maps with your feet.

Ladies. Has it ever occurred to you that fairy tales aren't easy on the feet?

So this is the story so far. You grew up, you fell in love with the boy next door, Kay, the one with blue eyes who brought you bird feathers and roses, the one who was so good at puzzles. You thought he loved you—maybe he thought he did, too. His mouth tasted so sweet, it tasted like love, and his fingers were so kind, they pricked like love on your skin, but three years and exactly two days after you moved in with him, you were having drinks out on the patio. You weren't exactly fighting, and you can't remember what he had done that had made you so angry, but you threw your glass at him. There was a noise like the sky shattering.

The cuff of his trousers got splashed. There were little fragments of glass everywhere. "Don't move," you said. You weren't wearing shoes.

He raised his hand up to his face. "I think there's something in my eye," he said.

His eye was fine, of course, there wasn't a thing in it, but later that night when he was undressing for bed, there were little bits of glass like grains of sugar, dusting his clothes. When you brushed your hand against his chest, something pricked your finger and left a smear of blood against his heart.

The next day it was snowing and he went out for a pack of cigarettes and never came back. You sat on the patio drinking something warm and alcoholic, with nutmeg in it, and the snow fell on your shoulders. You were wearing a short-sleeved T-shirt; you were pretending that you weren't cold, and that your lover would be back soon. You put your finger on the ground and then stuck it in your mouth. The snow looked like sugar, but it tasted like nothing at all.

The man at the corner store said that he saw your lover get into a long white sleigh. There was a beautiful woman in it, and it was pulled by thirty white geese. "Oh, her," you said, as if you weren't surprised. You went home and looked in the wardrobe for that cloak that belonged to your great-grandmother. You were thinking about going after him. You remembered that the cloak was woolen and warm, and a beautiful red—a traveler's cloak. But when you pulled it out, it smelled like wet dog and the lining was ragged, as if something had chewed on it. It smelled like bad luck: it made you sneeze, and so you put it back. You waited for a while longer.

Two months went by, and Kay didn't come back, and finally you left and locked the door of your house behind you. You were going to travel for love, without shoes, or cloak, or common sense. This is one of the things a woman can do when her lover leaves her. It's hard on the feet perhaps, but staying at home is hard on the heart, and you weren't quite ready to give him up yet. You told yourself that the woman in the sleigh must have put a spell on him, and he was probably already missing you. Besides, there are some questions you want to ask him, some true things you want to tell him. This is what you told yourself.

The snow was soft and cool on your feet, and then you found the trail of glass, the map.

After three weeks of hard traveling, you came to the city.

No, really, think about it. Think about the little mermaid, who traded in her tail for love, got two legs and two feet, and every step was like walking on knives. And where did it get her? That's a rhetorical question, of course. Then there's the girl who put on the beautiful red dancing shoes. The woodsman had to chop her feet off with an axe.

There are Cinderella's two stepsisters, who cut off their own toes, and Snow White's stepmother, who danced to death in red-hot iron slippers. The Goose Girl's maid got rolled down a hill in a barrel studded with nails. Travel is hard on the single woman. There was this one woman who walked east of the sun and then west of the moon, looking for her lover, who had left her because she spilled tallow on his nightshirt. She wore out at least one pair of perfectly good iron shoes before she found him. Take our word for it, he wasn't worth it. What do you think happened when she forgot to put the fabric softener in the dryer? Laundry is hard, travel is harder. You deserve a vacation, but of course you're a little wary. You've read the fairy tales. We've been there, we know.

That's why we here at Snow Queen Tours have put together a luxurious but affordable package for you, guaranteed to be easy on the feet and on the budget. See the world by goosedrawn sleigh, experience the archetypal forest, the winter wonderland; chat with real live talking animals (please don't feed them). Our accommodations are three-star: sleep on comfortable, guaranteed pea-free boxspring mattresses; eat meals prepared by world-class chefs. Our tour guides are friendly, knowledgeable, well-traveled, trained by the Snow Queen herself. They know first aid, how to live off the land; they speak three languages fluently.

Special discount for older sisters, stepsisters, stepmothers, wicked witches, crones, hags, princesses who have kissed frogs without realizing what they were getting into, etc.

You leave the city and you walk all day beside a stream that is as soft and silky as blue fur. You wish that your map was water, and not broken glass. At midday you stop and bathe your feet in a shallow place and the ribbons of red blood curl into the blue water.

Eventually you come to a wall of briars, so wide and high that you can't see any way around it. You reach out to touch a rose, and prick your finger. You suppose that you could walk around, but your feet tell you that the map leads directly through the briar wall, and you can't stray from the path that has been laid out for you. Remember what happened to the little girl, your great-grandmother, in her red woolen cape. Maps protect their travelers, but only if the travelers obey the dictates of their maps. This is what you have been told.

Perched in the briars above your head is a raven, black and sleek as the curlicued moustache of the guardsman. The raven looks at you and you look back at it. "I'm looking for someone," you say. "A boy named Kay."

The raven opens its big beak and says, "He doesn't love you, you know."

You shrug. You've never liked talking animals. Once your lover gave you a talking cat, but it ran away and secretly you were glad. "I have a few things I want to say to him, that's all." You have, in fact, been keeping a list of all the things you are going to say to him. "Besides, I wanted to see the world, be a tourist for a while."

"That's fine for some," the raven says. Then he relents. "If you'd like to come in, then come in. The princess just married the boy with the boots that squeaked on the marble floor."

"That's fine for some," you say. Kay's boots squeak; you wonder how he met the princess, if he is the one that she just married, how the raven knows that he doesn't love you, what this princess has that you don't have, besides a white sleigh pulled by thirty geese, an impenetrable wall of briars, and maybe a castle. She's probably just some bimbo.

"The Princess Briar Rose is a very wise princess," the raven says, "but she's the laziest girl in the world. Once she went to sleep for a hundred days and no one could wake her up, although they put one hundred peas under her mattress, one each morning."

This, of course, is the proper and respectful way of waking up princesses. Sometimes Kay used to wake you up by dribbling cold water on your feet. Sometimes he woke you up by whistling.

"On the one hundredth day," the raven says, "she woke up all by herself and told her council of twelve fairy godmothers that she supposed it was time she got married. So they stuck up posters, and princes and youngest sons came from all over the kingdom."

When the cat ran away, Kay put up flyers around the neighborhood. You wonder if you should have put up flyers for Kay. "Briar Rose wanted a clever husband, but it tired her dreadfully to sit and listen to the young men give speeches and talk about how rich and sexy and smart they were. She fell asleep and stayed asleep until the young man with the squeaky boots came in. It was his boots that woke her up.

"It was love at first sight. Instead of trying to impress her with everything he knew and everything he had seen, he declared that he had come all this way to hear Briar Rose talk about her dreams. He'd been studying in Vienna with a famous Doctor, and was deeply interested in dreams."

Kay used to tell you his dreams every morning. They were long and complicated and if he thought you weren't listening to him, he'd sulk. You never remember your dreams. "Other peoples' dreams are never very interesting," you tell the raven.

The raven cocks its head. It flies down and lands on the grass at your feet. "Wanna bet?" it says. Behind the raven you notice a little green door recessed in the briar wall. You could have sworn that it wasn't there a minute ago.

The raven leads you through the green door, and across a long green lawn towards a two-story castle that is the same pink as the briar roses. You think this is kind of tacky, but exactly what you would expect from someone named after a flower. "I had this dream once," the raven says, "that my teeth were falling out. They just crumbled into pieces in my mouth. And then I woke up, and realized that ravens don't have teeth."

You follow the raven inside the palace, and up a long, twisty staircase. The stairs are stone, worn and smoothed away, like old thick silk. Slivers of glass glister on the pink stone, catching the light of the candles on the wall. As you go up, you see that you are part of a great gray rushing crowd. Fantastic creatures, flat and thin as smoke, race up the stairs, men and women and snakey things with bright eyes. They nod to you as they slip past. "Who are they?" you ask the raven.

"Dreams," the raven says, hopping awkwardly from step to step. "The Princess's dreams, come to pay their respects to her new husband. Of course they're too fine to speak to the likes of us."

But you think that some of them look familiar. They have a familiar smell, like a pillow that your lover's head has rested upon.

At the top of the staircase is a wooden door with a silver keyhole. The dreams pour steadily through the keyhole, and under the bottom of the door, and when you open it, the sweet stink and cloud of dreams are so thick in the Princess's bedroom that you can barely breathe. Some people might mistake the scent of the Princess's dreams for the scent of sex; then again, some people mistake sex for love.

You see a bed big enough for a giant, with four tall oak trees for bedposts. You climb up the ladder that rests against the side of the bed to see the Princess's sleeping husband. As you lean over, a goose feather flies up and tickles your nose. You brush it away, and dislodge several seedy-looking dreams. Briar Rose rolls over and laughs in her sleep, but the man beside her wakes up. "Who is it?" he says. "What do you want?"

He isn't Kay. He doesn't look a thing like Kay. "You're not Kay," you tell the man in the Princess's bed.

"Who the fuck is Kay?" he says, so you explain it all to him, feeling horribly embarrassed. The raven is looking pleased with itself, the way your talking cat used to look, before it ran away. You glare at the raven. You glare at the man who is not Kay.

After you've finished, you say that something is wrong, because your map clearly indicates that Kay has been here, in this bed. Your feet are leaving bloody marks on the sheets, and you pick a sliver of glass off the foot of the bed, so everyone can see that you're not lying. Princess Briar Rose sits up in bed, her long pinkish-brown hair tumbled down over her shoulders. "He's not in love with you," she says, yawning.

"So he was here, in this bed, you're the icy slut in the sleigh at the corner store, you're not even bothering to deny it," you say.

She shrugs her pink-white shoulders. "Four, five months ago, he came through, I woke up," she says. "He was a nice guy, okay in bed. She was a real bitch, though."

"Who was?" you ask.

Briar Rose finally notices that her new husband is glaring at her. "What can I say?" she says, and shrugs. "I have a thing for guys in squeaky boots."

"Who was a bitch?" you ask again.

"The Snow Queen," she says, "the slut in the sleigh."

This is the list you carry in your pocket, of the things you plan to say to Kay, when you find him, if you find him:

> 1. I'm sorry that I forgot to water your ferns while you were away that time.
> 2. When you said that I reminded you of your mother, was that a good thing?
> 3. I never really liked your friends all that much.
> 4. None of my friends ever really liked you.
> 5. Do you remember when the cat ran away, and I cried and cried and made you put up posters, and she never came back? I wasn't crying because she didn't come back. I was crying because I'd taken her to the woods, and I was scared she'd come back and tell you what I'd done, but I guess a wolf got her, or something. She never liked me anyway.
> 6. I never liked your mother.
> 7. After you left, I didn't water your plants on purpose. They're all dead.
> 8. Goodbye.
> 9. Were you ever really in love with me?
> 10. Was I good in bed, or just average?

11. What exactly did you mean, when you said that it was fine that I had put on a little weight, that you thought I was even more beautiful, that I should go ahead and eat as much as I wanted, but when I weighed myself on the bathroom scale, I was exactly the same weight as before, I hadn't gained a single pound?

12. So all those times, I'm being honest here, every single time, and anyway I don't care if you don't believe me, I faked every orgasm you ever thought I had. Women can do that, you know. You never made me come, not even once.

13. So maybe I'm an idiot, but I used to be in love with you.

14. I slept with some guy, I didn't mean to, it just kind of happened. Is that how it was with you? Not that I'm making any apologies, or that I'd accept yours, I just want to know.

15. My feet hurt, and it's all your fault.

16. I mean it this time, goodbye.

The Princess Briar Rose isn't a bimbo after all, even if she does have a silly name and a pink castle. You admire her dedication to the art and practice of sleep. By now you are growing sick and tired of traveling, and would like nothing better than to curl up in a big featherbed for one hundred days, or maybe even one hundred years, but she offers you to loan you her carriage, and when you explain that you have to walk, she sends you off with a troop of armed guards. They will escort you through the forest, which is full of thieves and wolves and princes on quests, lurking about. The guards politely pretend that they don't notice the trail of blood that you are leaving behind. They probably think it's some sort of female thing.

It is after sunset, and you aren't even half a mile into the forest, which is dark and scary and full of noises, when bandits ambush your escort, and slaughter them all. The bandit queen, who is grizzled and gray, with a nose like an old pickle, yells delightedly at the sight of you. "You're a nice plump one for my supper!" she says, and draws her long knife out of the stomach of one of the dead guards. She is just about to slit your throat, as you stand there, politely pretending not to notice the blood that is pooling around the bodies of the dead guards, that is now obliterating the bloody tracks of your feet, the knife that is at your throat, when a girl about your own age jumps onto the robber queen's back, pulling at the robber queen's braided hair as if it were reins.

There is a certain family resemblance between the robber queen and the girl who right now has her knees locked around the robber queen's throat. "I don't want you to kill her," the girl says, and you realize that she means you, that you were about to die a minute ago, that travel is much more dangerous than you had ever imagined. You add an item of complaint to the list of things that you plan to tell Kay, if you find him.

The girl has half-throttled the robber queen, who has fallen to her knees, gasping for breath. "She can be my sister," the girl says insistently. "You promised I could have a sister and I want her. Besides, her feet are bleeding."

The robber queen drops her knife, and the girl drops back onto the ground, kissing her mother's hairy gray cheek. "Very well, very well," the robber queen grumbles, and the girl grabs your hand, pulling you farther and faster into the woods, until you are running and stumbling, her hand hot around yours.

You have lost all sense of direction; your feet are no longer set upon your map. You should be afraid, but instead you are strangely exhilarated. Your feet don't hurt anymore, and although you don't know where you are going, for the very first time you are moving fast enough, you are almost flying, your feet are skimming over the night-black forest floor as if it were the smooth, flat surface of a lake, and your feet were two white birds. "Where are we going?" you ask the robber girl.

"We're here," she says, and stops so suddenly that you almost fall over. You are in a clearing, and the full moon is hanging overhead. You can see the robber girl better now, under the light of the moon. She looks like one of the bad girls who loiter under the street lamp by the corner shop, the ones who used to whistle at Kay. She wears black leatherette boots laced up to her thighs, and a black, ribbed T-shirt and grape-colored plastic shorts with matching suspenders. Her nails are painted black, and bitten down to the quick. She leads you to a tumbledown stone keep, which is as black inside as her fingernail polish, and smells strongly of dirty straw and animals.

"Are you a princess?" she asks you. "What are you doing in my mother's forest? Don't be afraid. I won't let my mother eat you."

You explain to her that you are not a princess, what you are doing, about the map, who you are looking for, what he did to you, or maybe it was what he didn't do. When you finish, the robber girl puts her arms around you and squeezes you roughly. "You poor thing! But what a silly way to travel!" she says. She shakes her head and makes you sit down on the stone floor of the keep and show her your feet. You explain that they always heal, that really your feet are quite tough, but she takes off her leatherette boots and gives them to you.

The floor of the keep is dotted with indistinct, motionless forms. One snarls in its sleep, and you realize that they are dogs. The robber girl is sitting between four slender columns, and when the dog snarls, the thing shifts restlessly, lowering its branchy head. It is a hobbled reindeer. "Well go on, see if they fit," the robber girl says, pulling out her knife. She drags it along the stone floor to make sparks. "What are you going to do when you find him?"

"Sometimes I'd like to cut off his head," you say. The robber girl grins, and thumps the hilt of her knife against the reindeer's chest.

The robber girl's feet are just a little bigger, but the boots are still warm from her feet. You explain that you can't wear the boots, or else you won't know where you are going. "Nonsense!" the robber girl says rudely.

You ask if she knows a better way to find Kay, and she says that if you are still determined to go looking for him, even though he obviously doesn't love you, and he isn't worth a bit of trouble, then the thing to do is to find the Snow Queen. "This is Bae. Bae, you mangy old, useless old thing," she says. "Do you know where the Snow Queen lives?"

The reindeer replies in a low, hopeless voice that he doesn't know, but he is sure that his old mother does. The robber girl slaps his flank. "Then you'll take her to your mother," she says. "And mind that you don't dawdle on the way."

She turns to you and gives you a smacking wet kiss on the lips and says, "Keep the shoes, they look much nicer on you than they did on me. And don't let me hear that you've been walking on glass again." She gives the reindeer a speculative look. "You know, Bae, I almost think I'm going to miss you."

You step into the cradle of her hands, and she swings you over the reindeer's bony back. Then she saws through the hobble with her knife, and yells "Ho!" waking up the dogs.

You knot your fingers into Bae's mane, and bounce up as he stumbles into a fast trot. The dogs follow for a distance, snapping at his hooves, but soon you have outdistanced them, moving so fast that the wind peels your lips back in an involuntary grimace. You almost miss the feel of glass beneath your feet. By morning, you are out of the forest again, and Bae's hooves are churning up white clouds of snow.

Sometimes you think there must be an easier way to do this. Sometimes it seems to be getting easier all on its own. Now you have boots and a reindeer, but you still aren't happy. Sometimes you wish that you'd stayed at home. You're sick and tired of traveling towards the happily ever after, whenever the fuck that is—you'd like the happily right now. Thank you very much.

When you breathe out, you can see the fine mist of your breath and the breath of the reindeer floating before you, until the wind tears it away. Bae runs on.

The snow flies up, and the air seems to grow thicker and thicker. As Bae runs, you feel that the white air is being rent by your passage, like heavy cloth. When you turn around and look behind you, you can see the path shaped to your joined form, woman and reindeer, like a hall stretching back to infinity. You see that there is more than one sort of map, that some forms of travel are indeed easier. "Give me a kiss," Bae says. The wind whips his words back to you. You can almost see the shape of them hanging in the heavy air.

"I'm not really a reindeer," he says. "I'm an enchanted prince."

You politely decline, pointing out that you haven't known him that long, and besides, for traveling purposes, a reindeer is better than a prince.

"He doesn't love you," Bae says. "And you could stand to lose a few pounds. My back is killing me."

You are sick and tired of talking animals, as well as travel. They never say anything that you didn't already know. You think of the talking cat that Kay gave you, the one that would always come to you, secretly, and looking very pleased with itself, to inform you when Kay's fingers smelled of some other woman. You couldn't stand to see him pet it, his fingers stroking its white fur, the cat lying on its side and purring wildly, "There, darling, that's perfect, don't stop," his fingers on its belly, its tail wreathing and lashing, its pointy little tongue sticking out at you. "Shut up," you say to Bae.

He subsides into an offended silence. His long brown fur is rimmed with frost, and you can feel the tears that the wind pulls from your eyes turning to ice on your cheeks. The only part of you that is warm are your feet, snug in the robber girl's boots. "It's just a little farther," Bae says, when you have been traveling for what feels like hours. "And then we're home."

You cross another corridor in the white air, and he swerves to follow it, crying out gladly, "We are near the old woman of Lapmark's house, my mother's house."

"How do you know?" you ask.

"I recognize the shape that she leaves behind her," Bae says. "Look!"

You look and see that the corridor of air you are following is formed like a short, stout, petticoated woman. It swings out at the waist like a bell.

"How long does it last?"

"As long as the air is heavy and dense," he says, "we burrow tunnels through the air like worms, but then the wind will come along and erase where we have been."

The woman-tunnel ends at a low red door. Bae lowers his head and knocks his antlers against it, scraping off the paint. The old woman of Lapmark opens the door, and you clamber stiffly off Bae's back. There is much rejoicing as mother recognizes son, although he is much changed from how he had been.

The old woman of Lapmark is stooped and fat as a grub. She fixes you a cup of tea, while Bae explains that you are looking for the Snow Queen's palace.

"You've not far to go now," his mother tells you. "Only a few hundred miles and past the house of the woman of Finmany. She'll

113

tell you how to go—let me write a letter explaining everything to
her. And don't forget to mention to her that I'll be coming for tea
tomorrow; she'll change you back then, Bae, if you ask her nicely."

The woman of Lapmark has no paper, so she writes the letter on
a piece of dried cod, flat as a dinner plate. Then you are off again.
Sometimes you sleep as Bae runs on, and sometimes you aren't sure if
you are asleep or waking. Great balls of greenish light roll cracking
across the sky above you. At times it seems as if Bae is flying alongside the lights, chatting to them like old friends. At last you come to
the house of the woman of Finmany, and you knock on her chimney,
because she has no door.

Why, you may wonder, are there so many old women living out here?
Is this a retirement community? One might not be remarkable, two is
certainly more than enough, but as you look around, you can see little
heaps of snow, lines of smoke rising from them. You have to be careful
where you put your foot, or you might come through someone's roof.
Maybe they came here for the quiet, or because they like ice fishing,
or maybe they just like snow.

It is steamy and damp in the house, and you have to climb down the
chimney, past the roaring fire, to get inside. Bae leaps down the
chimney, hooves first, scattering coals everywhere. The Finmany
woman is smaller and rounder than the woman of Lapmark. She
looks to you like a lump of pudding with black currant eyes. She
wears only a greasy old slip, and an apron that has written on it, "If
you can't stand the heat, stay out of my kitchen."

She recognizes Bae even faster than his mother had, because, as
it turns out, she was the one who turned him into a reindeer for
teasing her about her weight. Bae apologizes, insincerely, you think,
but the Finmany woman says she will see what she can do about

turning him back again. She isn't entirely hopeful. It seems that a kiss is the preferred method of transformation. You don't offer to kiss him, because you know what that kind of thing leads to.

The Finmany woman reads the piece of dried cod by the light of her cooking fire, and then she throws the fish into her cooking pot. Bae tells her about Kay and the Snow Queen, and about your feet, because your lips have frozen together on the last leg of the journey, and you can't speak a word.

"You're so clever and strong," the reindeer says to the Finmany woman. You can almost hear him add *and fat* under his breath. "You can tie up all the winds in the world with a bit of thread. I've seen you hurling the lightning bolts down from the hills as if they were feathers. Can't you give her the strength of ten men, so that she can fight the Snow Queen and win Kay back?"

"The strength of ten men?" the Finmany woman says. "A lot of good that would do! And besides, he doesn't love her."

Bae smirks at you, as if to say, I told you so. If your lips weren't frozen, you'd tell him that she isn't saying anything that you don't already know. "Now!" the Finmany woman says, "take her up on your back one last time, and put her down again by the bush with the red berries. That marks the edge of the Snow Queen's garden; don't stay there gossiping, but come straight back. You were a handsome boy—I'll make you twice as good-looking as you were before. We'll put up flyers, see if we can get someone to come and kiss you."

"As for you, missy," she says. "Tell the Snow Queen now that we have Bae back, that we'll be over at the Palace next Tuesday for bridge. Just as soon as he has hands to hold the cards."

She puts you on Bae's back again, giving you such a warm kiss that your lips unfreeze, and you can speak again. "The woman of Lapmark is coming for tea tomorrow," you tell her.

The Finmany woman lifts Bae, and you upon his back, in her strong, fat arms, giving you a gentle push up the chimney.

Good morning, ladies, it's nice to have you on the premiere Snow Queen Tour. I hope that you all had a good night's sleep, because today we're going to be traveling quite some distance. I hope that everyone brought a comfortable pair of walking shoes. Let's have a head count, make sure that everyone on the list is here, and then we'll have introductions. My name is Gerda, and I'm looking forward to getting to know all of you.

Here you are at last, standing before the Snow Queen's palace, the palace of the woman who enchanted your lover and then stole him away in her long white sleigh. You aren't quite sure what you are going to say to her, or to him. When you check your pocket, you discover that your list has disappeared. You have most of it memorized, but you think maybe you will wait and see, before you say anything. Part of you would like to turn around and leave before the Snow Queen finds you, before Kay sees you. You are afraid that you will burst out crying or even worse, that he will know that you walked barefoot on broken glass across half the continent, just to find out why he left you.

The front door is open, so you don't bother knocking, you just walk right in. It isn't that large a palace, really. It is about the size of your own house and even reminds you of your own house, except that the furniture, Danish modern, is carved out of blue-green ice—as are the walls and everything else. It's a slippery place and you're glad that you are wearing the robber girl's boots. You have to admit that the Snow Queen is a meticulous housekeeper, much tidier than you ever were. You can't find the Snow Queen and you can't find Kay, but in every room there are white geese who, you are in equal parts relieved and surprised to discover, don't utter a single word.

"Gerda!" Kay is sitting at a table, fitting the pieces of a puzzle together. When he stands up, he knocks several pieces of the puzzle off the table, and they fall to the floor and shatter into even smaller fragments. You both kneel down, picking them up. The table is blue, the puzzle pieces are blue, Kay is blue, which is why you didn't see him when you first came into the room. The geese brush up against you, soft and white as cats.

"What took you so long?" Kay says. "Where in the world did you get those ridiculous boots?" You stare at him in disbelief.

"I walked barefoot on broken glass across half a continent to get here," you say. But at least you don't burst into tears. "A robber girl gave them to me."

Kay snorts. His blue nostrils flare. "Sweetie, they're hideous."

"Why are you blue?" you ask.

"I'm under an enchantment," he says. "The Snow Queen kissed me. Besides, I thought blue was your favorite color."

Your favorite color has always been yellow. You wonder if the Snow Queen·kissed him all over, if he is blue all over. All the visible portions of his body are blue. "If you kiss me," he says, "you break the spell and I can come home with you. If you break the spell, I'll be in love with you again."

You refrain from asking if he was in love with you when he kissed the Snow Queen. Pardon me, you think, when *she* kissed him. "What is that puzzle you're working on?" you ask.

"Oh, that," he says. "That's the other way to break the spell. If I can put it together, but the other way is easier. Not to mention more fun. Don't you want to kiss me?"

You look at his blue lips, at his blue face. You try to remember if you liked his kisses. "Do you remember the white cat?" you say. "It didn't exactly run away. I took it to the woods and left it there."

"We can get another one," he says.

"I took it to the woods because it was telling me things."

"We don't have to get a talking cat," Kay says. "Besides, why did you walk barefoot across half a continent of broken glass if you aren't going to kiss me and break the spell?" His blue face is sulky.

"Maybe I just wanted to see the world," you tell him. "Meet interesting people."

The geese are brushing up against your ankles. You stroke their white feathers and the geese snap, but gently, at your fingers. "You had better hurry up and decide if you want to kiss me or not," Kay says. "Because she's home."

When you turn around, there she is, smiling at you like you are exactly the person that she was hoping to see.

The Snow Queen isn't how or what you'd expected. She's not as tall as you—you thought she would be taller. Sure, she's beautiful, you can see why Kay kissed her (although you are beginning to wonder why she kissed him), but her eyes are black and kind, which you didn't expect at all. She stands next to you, not looking at Kay at all, but looking at you. "I wouldn't do it if I were you," she says.

"Oh come on," Kays says. "Give me a break, lady. Sure it was nice, but you don't want me hanging around this icebox forever, any more than I want to be here. Let Gerda kiss me, we'll go home and live happily ever after. There's supposed to be a happy ending."

"I like your boots," the Snow Queen says.

"You're beautiful," you tell her.

"I don't believe this," Kay says. He thumps his blue fist on the blue table, sending blue puzzle pieces flying through the air. Pieces lie like nuggets of sky-colored glass on the white backs of the geese. A piece of the table has splintered off, and you wonder if he is going to have to put the table back together as well.

"Do you love him?"

You look at the Snow Queen when she says this and then you look at Kay. "Sorry," you tell him. You hold out your hand in case he's willing to shake it.

"Sorry!" he says. "You're sorry! What good does that do me?"

"So what happens now?" you ask the Snow Queen.

"Up to you," she says. "Maybe you're sick of traveling. Are you?"

"I don't know," you say. "I think I'm finally beginning to get the hang of it."

"In that case," says the Snow Queen, "I may have a business proposal for you."

"Hey!" Kay says. "What about me? Isn't someone going to kiss me?"

You help him collect a few puzzle pieces. "Will you at least do this much for me?" he asks. "For old time's sake. Will you spread the word, tell a few single princesses that I'm stuck up here? I'd like to get out of here sometime in the next century. Thanks. I'd really appreciate it. You know, we had a really nice time, I think I remember that."

The robber girl's boots cover the scars on your feet. When you look at these scars, you can see the outline of the journey you made. Sometimes mirrors are maps, and sometimes maps are mirrors. Sometimes scars tell a story, and maybe someday you will tell this story to a lover. The soles of your feet are stories—hidden in the black boots, they shine like mirrors. If you were to take your boots off, you would see reflected in one foot-mirror the Princess Briar Rose as she sets off on her honeymoon, in her enormous four-poster bed, which now has wheels and is pulled by twenty white horses.

It's nice to see women exploring alternative means of travel.

In the other foot-mirror, almost close enough to touch, you could see the robber girl whose boots you are wearing. She is setting off to find Bae, to give him a kiss and bring him home again. You wouldn't presume to give her any advice, but you do hope that she has found another pair of good sturdy boots.

Someday, someone will probably make their way to the Snow Queen's palace, and kiss Kay's cold blue lips. She might even manage a happily ever after for a while.

You are standing in your black laced boots, and the Snow Queen's white geese mutter and stream and sidle up against you. You are beginning to understand some of what they are saying. They grumble about the weight of the sleigh, the weather, your hesitant jerks at their reins. But they are good-natured grumbles. You tell the geese that your feet are maps *and* your feet are mirrors. But you tell them that you have to keep in mind that they are also useful for walking around on. They are perfectly good feet.

VANISHING ACT

The three of them were sitting in a boat. When she closed her eyes, she could almost picture it. A man and a woman and a girl, in a green boat on the green water. Her mother had written that the water was an impossible color; she imagined the mint color of the Harmons' Tupperware. But what did the boat look like? Was it green? How she wished her mother had described the boat!

The boat refused to settle upon the water. It was too buoyant, sliding along the mint surface like a raindrop on a pane of glass. It had no keel, no sail, no oars. And if they fell in, no lifejackets (at least she knew of none). The man and the woman, unaware, smiled at each other over the head of the girl. And the girl was holding on to both sides of the boat for dear life, holding it intact and upright on the tilting Tupperware-colored water.

She realized that not only had the boat been left out of the letter; after so long she could hardly trust her parents to resemble her memories of them. That was the great tragedy, the inconvenient unseaworthiness of memories and boats and letters, that events never remained themselves long enough for you to insert yourself into them. . . . The girl fell out of the boat into the green water.

Was it cold? She didn't know.

Hildegard and Myron are spying on Hildy's cousin, Jenny Rose. It is Thursday afternoon, October the fifth, 1970, and Jenny Rose is lying on her bed in the room she shares with Hildy. She hasn't moved once in the fifteen minutes that Hildy and Myron have been watching her. Hildy can't explain why she watches Jenny Rose: Jenny Rose never picks her nose or bursts into tears. She mostly lies on her bed with her eyes closed, but not asleep. She's the same age as Hildy—ten—and an utter freak.

Myron says, "I think she's dead," and Hildy snorts.

"I can see her breathing," she says, handing him the binoculars.

"Is she asleep, then?"

"I don't think so," Hildy says, considering. "I think she just turns herself off, like a TV or something."

They are sitting in the gazebo that Hildy's older brother James made in woodworking the year before. The gazebo is homely and ramshackle. The white paint has peeled away in strips, and bees float in the warm air above their heads. With the aid of a borrowed set of binoculars, Hildy and Myron can spy privately upon Jenny Rose upon her bed. Hildy picks at the paint and keeps an eye out for James as well, who considers the gazebo to be exclusively his.

The three of them sat in the boat on the water. They weren't necessarily people, and it wasn't necessarily a boat either. It could be three knots tied in her shoelace; three tubes of lipstick hidden in Hildy's dresser; three pieces of fruit, three oranges in the blue bowl beside her bed.

What was important, what she yearned for, was the trinity, the triangle completed and without lack. She lay on the bed, imagining this: the three of them in the boat upon the water, oh! sweet to taste.

Jenny Rose is the most monosyllabic, monochromatic person Hildy has ever laid eyes on. She's no-colored, like a glass of skim milk, or a piece of chewed string. Lank hair of indeterminate length, skin neither pale nor sunny, and washed-out no-color eyes. She's neither tall nor short, fat or skinny. She smells weird, sad, *electric*, like rain on asphalt. Does she resemble her parents? Hildy isn't sure, but Jenny Rose has nothing of Hildy's family. Hildy's mother is tall and glamorous with red hair. Hildy's mother is a Presbyterian minister. Her father teaches at the university.

The Reverend Molly Harmon's brother and sister-in-law have been missionaries in the Pacific since before Hildy and Jenny Rose were born. When Hildy was little, the adventures of her cousin were like an exotic and mysterious bedtime story. She used to wish she was Jenny Rose.

During the 1965 coup in Indonesia, Hildy's aunt and uncle and Jenny Rose spent a few months in hiding and then a short time in prison, suspected of being Communist sympathizers. This is the way the rumors went: they were dead; they were hidden in Ubud in the house of a man named Nyoman; they were in prison in Jakarta; they had been released, they were safely in Singapore. Hildy always knew that Jenny Rose would be fine. Stories have happy endings. She still believes this.

Jenny Rose was in Singapore for the next four and a half years. When her parents went back to Indonesia, it was proposed that Jenny Rose would come to stay with the Harmons, in order to receive a secondary school education. Hildy helped her mother prepare for the arrival of her cousin. She went to the library and found a book on Indonesia. She went shopping with her mother for a second bed and a second desk, extra clothes, hangers, and sheets. The day before her cousin arrived, Hildy used a ruler, divided her own room into two equal halves.

Hildy hugged Jenny Rose at the airport, breathed her in, that strange hot and cold smell. She hauled Jenny Rose's luggage to the car single-handedly. "What is Indonesia like?" she asked her cousin. "Hot," Jenny Rose said. She closed her eyes, leaned her head against the back of the car, and for the next three weeks said nothing that required more than one syllable. So far, the most meaningful words her cousin has spoken to Hildy are these: "I think I wet the bed."

"Give her time," Hildy's mother advised, putting the sheets into the washer. "She's homesick."

"How can she be homesick?" Hildy said. "She's never lived in a single place for longer than a year."

"You know what I mean," said the Reverend Molly Harmon. "She misses her parents. She's never been away from them before. How would you like it if I sent you to live on the other side of the world?"

"It wouldn't turn me into a mute, stunted turnip-person," Hildy said. But she thinks she understands. She read the library book. Who wouldn't prefer the emerald jungles of Bali to the suburbs of Houston, the intricate glide and shadow jerk of *wayang kulit* puppets on a horn screen to the dollar matinee, *nasi goreng* to a McDonald's hamburger?

Hildy and Myron come inside to make hot chocolate and play Ping-Pong. They go to Hildy and Jenny Rose's room first, and Myron stands over Jenny Rose on her bed, trying to make conversation. "Hey, Sleeping Beauty, whatcha doing?" he says.

"Nothing."

He tries again. "Would you like to play Ping-Pong with us?"

"No." Her eyes don't even open as she speaks.

There is a bowl of oranges on the night table. Myron picks one up and begins to peel it with his thumbnail.

Jenny Rose's eyelids open, and she jackknifes into a sitting position. "Those are my oranges," she says, louder than Hildy has ever heard her speak.

"Hey!" Myron says, backing up and cradling the orange in his palm. He is afraid of Jenny Rose, Hildy realizes. "It's just an orange.

I'm hungry, I didn't mean anything."

Hildy intervenes. "There are more in the refrigerator," she says diplomatically. "You can replace that one—if it's such a big deal."

"I wanted that one," Jenny Rose says, more softly.

"What's so special about that orange?" Myron says. Jenny Rose doesn't say anything. Hildy stares at her, and Jenny Rose stares, without expression, at the orange in Myron's hand. The front door bangs open, and James, the Reverend Harmon, and Dr. Orzibal are home.

Myron's mother, Mercy Orzibal, is a professor of English and a close friend of the Harmons. She is divorced, and teaches night classes. Myron spends a lot of time at the Harmons under the harried attention of Hildy's mother, known as the Reverend Mother.

This afternoon was a wedding, and the Reverend Mother is still in the white robes of a divine: the R.M. and Mercy Orzibal, in her sleeveless white dress, look like geese, or angels.

James is wearing black. James is almost seventeen years old and he hates his family. Which is all right. Hildy doesn't care much for him. His face is sullen, but this is his usual expression. His hair is getting long. His hair is red like his mother's hair. How Hildy wishes that she had red hair.

A cigarette dangles from the lips of the Reverend Mother. She's reached an agreement with Hildy: two cigarettes on weekdays, four on Saturday, and none on Sunday. Hildy hates the smell, but loves the way that the afternoon light falters and falls thickly through the smoke around her mother's beautiful face.

"Do we have any more oranges?" Hildy asks her mother. "Myron ate Jenny Rose's." There are several in the refrigerator, when Hildy looks. She picks out the one that is the most shriveled and puny. She tells herself that she feels sorry for this orange. Jenny Rose will take good care of it. The good oranges are for eating. Jenny Rose has followed Myron and Hildy, she stands just inside the doorway.

"Oh, Jenny!" says the Reverend Mother, as if surprised to find her niece here, in her kitchen. "How was your day, sweetheart?"

Jenny Rose says something inaudible as she takes the orange from Hildy. The R.M. has turned away already and is tapping her ash into the kitchen sink.

Hildy retrieves three more oranges out of the refrigerator. She juggles them, smacking them in her palms, tossing them up again. "Hey, look at me!" James rolls his eyes, the mothers and Myron applaud dutifully—Hildy looks, but Jenny Rose has left the room.

Hildy plays Ping-Pong in the basement every night with her father, uncrowned Ping-Pong champion of the world. He tells silly jokes as he serves, to make Hildy miss her return. "What's brown and sticky?" he says. "A stick."

When Hildy groans, he winks at her. "You can't disguise it," he says. "I know you think I'm the handsomest man in the world, the funniest man in the world, the smartest man in the whole world."

"Yeah, right," Hildy tells him. The sight of his white teeth across the table, floating in the mild, round pink expanse of his face, makes her sad for a moment, as if she is traveling a great distance away, leaving her father pinned down under the great weight of that distance. "You're silly." She spins the ball fast across the net.

"That's what all the ladies tell me," he says. "The silliest man in the world, that's me."

The basement is Hildy's favorite room in the whole house, now that Jenny Rose has taken over her bedroom. The walls are a cheerful yellow, and fat stripey plants in macramé hangers dangle from the ceiling like green and white snakes. Hildy lobs a Ping-Pong ball into the macramé holders—it takes more effort to retrieve these balls than it does to place them, and at night when Hildy watches television in the basement, the Ping-Pong balls glow with reflected TV light like tiny moons and satellites.

She lets her father beat her in the next game, and when he goes back upstairs, she ducks under the table. This is where Hildy sits whenever she needs to think. This is where she and Myron do their homework, cross-legged on the linoleum floor of their own personal cave. Myron is better at social studies, but Hildy is better at math. Hildy is better at spying on Jenny Rose. She shifts on the cold linoleum floor. She is better at hiding than her cousin. No one can spy on her under the table, although she can see anyone who comes into the basement.

She has learned to identify people from the waist down: brown corduroy would be her father; James and Myron wear blue jeans. Her mother's feet are very small. The R.M. never wears shoes in the house, and her toenails are always red, like ten cherries in a row. Hildy doesn't need to remember Jenny Rose's legs or toes—she would know her cousin by the absolute stillness. Jenny Rose's legs would suddenly appear above two noiseless feet, pale and otherworldly as two ghost trees. Hildy imagines jumping out from under the table, yelling "Boo!" Jenny Rose would have to see her then, but would she see Jenny Rose?

Last night at dinner, the R.M. set four places at the table, the blue plate for James, red for Hildy, orange for her husband, purple for herself. The R.M. likes routine, and her family accommodates. No one would ever eat off the wrong-colored plate—surely the food would not taste the same.

Hildy set a fifth place, yellow for Jenny Rose, while her mother was in the kitchen, and retrieved the fifth chair with the wobbly leg from her mother's study. She did these things without saying anything: it seemed unthinkable to say anything to the R.M., who in any case, neither noticed her error nor saw that it had been corrected. At dinner, Jenny Rose did not speak—she hardly ate. No one spoke to her and it seemed to Hildy that no one even noticed her cousin.

She was as invisible as Hildy is now, under the green roof of the Ping-Pong table. She almost feels sorry for Jenny Rose.

Jenny Rose's parents write her every week. Hildy knows this because Jenny Rose donates the stamps to Mr. Harmon's stamp collection. Her father currently has 18 stamps, neatly cut out of the airmail envelopes, lying on his desk in the basement.

As for the letters themselves, they are limp and wrinkled, like old pairs of cotillion gloves. They are skinny as feathers, and light, and Jenny Rose receives them indifferently. They disappear, and when the R.M. or Mr. Harmon asks, "How are your parents doing?" Jenny Rose says, "They're fine," and that's that.

October 10th, 1970

Darling Jenny,

We have been staying in Ubud for three weeks now, visiting Nyoman's church. Every night as we fall asleep the lizards tick off the minutes like pocket watches, and every morning Nyoman brings us pancakes with honey. Do you remember Nyoman? Do you remember the lizards, the length of your pinky? They are green and never blink, watching us watching them.

Nyoman asks how you are doing, so far away. He and his wife are having their second baby. They have asked us to be their child's godparents, and to pick the baptismal name. Would you like the baby to have your name, Rose, if it is a girl?

It is sticky here, and we go for walks in the Monkey Forest, where the old woman sits with her bunches of bananas and her broom, swatting the monkeys away. Do you remember how they scream and fly up into the trees?

Aunt Molly wrote that you are quiet as a mouse, and I don't blame you, in that noisy family!

Love you,
Mom and Dad

Hildy knocks on the door of her mother's study. When she opens the door, she can see a cigarette, hastily stubbed out, still smoldering in the ashtray. "It's only my second," the R.M. says automatically.

Hildy shrugs. "I don't care what you do," she says. "I wanted to know if you'd take me to the library. I already asked Jenny Rose—she doesn't need to go."

The R.M.'s face is momentarily blank. Then she frowns and taps another cigarette out of the pack.

"Three," she says. "I promise that's it, okay? She's so quiet, it's easy to forget she's here. Except for the wet sheets. I must be the worst guardian in the world—I got a call from one of Jenny Rose's teachers yesterday, and when I put down the phone, it flew straight out of my head. She hasn't turned in her assignments recently, and they're worried that the work might be too much for her. Does she seem unhappy to you?"

Hildy shrugs. "I don't know, I guess so. She never says anything."

"I keep forgetting to write and ask your aunt and uncle if she wet the bed before," the R.M. says. She waves her cigarette and a piece of ash floats down onto her desk. "Has Jenny Rose made any friends at school, besides you and Myron?"

Hildy shrugs again. She is mildly jealous, having to share her absent-minded mother with Jenny Rose. "No, I mean I'm not sure she wants any friends. Mostly she likes to be alone. Can you take me to the library?"

"Sweetie," her mother says. "I would, but I have to finish the sermon for tomorrow. Ask your dad when he gets home."

"OK," Hildy says. She turns to leave.

"Will you keep an eye on your cousin?" the R.M. says, "I mean, on Jenny Rose? I'm a little concerned."

"OK," Hildy says again. "When is Dad coming home?"

"He should be here for dinner," her mother says. But Mr. Harmon doesn't come home for dinner. He doesn't come home until Hildy is already in bed, hours after the library has closed.

She lies in bed and listens to her mother shout at him. She wonders if Jenny Rose is awake too.

So Hildy and Myron are watching Jenny Rose again, as she lies on her bed. They scoot their bare feet along the warm, dusty plank floor of the gazebo, taking turns peering through the binoculars.

"She hasn't been turning in her homework?" Myron asks. "Then what does she do all the time?"

"That's why we're watching her," Hildy says. "To find out."

Myron lifts the binoculars. "Well, she's lying on her bed. And she's flipping the light switch on and off."

They sit in silence for a while.

"Give me the binoculars," Hildy demands. "How can she be turning off the light if she's lying on the bed?"

But she is. The room is empty, except for Jenny Rose, who lies like a stone upon her flowered bedspread, her arms straight at her side. There are three oranges in the bowl beside the bed. The light flashes on and off, on and off. Myron and Hildy sit in the gazebo, the bared twigs of the oak tree scratching above their heads.

Myron stands up. "I have to go home," he says.

"You're afraid!" Hildy says. Her own arms are covered in goose pimples, but she glares at him anyway.

He shivers. "Your cousin is creepy." Then he says, "At least I don't have to share a room with her."

Hildy isn't afraid of Jenny Rose. She tells herself this over and over again. How can she be afraid of someone who still wets the bed?

It seems to Hildy that her parents fight more and more.

Their fights begin over James mostly, who refuses to apply to college. The R.M. is afraid that he will pick a low lottery number, or even volunteer, to spite his family. Mr. Harmon thinks that the war will be over soon, and James himself is closemouthed and noncommittal.

Hildy is watching the news down in the basement. The newscaster is listing names, and dates, and places that Hildy has never heard of. It seems to Hildy that the look on his face is familiar. He holds his hands open and empty on the desk in front of him, and his face is carefully blank, like Jenny Rose's face. The newscaster looks as if he wishes he were somewhere else.

Hildy's mother sits on the couch beside her, smoking. When Mr. Harmon comes downstairs, her nostrils flare but she doesn't say anything.

"Do Jenny Rose's parents miss her?" Hildy asks.

Her father stands behind her, tweaks her ear. "What made you think of that?"

She shrugs. "I don't know, I just wondered why they didn't take her with them."

The R.M. expels a perfect smoke ring at the TV set. "I don't know why they went back at all," she says shortly. "After what happened, your uncle felt that Jenny Rose shouldn't go back. They spent a week in a five-by-five jail cell with seven other missionaries, and Jenny Rose woke up screaming every night for two years afterwards. I don't know why he wanted to go back at all, but then I guess in the long run, it wasn't his child or his wife he was thinking about."

She looks over Hildy's head at her husband. "Was it?" she says.

November 26, 1970

Darling Jenny,

We passed a pleasant Thanksgiving, thinking of you in America, and making a pilgrimage ourselves. We are traveling across the islands now, to Flores, where the villagers have rarely heard a sermon, rarely even met people so pale and odd as ourselves.

131

We took a ferry from Bali to Lombok, where the fishermen hang glass lanterns from their boats at night. The lantern light reflects off the water and the fish lose direction and swim upwards towards the glow and the nets. It occurred to your father that there is a sermon in this, what do you think?

From the shore you can see the fleet of boats, moving back and forth like tiny needles sewing up the sea. We rode in one, the water an impossible green beneath us. From Lombok we took the ferry to Sumbawa, and your father was badly seasick. We made a friend on the ferry, a student coming home from the university in Java.

The three of us took the bus from one end of the island to Sumbawa at the other end, and as we passed through the villages, children would run alongside the bus, waving and calling out "Orang bulan bulan!"

We arrived on Flores this morning, and are thinking of you, so far away.

Love,

Mom and Dad

Hildy keeps an eye on Jenny Rose. She promised her mother she would. It isn't spying anymore. It seems to her that Jenny Rose is slowly disappearing. Even her presences, at dinners, in class, are not truly *presences*. The chair where she sits at the dinner table is like the space at the back of the mouth, where a tooth has been removed, where the feeling of possessing a tooth still lingers. In class, the teachers never call on Jenny Rose.

Only when Hildy looks through the binoculars, watching her cousin turn the bedroom light on and off without lifting a hand, does Jenny Rose seem solid. She is training her eyes to see Jenny Rose. Soon Hildy will be the only person who can see her.

No one else sees the way Jenny Rose's clothes have grown too big, the way she is sealing up her eyes, her lips, her face, like a person shutting the door of a house to which they will not return. No one else seems to see Jenny Rose at all.

The R.M. worries about James, and Mr. Harmon worries about the news; they fight busily in their spare time, and who knows what James worries about? His bedroom door is always shut and his clothes have the sweet-sour reek of marijuana, a smell that Hildy recognizes from the far end of the school yard.

Jenny Rose doesn't wet the bed anymore. At nine-thirty, she goes to the bathroom and then climbs into bed and waits for Hildy to turn out the light. Which is pretty silly, Hildy thinks, considering how Jenny Rose spends her afternoons. As she walks back to her bed in the darkness, she thinks of Jenny Rose lying on her bed, eyes open, mouth closed, like a dead person, and she thinks she would scream if the lights came back on. She refuses to be afraid of Jenny Rose. She wonders if her aunt and uncle are afraid of Jenny Rose.

This is a trick that her father taught her in the blackness of the prison cell, when she cried and cried and asked for light. He said, close your eyes and think about something good. From before. (What? she said.)

Are your eyes closed? (Yes.) Good. Now do you remember when we spent the night on the Dieng Plateau? (Yes.) It was cold, and when we walked outside, it was night and we were in the darkness, and the stars were there. Think about the stars. (Light.)

In this darkness, like that other darkness which was full of the breathing of other people, she remembers the stars. There was no moon, and in the utter darkness the stars were like windows, hard bits of glass and glitter where the light poured through. What she remembers is not how far away they seemed, but how different they were from any other stars she had seen before, so bright-burning and close. (Darkness.)

Do you remember the Southern Cross? (Yes.) Do you remember the birds? (Yes.)

She had walked between her father and mother, passing under the bo trees, looking always upward at the stars. And the bo trees had risen upward, in a great beating of wings, nested birds waking and rising as she walked past. The sound of the breathing of the cell around her became the beautiful sound of the wings.

(Light.)

Do you remember the four hundred stone buddhas of Borobodur, the seventy-two buddhas that were calm within their bells, their cages? (Yes.) Be calm, Jenny Rose, my darling, be calm.

(Darkness.)

Do you remember the guard that gave you bubur ayam? (Yes.) Do you remember Nyoman? (Yes.) Do you remember us, Jenny Rose, remember us.

(Light.)

"What are you doing?" James says, coming upon Hildy in the gazebo.

She puts down the binoculars, and shrugs elaborately. "Just looking at things."

James's eyes narrow. "You better not be spying on me, you little brat." He twists the flesh of her arm above the elbow, hard enough to leave a bruise.

"Why would I want to watch you?" Hildy yells at him. "You're the most boring person I know! You're more boring than *she* is."

She means Jenny Rose, but James doesn't understand. "You must be the most hopeless spy in the world, you little bitch. You wouldn't even notice the end of the world. She's going to kick him out of the house soon, and you probably won't even notice that."

"What?" Hildy says, stunned, but James stalks off. She doesn't understand what James just said, but she knows that marijuana affects the brains of the people who use it. Poor James.

The lights in her bedroom flick on and off, on and off.

Light, darkness, light.

Myron and Hildy are in the basement. In between studying for biology, and cutting out articles for current events, they play desultory Ping-Pong. "Is your cousin a mutant?" Myron says. "Or is she just a mute ant?"

Hildy serves. "She can talk fine, she just doesn't want to."

"Huh. Just like she doesn't bother to turn the lights on and off the way normal people do." He misses again.

"She's not that bad," Hildy says.

"Yeah, sure. That's why we spy on her all the time. I bet she's really a communist spy and that's why you have to keep an eye on her, spying on a spy. I bet her parents are spies, too."

"She's not a spy!" Hildy yells, and hits the ball so hard that it bounces off the wall. It's moving much faster than it should. It whizzes straight for the back of Myron's head, veering off at the last minute to smash into one of the spider plants.

The macramé plant holder swings faster and faster, loops up and drops like a bomb on the carpet. Untouched, the other macramé plant holders explode like tiny bombs, spilling dirt, spider plants, old Ping-Pong balls all over the basement floor.

Hildy looks over and sees Jenny Rose standing on the bottom step. She's come down the stairs as silently as a cat. Myron sees her too. She's holding a postage stamp in her hand. "I'm sorry," Myron says, his eyes wide and scared. "I didn't mean it."

Jenny Rose turns and walks up the stairs, still clutching the postage stamp. Her feet on the stairs make no sound and her legs are as white and thin as two ghosts.

Hildy collects lipsticks. She has two that her mother gave her, and a third that she found under the seat of her father's car. One is a waxy red, so red that Hildy thinks it might taste like a candy apple. One is pink, and the one that she found in the car is so dark that when she puts it on, her mouth looks like a small fat plum. She practices saying

135

sexy words, studying her reflection in the bathroom mirror, her mouth a glossy, bright O. *Oh darling,* she says. *You're the handsomest, you're the funniest, you're the smartest man I know. Give me a kiss, my darling.*

She wants to tell Jenny Rose that if she—if Jenny Rose—wore lipstick, maybe people would notice her. Maybe people would fall in love with her, just as they will fall in love with Hildy. Hildy kisses her reflection; the mirror is smooth and cool as water. She keeps her eyes open, and she sees the mirror face, yearning and as close to her own face as possible, the slick cheek pressed against her own warm cheek.

In the mirror, she looks like Jenny Rose. Or maybe she has watched Jenny Rose for too long, and now Jenny Rose is all she can see. She leans her forehead against the mirror, suddenly dizzy.

Myron won't come over to the Harmons' house anymore. He goes to the Y instead, plays basketball, until his mother comes to pick him up. He avoids Hildy at school, and finally Hildy calls and explains that she needs him, that it's an emergency.

They meet in the gazebo, of course. Myron won't go inside the house, he says, even to pee.

"How are things?" Myron says.

"Fine," Hildy says. They are formal as two ambassadors.

"I'm sorry I called your cousin a communist."

"That's okay. Look," Hildy says. She presses the heel of her Ked against a loose board until the other end pops up. In the hollow there is a stack of white envelopes with square holes where the stamps have been cut out. She picks up the top one, dated July 19, 1970. "It's her secret place. These are her letters."

"I hope you didn't read them," Myron says. He sounds prim, as if he thinks they shouldn't read other people's letters, not even letters from spies.

"Of course I did," she tells him. "And she's not a spy. She just misses her parents."

"Oh. Is that all?" he asks sarcastically.

Hildy remembers the cool surface of the mirror, the way it almost gave way against her forehead, like water. "She wants to go home. She's going to disappear herself. She's been practicing with the light switch, moving it up and down. She's going to disappear herself back to Indonesia and her parents."

"You're kidding," he says, but Hildy is sure. She knows this as plainly as if Jenny Rose had told her. The letters are a history of disappearance, reappearance, of travelling. It is what they don't say that is important.

"Her parents always tell her how much they love her, they tell her the things that they've seen and done, and they ask her to be happy. But they never tell her they miss her, that they wish she was with them."

"I wouldn't miss her," Myron says, interrupting. Hildy ignores him.

"They don't tell her they miss her, because they know that she would come to them. She's the most stubborn person I know. She's still waiting for them to say it, to say she can come home."

"You're getting as weird as she is," Myron says. "Why are you telling *me* all this?"

Hildy doesn't say, *Because you're my best friend.* She says, "Because you have terrible handwriting. You write like an adult."

"So what?"

"I want you to help me steal her next letter. I want you to write like them, write that she can go home now. I can't do it. What if she recognized my handwriting?"

"You want me to get rid of her for you?" Myron says.

"I think that if she doesn't go home soon, she'll get sick. She might even die. She never eats anything anymore."

"So call the doctor." Myron says, "No way. I can't help you."

But in the end he does. It is December, and the R.M. has canceled two conferences with Jenny Rose's teachers, busy with her church duties. It doesn't really matter. The teachers don't notice Jenny Rose; they call on other students, check off her name at attendance without looking to see her. Hildy watches Jenny Rose, she looks away to see Myron watching her. He passes her a note in class on Tuesday. *I can't keep my eyes on her. How can you stand it?* Hildy can barely decipher his handwriting, but she knows Jenny Rose will be able to read it. Jenny Rose can do anything.

This morning the R.M. almost walked right into Jenny Rose. Hildy was sitting at the breakfast table, eating cereal. She saw the whole thing. Jenny Rose opened the refrigerator door, picked out an orange, and then as she left the kitchen, the R.M. swerved into the room around her, as if Jenny Rose were an inconveniently placed piece of furniture.

"Mom," Hildy said. The R.M. picked up Hildy's cereal bowl to wash it, before Hildy was finished.

"What?" the R.M. said.

"I want to talk to you about Jenny Rose."

"Your cousin?" said the R.M. "It was nice having her stay with us, wasn't it?"

"Never mind," Hildy said. She went to get ready for school.

The three of them sit in the boat. The water is green, the boat is green, she is surprised sometimes when she opens her eyes, that her skin isn't green. Sometimes she is worried because her parents aren't there. Sometimes there is another girl in the boat, bigger than her, always scowling. She wants to tell this girl not to scowl, but it's better to ignore her, to concentrate on putting her parents back in the boat. Go away, she tells the girl silently, but that isn't right. She's the one who has to go away. What is the girl's name? The girl refuses to sit still, she stands up and waves her arms and jumps around and can't even see that she is in danger of falling into the water.

Go away, she thinks at the girl, I'm busy. I blew the roof off a prison once, I knocked the walls down, so I could look at the stars. Why can't I make you go away? I can walk on water, can you? When I leave, I'm taking the boat with me, and then where will you be, silly girl?

Hildy loves her mother's preaching voice, so strong and bell-clear. The R.M. and Hildy's father fight all the time now; the R.M. stays in the kitchen until late at night, holding conversations in a whisper with Mercy Orzibal, Myron's mother, over the phone. Hildy can't hear what the R.M. is saying when she whispers, but she's discovered that if she stands very quietly, just inside the kitchen door, she can make herself as invisible as Jenny Rose. It is just like hiding under the Ping-Pong table. No one can see her.

At night, when the R.M. screams at her husband, Hildy covers her ears with her hands. She sticks the pillow over her head. Lately Hildy never loses at Ping-Pong, although she tries to let her father win. The skin under her father's eyes is baggy and too pink. Next week, he is going away to a conference on American literature.

The R.M. stands straight as a pin behind the pulpit, but this is what Hildy remembers: her mother sitting curled on the kitchen floor, the night before, cupping the phone to her ear, smoking cigarette after cigarette. Hildy waited for her mother to see her, standing in the doorway. The R.M. slammed the phone down on the hook. *That bitch,* she said, and sat sucking smoke in and looking at nothing at all.

Hildy's father sits with the choir, listening attentively to his wife's sermon. This is what Hildy remembers: at dinner, the spoon trembling in his hand as he lifted it to his mouth, his wife watching him. Hildy looked at her father, then at her mother, then at Jenny Rose who never seems to look at anything, whom no one else sees, except Hildy.

It is easier now, looking at Jenny Rose; Hildy finds it hard to look at anyone else for very long. Jenny Rose sits beside her on the wooden pew bench, her leg touching Hildy's leg. Hildy knows that Jenny Rose

139

is only holding herself upon the bench by great effort. It is like sitting beside a struck match that waits and refuses to ignite. Hildy knows that Jenny Rose is so strong now that if she wanted, she could raise the roof, turn the communion grape juice into wine, walk on water. How can the R.M. not see this, looking down from the pulpit at Hildy, her eyes never focusing on her niece, as if Jenny Rose has already gone? As if Jenny Rose was never there?

Even with her eyes closed for the benediction, Hildy can still see Jenny Rose. Jenny Rose's eyes remain open, her hands are cupped and expectant: her leg trembles against Hildy's leg. Or maybe it is Hildy's leg that trembles, beneath the weight of her mother's voice, her father's terrible, pleading smile. For a moment she longs to be as invisible as Jenny Rose, to be such a traveler.

When the mail comes on Monday, there is a letter from Jenny Rose's parents. Hildy extracts the letter from the pile. Myron watches, shifting his weight from one foot to the other. He is not happy about being in the same house as Jenny Rose.

All weekend Myron has been practicing two short phrases, with the aid of one of the original letters. Hildy steams open the letter over the teakettle, while Myron watches. The light in Hildy's bedroom flicks on, flicks off, flicks on again. Hildy can feel it pulling at her: for a moment, she feels as if she were tumbling down the spout, falling into the kettle. She might drown in the kettle water. It's that deep. She's gotten too small. She shakes her head, takes a breath.

They take the letter down to the basement, and sit under the Ping-Pong table while Hildy quickly scans it. Myron, who has gone to the trouble of collecting an assortment of pens, adds a postscript in black ballpoint. *We miss you so much, darling Jenny. Please, please come home.*

"It doesn't match," Myron says, handing the letter to Hildy. She folds it back into the envelope and glues the envelope shut again. It really doesn't matter: Jenny Rose is ready to go. Hildy realizes that she wasn't worried Jenny Rose would recognize her handwriting, it wasn't because of that—Hildy just wants a witness, someone who will see what she has done, what Jenny Rose will do.

"I saw your father," Myron says. "He was at my house last night."

"He's out of town," Hildy says. "He went to a conference."

"He stayed all night long," Myron says. "I know because when I went to school this morning, he was hiding. In my mother's bedroom."

"You're such a liar," Hildy says. "My father is in Wisconsin. He called us from the hotel. How do you think he got from Wisconsin to your house? Do you think he flew?"

"You think Jenny Rose can fly," Myron says. His face is very red.

"Get out of my house," Hildy says. Her hand floats at her side, longing to slap him.

"I think you're nuts," Myron says. "Just like her." And he leaves. His back is stiff with outrage.

Hildy rocks back and forth, sitting under the Ping-Pong table. She holds the letter in her hand as if it were a knife. She thinks about Jenny Rose, and what is going to happen.

Hildy is theatrical enough to want a bang at the end of all her labors. She wants to see Jenny Rose restored to herself. Hildy wants to see the mythical being that she is sure her cousin contains, like a water glass holding a whole ocean. She wants to see Jenny Rose's eyes flash, hear her voice boom, see her fly up the chimney and disappear like smoke. After all, she owes Hildy something, Hildy who generously divided her room in half, Hildy who has arranged for Jenny Rose to go home.

No one is in the house now. James, two months away from his birthday, has gone to register for the draft. Her father is still in Wisconsin (Myron is such a liar!), and her mother is at the church. So after a while, Hildy brings the letter to Jenny Rose, gives it to her cousin, who is lying on her bed.

Hildy sits on her own bed and waits while Jenny Rose opens the letter. At first it seems that Hildy has miscalculated, that the post-script is not enough. Jenny Rose sits, her head bent over the letter. She doesn't move or exclaim or do *anything*. Jenny Rose just sits and looks down at the letter in her lap.

Then Hildy sees how tightly Jenny Rose holds the letter. Jenny Rose looks up, and her face is beautiful with joy. Her eyes are green and hot. All around Jenny Rose the air is hot and bright. Hildy inhales the air, the buzzing rain and rusted metal smell of her cousin.

Jenny Rose stands up. The air seems to wrap around her like a garment. It sounds like swarms and swarms of invisible bees. Hildy's hair raises on her scalp. All around them, drawers and cabinets dump their contents on the floor, while T-shirts whoosh up, slapping sleeves against the ceiling. Schoolbooks open and flap around the room like bats, and one by one the three oranges lift out of the blue bowl on the bedside table. They roll through the air, faster and faster, circling around Jenny Rose on her bed. Hildy ducks as tubes of lipstick knock open the bureau drawer, and dart towards her like little chrome-and-tangerine-, flamingo-and-ebony-colored bees. Everything is buzzing, humming, the room is full of bees.

And then—

"I'm making a mess," Jenny Rose says. She tears the stamp from the envelope, gives it to Hildy. Only their two hands touch, but Hildy falls back on the bed—as if she has stuck her fingers into an electrical outlet—she flies backwards onto her bed.

Jenny Rose walks into the bathroom, and Hildy can see the bath-tub full of water, the silly little boat (is that what she wanted?), the green water spilling over the lip of the tub and rushing over Jenny Rose's feet. Be careful! Hildy thinks. The door slams shut. As Hildy catches her breath, the air in the room becomes thin, and her ears pop. The magic trick is over, the bathroom is empty: Jenny Rose has gone home. Hildy bursts into tears, sits on her bed and waits for her mother to come home. After a while, she begins to pick up her room.

This is the first and most mysterious of three vanishings. No one but Hildy seems to notice that Jenny Rose is gone. A few months later, James goes to Canada. He is dodging the draft. He tells no one he is going, and Hildy finds the brief, impersonal note. He is failing his senior classes, he is afraid, he loves them but they can't help him. Please take care of his fish.

When Mr. Harmon moves out of the house, Hildy has resigned herself to this, that life is a series of sudden disappearances, leave-takings without the proper goodbyes. Someday she too might vanish. Some days she looks forward to learning this trick.

What sustains her is the thought of the better place in which one arrives. This is the R.M.'s heaven; the Canada that James has escaped to; it is in the arms of Mercy Orzibal with her bright, glossy mouth, who tells Mr. Harmon *how witty, how charming, how handsome* he is. It is the green lake in the photograph Jenny Rose has sent Hildy from the island of Flores.

In the photograph Jenny Rose sits between her mother and father, in a funny little white boat with a painted red eye. On the back of the photograph is an enigmatic sentence. There is a smudge that could be a question mark; the punctuation is uncertain. *Wish you were here.*

Wish you were here?

SURVIVOR'S BALL, OR, THE DONNER PARTY

I. Travel.

They had been traveling together for three days in Jasper's rented car when they came to the dark mouth of the tunnel into Milford Sound. Serena was telling Jasper something very important. What did Jasper know about Serena after three days? That she didn't wear underwear. That she was allergic to bees. That she liked to talk. (She said the strangest things.) That she was from Pittsburgh. Listening to her voice made him feel less homesick.

Jasper was driving on the wrong side of the road, in a place where water spun down the wrong way in the drain, on a continent that was on what he thought of as the upside-down part of the globe, where they celebrated Christmas on the beach and it snowed in the summer, which was the winter. A girl from Pittsburgh was a good thing, like an anchor. Every homesick traveler should have one.

"That thing you said to me in the bar was so cute," Serena said.

"You know, when we met?" Jasper said nothing. His tooth hurt. He mimed, to show that it was hurting. "Poor guy," Serena said.

They drove down the Avenue of the Disappearing Mountain through groves of swordlike cabbage trees. The road circled up between cracked gray boulders and the little red car went up the road like a toy pulled on a string.

"There was a guy in Auckland who had been to Milford Sound," Serena said. "He told me it was like standing at the edge of the world. It's funny. I'd met him before, in Tokyo, I think. Once you've been traveling for a while, you run into the same people everywhere you go. But I never remember their names. You end up saying things to each other like, 'Do I know you? Were you the guy at that restaurant, that one with the huge fish tank, in Amsterdam?' You end up writing down your addresses on little pieces of paper for each other, and then you always lose the pieces of paper, but it's okay, because you'll run into each other again.

"It's not a very big world," she said sadly.

They had been late leaving the youth hostel in Te Anau because Serena slept past noon, and then she thought she might like a shower. There was no hot water left, but she spent a long time in the bathroom anyway, writing in her journal. Jasper hoped she wasn't writing about him. He consulted his guidebook and then the hostel manager and still managed to get lost on his way to the corner dairy to buy aspirin for his tooth, and then lost again on the way back. In the end, he had to ask a little girl wearing a red parka and striped black-and-white stockings for directions. When he came back, Serena was sitting on the bed, writing postcards. Her clothes and her books and other things were scattered all around her. She looked completely at home in the hostel room, as if she had lived here for years, but everything went back into her backpack, snip-snap, and then the room looked very empty, nothing but a lonely bed and a heap of sheets.

146

Before they left Te Anau, they stopped at a pub for lunch. Jasper couldn't eat, but he paid for Serena's meal. She flirted with the barman, sticking strands of her hair into her wide red mouth, and licking them into dark, glossy tips. She told the barman that she was running away from home, that she was going to travel all the way around the world and just keep on going, that she liked New Zealand beer. She didn't say anything at all about Jasper who was standing at the bar right there beside her, but her hand had been curled in a comfortable way in his pocket, down under the counter.

They hadn't seen a single car since they'd left the main road and headed for the pass into Milford Sound. After enduring ominous weather reports all the way from Queenstown to Te Anau, he guessed it wasn't surprising. Alone, Jasper would have headed up the east coast to Dunedin, rather than making the long drive into the West and Fiordland, but Serena had a great desire to see Milford Sound and he was quickly learning that Serena was seldom thwarted in her great desires.

Two nights ago he had been sitting in bed, watching her sleep. Dust floated in the cold moon-lighted air and he sneezed. A piece of his tooth, a back molar, fell into his hand. In the morning when Serena woke up, she had put it in an airmail envelope, sealed the envelope, and written "Jasper's tooth" on it.

He had the envelope in his pocket now and every once in a while his tongue went up to touch the changed, broken place in his mouth. "I've never met anyone named Jasper before," Serena said, "It's old-fashioned."

Jasper looked at her. She looked back, smirking, black hair tucked into her mouth. She was doodling on the back of her own hand with a fountain pen, making thin jagged lines. It was an expensive pen. His name was engraved on it.

"So's Serena," he said carefully, around the tooth. "My grandmother's youngest brother's name was Jasper. He died in a war."

"I'm not named after anybody," Serena said. "In fact, I've always hated my name. It makes me sound like a lake or something. Lake Serena. Lake Placid. I don't even like to swim."

Jasper kept his eyes on the road. "I never learned how to swim," he said.

"Then hope that there will always be enough lifeboats," she said, and closed one eye slowly. He watched her in the rear-view mirror. It was not an altogether friendly wink. She put the pen down on the dashboard.

"My grandmother gave me that pen," he said. He'd lent it to Serena in the bar in Queenstown when they met. She hadn't given it back yet, although he had bought her a ballpoint at a chemist's the next day. He'd also bought her a bright red lipstick, which he had thought was funny for some reason, a bar of chocolate, and a tiny plastic dinosaur because she said she didn't like flowers. He wasn't really sure what you were supposed to buy for a girl you met in the bar, but she had liked the dinosaur.

"I never had a grandmother," Serena said, "Not a single one. Not a mother, not a brother, not a sister, not a cousin. In fact, there was a general drought of relatives where I was concerned. A long dry spell. Although once I brought home a kitten, and my father let me keep it for a while. That kitten was the only relative who ever purely loved me. Does your grandmother love you?"

"I guess," Jasper said. "We have the same ears. That's what everyone says. But I have my father's crummy teeth."

"My father's dead," Serena said, "and so is the kitten."

"I'm sorry," Jasper said, and Serena shrugged. She held her left hand away from her, examining her drawing. It looked like a map to Jasper—pointy stick-drawings of mountains, and lines for roads. She stuck a finger in her mouth and began to smudge the lines away carefully, one by one. "Your ears aren't so bad," she said.

The radio went on and off in a blur of static. *Unseasonable weather . . . party of trekkers on the Milford Track . . . missing for nearly . . . between Dumpling and Doughboy Huts . . . rescue teams . . . .* Then nothing but static. Jasper turned off the radio.

"They might as well give up," Serena said. "They're all dead by now, buried under an avalanche somewhere. They'll find the bodies in a couple of weeks when the snow melts." She sounded almost cheerful.

There were tall drifts of snow on either side of the road. Every 500 meters they passed black-and-yellow signs reading: "Danger! Avalanche Area: Do Not Stop Vehicle!" Every sign said exactly the same thing, but Serena read them out loud anyway, in different voices—Elmer Fudd, Humphrey Bogart, the barman's flirty New Zealand sing-song.

"Danger, Will Robinson Crusoe!" she said, "Killer robots and tsunamis from Mars ahead. Also German tourists. Do not stop your vehicle. Do not roll down your window to feed the lions. Remain inside your vehicle at all times. Do not pass go. Do not pick up hitchhikers—oops, too late."

All day the sky had been the color of a blue china plate, flat and suspended upon the narrow teeth of the mountains. The road wound precariously between the mountains, and the car threaded the road. The sun was going down. Just where the road seemed about to lift over the broken mountain rim, where the sun was sliding down to meet them, a black pinprick marked the tunnel into Milford Sound. As Jasper drove, the pinprick became a door and the door became a mouth that ate up first the road and then the car.

Serena was reading out of Jasper's guidebook. "Started in 1935," she said. "Did you know it took twenty years to complete? It's almost a mile long. Four men died in rock falls during the blasting. You should always call a mountain *Grandmother*, to show respect. Did you know that? Turn on the headlights—"

They went from the pink-gray of the snowdrifts into sudden dark. The road went up at a 45-degree angle, the car laboring against the steep climb. The headlights were sullen and small reflecting off the greasy black swell of the tunnel walls. The walls were not smooth; they bulged and pressed against the tarmac road.

In the headlights, the walls ran with condensation. Over the noise of the car Jasper could hear the plink-plink of fat droplets falling down the black rock. He touched his tongue to his tooth.

"Why, Grandmother, what a big dark tunnel you have," he said. The terrible weight of the mountain above him, the white snow shrouding the black mountain, the stale wet air in the tunnel, all pressed down inexorably upon him in the dark. He felt strangely sad, he felt lost, he felt dizzy. He sank like a slow stone in a cold well.

"Hello sailor," Serena said. "Welcome to Grandmother's Tunnel of Love." She put her long white hand on his leg and looked at him sidelong. He sank down, was pressed down, heavy. His tooth whining like a dog. He couldn't bear the weight of Serena's black eyes, her thin shining face. "Are you all right?"

He shook his head. "Claustrophobic," he managed to say. He could hardly keep his foot on the gas pedal. He saw them spinning through the dark towards a black wall, a frozen door of ice.

And then he had to stop the car. "You drive," he said, and fumbled the door open and went stumbling over to the passenger's door. Serena shifted to the driver's side and he sat down in her warm seat. It took all his strength to shut the door again.

"Please," he said. "Hurry."

She drove competently, talking at him the whole time. "You never told me you were claustrophobic. Lucky for you I came along. We should be out soon."

They came out into night. There was nothing to distinguish one darkness from the other but dirty snow in the headlights. Yet Jasper felt the great clinging weight fall away from him. His tongue went up to touch his broody tooth. "Stop the car," he said. He threw up kneeling beside the road. When he stood up, his knees were wet with melted snow. "I think I'm all right again," he said.

"You drive if you want to," she said. "Your call, pal. It's about another forty-five minutes to the hotel, and you can't miss it. There's only one road and one hotel."

Iced pinecones shattered like glass under the wheels of the car. The road was steeper, circling down this time.

"What does the guidebook say about the hotel?" he asked.

Serena said, "Well, it's an interesting story. This is funny. When I called to make the reservation, the man said they were booked solid. It's a private party or something. But I talked sweet, told him we had come a long way, a *really* long way." She stuck her feet up on the dashboard and leaned her head on his shoulder. He could see her in the mirror, looking pleased with herself.

Jasper said, "The hotel is full?" He pulled over to the side of the road and put his head against the steering wheel. Serena said, "This is the third time you've stopped the car. I have to pee."

"Is the hotel full or isn't it?" Jasper said.

"Have some chewing gum," Serena said. "Your breath smells like vomit. Don't worry so much."

He couldn't chew the gum, but he sucked on it. He started the car again.

"Is your tooth killing you?" she said.

"Yeah," he said. "Revenge of the sugar cereal."

They went another five hundred yards when something ran across the road. It looked like a small person, scrambling across the road on all fours. It had a long bony tail. Jasper slammed on the brakes and swerved. Serena's arm flailed out and walloped him, catching his jaw precisely upon the broken tooth. He howled. Serena fell forward, knocking her skull loudly against the dashboard. The car came to a stop, and after a moment, during which neither of them was capable of speech, he said, "Are you okay? Did we hit it?"

"What was it?" she said. "A possum? My head hurts. And my hand."

"It wasn't a possum," he said. "Too big. Maybe a deer."

"There are no deer in New Zealand," she said. "The only native mammal is the bat. It's just us poor unsuspecting marsupials around here. Marsupials."

Then she snorted. He was amazed to see that tears were streaming down her face. She was laughing so hard she couldn't speak. "What's a marsupial?" he said. "Are you laughing at me? What's so funny?"

She punched his shoulder. "A possum is a marsupial. It carries its young in a pouch. It's just the word marsupial. It always cracks me up. It's like pantyhose or crumhorn."

It didn't seem that funny to him, but he laughed experimentally. "Marsupial," he said. "Ha."

"Your mouth is bleeding," she said, and snorted again. "Here." She took a dirty Kleenex out of her bag and licked it. Then she applied it to his lower lip. "Let me drive."

"Maybe it was a dog," he said. There was nothing on the road now.

2. Arrival

Milford Sound curls twenty-two kilometers inland, like a dropped boot. Its heel points north, kicking at the belly of South Island. The Tasman Sea fills the boot, slippery and cold and dark. Abel Tasman, the first European to set foot on shore, sailed away in a hurry again after several of his crew were cooked and eaten. He left behind him

Breaksea, Doubtful and George Sounds, and Milford Sound, which is now accessible by sea, by air, by foot across the Milford Track, or along the Milford Road by car, through Homer Tunnel.

In winter, the road is sometimes closed by avalanches. In summer there are sometimes unseasonable storms. Even blizzards, sometimes. Was it winter or was it summer? There was snow on the ground. Jasper's tooth hurt. He didn't remember.

The Milford Hotel is a tall white colonial building. It has a veranda for warm weather use in December. From the front bedrooms, guests look out on the Mitre, rising up from the Sound 1,695 meters, thin and pointed, doubled in the looking-glass water below. At the back of the hotel, lesser mountains march down to a flat broad meadow. The Milford Road ends at the hotel's front door; the Milford Track begins at the back door.

What happens when you get to the end of the world? Sometimes you find a party. This party has been going on for a long time. There is music, lights, people drinking and dancing. Strange things happen at these parties. It is the end of the world, after all.

There is a small guest parking lot behind the Milford Hotel. To Jasper's dismay, it was nearly full when they pulled in. As they got out of the car they could hear a band playing jazz. Two windows stood open on the veranda and they could see into an enormous room. There was a crowd of people, some dancing, some sitting and eating at small tables. Someone was singing, "I'd, like to get you, on a, slow boat, to China," in a low croony alto. They could hear wine glasses being tapped against each other, knives skittering across plates—all this through the two French doors that stood open to the veranda, to Jasper and Serena as they stood there, and to the Milford Track.

Jasper's tooth, his whole body, burned in the fresh cold air. He looked doubtfully at Serena, at her uncombed spit-curled tails of hair, parted haphazardly over the new livid bruise. Her jeans had holes in them. He was wearing his college fraternity sweatshirt with a cartoon of two dogs fucking on it. His tennis shoes were covered in gray caked mud and his knees were still wet. "Serena," he said, "They're having a party."

"Well, that's what I said," Serena said. "Come on. I love parties like this. Everything's always so fancy. Cocktails and little napkins and weird shit on toothpicks."

Inside, the women wore elegant dresses. The men wore dinner jackets. They were probably wearing cummerbunds. Jasper's tooth ached.

Serena turned and made a face at him. "Come on," she hissed.

"Serena," he said. "Wait for a second. Let's find another door. "

The farther she moved away from him—the closer to the veranda she got—the more the weight of the tunnel fell back on him. His tooth was twanging wildly now, like a dowser's rod. He ran after her.

A tall man met them in the open window. The man was all in black. He had a hairy face. "Here you are," the man said. His clothes were old-fashioned, the collar of his shirt narrow and starched. He smiled at them as if they were long-lost acquaintances. His lips in the black beard were red, as if he were wearing lipstick.

"You were expecting us?" Jasper said.

"Of course," the man said, still smiling. "The young lady was most insistent we make room for you both when she called."

Serena said, looking slyly at Jasper, "You do have a room available."

"We made arrangements," the man said. "But you must come in out of this weather. My name is Mr. Donner."

"I'm Serena Silkert, and this is Jasper Todd," Serena said. Mr. Donner held out his hand. It was neither warm nor cold and his grasp was not too firm nor too limp, but Jasper jerked his own hand away as if he had touched a live coal, or an eel. Mr. Donner smiled at him and took Serena's hand, leading her into the hotel.

They came into the room full of people. At that instant the music broke off. The dancers turned and stared at Jasper and Serena. A woman laughed as pages of sheet music lifted off the musicians' stands and came drifting and scuttering across the floor.

The room was longer than it was wide, with two enormous fireplaces set into the wall that faced the windows. From the fireplaces came a gnawing noise; gradually other small noises sprang up among the tables as the diners collected the scattered sheets of music. There were chandeliers and candles on the tables and the wind passing down the room caused the lights to flicker and dim. Between the greasy yellow light of the candles and the chandeliers, faces seemed to float like white masks. A man stumbled against Jasper. He smiled. His teeth were filed down to sharp points and Jasper flinched away. All the people that he saw had ruddy glowing cheeks and shining eyes—*Why, Grandmother, what big eyes you have!* The firelight elongated and warped their shadows, draped like tails across the floor.

"What kind of convention is this?" Jasper said as Serena said, "You're American, aren't you, Mr. Donner?"

"Yes," he said. He looked at them, his eyes lingering on Serena's forehead. "First thing, why don't you go freshen up? We've put you upstairs in Room 43. The key is in the door," he said almost apologetically, giving them a photocopied sheet of directions. "I'm afraid the hotel is a bit of a maze. Just keep turning left when you go up the stairs. Try not to get lost."

Jasper followed Serena through a nest of staircases and corridors. Sometimes they passed through doors which led to more stairs. From the outside, the hotel had not seemed this large or twisty. Serena walked purposefully, consulting the map, and Jasper stumbled after her, afraid that if they were separated, he would never find his way up or back down again to the dining room. Little drifts of plaster fallen from the ceiling lay upon the faded red carpet. Serena muttered under her breath, navigating. They went left, left, and left again.

Jasper, following Serena, had a sudden familiar feeling. He was following his grandmother, her beehive hairdo looming ahead of him. They were somewhere, he didn't know where. He was a small child. He fell further and further behind, and suddenly she turned around—her face—Serena put her head around the corner of a hall. "Hurry up," she said. "I have to pee."

At last they came to a hallway where none of the doors had numbers. They passed a door where inside someone paced back and forth, breathing loudly. Their own footsteps sounded sly to Jasper, and the person behind the door sucked in air with a hiss as they went by. Jasper pictured the occupant, ear against the door, listening carefully, putting eye to spyhole, peeking out.

The last door on the corridor had a tarnished key in the lock. The door was small and narrow, and Jasper stooped to enter. The ceiling sloped toward the floor, and beneath the white bolsters and comforter, the double bed sank in the middle like a collapsed wedding cake. It smelled fusty and damp. Jasper threw his pack down. "Did you see that man's teeth?" he asked.

"Mr. Donner? Teeth?" she said. "How is your tooth?"

"There was a man down the hall," he said. "He was breathing."

Serena pushed at his shoulders. "Lie down for a minute," she said. "You haven't eaten all day, have you?"

"This is a strange place." He sat on the bed. He lay down and his feet hung over the mattress.

"It's a foreign country," she said, and pulled her sweater over her head. Underneath, she was naked. A thick pink line of scar ran down under her collarbone. There was a faint mark on her breast as if someone had bitten her.

"I did that," he said.

"Mmm," Serena said. "You did. Maybe you broke your tooth on me."

"You have a scar," he said. He had traced his finger along the line of that scar, and she had exhaled slowly and smiled and said, "Warmer, you're getting warmer." He had bitten her experimentally, to see what she tasted like, to make his own small impermanent mark on her.

"That? I thought you were too polite to ask. That was a fire. My father's house burned down. I had to break a window to get out and I landed on the glass."

"Oh, sorry." He reached out a finger to trace that line again, to see if they ended up in the same place again, but she was standing too far away. He was too far away, lying on the bed.

"Don't be," she said. "First I took all the money out of the hiding place under the sink. Always look under the mattress, and under the sink." She pulled something velvety and stretchy out of the pack, held it up against her body. "Are you going to change into something clean?"

"These are my cleanest pants," Jasper said. But he took a woolly sweater out of his bag and put it on. He lay on the bed looking at her. As usual, she looked utterly at home, even in this strange place. He tried to think of Serena in her home, her real home in Pittsburgh. A house was burning down. She sat, domesticated and tame, nestled on a burning couch, watching a burning television, the kitten on her lap all made of flames. She was holding a map, he saw, a book of maps. The fire was erasing the roads, the continents, all of the essential information. Now they would never get home again. He tried opening his mouth as far as he could.

Serena pulled at his feet and he sat up and fumbled the bottle of aspirin out of his pocket. He poured a heap into his hand and swallowed them one by one.

The other thing from his pocket was the envelope with his tooth in it. Serena took it away from him. She stuck her finger in a corner, and ripped the envelope open. She held the tiny bit of tooth in her palm for a minute and then popped it into her mouth.

"Yuck!" he said, "Why did you do that?" But at the same time he was almost flattered.

"Tasty," Serena said. "Like candy corn. Yum. Go on down," she said. "You take the map. Don't wait for me—I never get lost. I'm going to have a quick shower." She left the bathroom door open.

In the hallway, he studied the map, his ears pricked, listening for the occupant of the room down the hall. He heard only music, very faint. In the end he followed the music down the many staircases to the dining room. All the way down, just behind his eyelids, he could see the thing from the road running alongside him, crouched and naked and anxious. It was burning. Small, heatless flames licked along its back like fur and dripped onto the carpet. His grandmother, somewhere behind him, was sweeping up the flames into a dustpan. *Someone should put that dog out,* she said. *It isn't house-trained.* Somewhere upstairs a door opened and slammed shut and then opened again.

In the dining room a table had been newly laid for two and he sat down with his back to the fireplace. At the front of the room Mr. Donner was dancing with a stout woman in red.

The fire behind him traced black figures on the walls and wavered over the faces of the diners around him. When he looked at them, they looked away. But they had been looking at him in the first place, he was certain. He wished that he'd taken a bath or at least combed his hair.

The heat beat at his skull and the snap of the fire lulled him, while the cold streaming in through the open doors stung his eyes and plucked at his jaw. Half of him burned cold, the other half hot. He thought of going up to the tiny room again, to wait until it was time to go to sleep. There would be the same discomfort: the damp cool sheets and between them the sticky warmth of Serena's body. Jasper thought of the white eyeless walls and shuddered. It was preferable to sit here between the fireplace and the open windows.

Framed in the window closest to him was a mountain, blunt and crooked like a ground-down incisor. Halfway down its slope he could see a procession of lights. He saw that others around him were intently watching the mountain and the moving lights.

A waiter emerged from a service door beside the fireplace and began arranging another table. He set seven places and silently disappeared again. Jasper looked back towards the mountain. His tongue went up to touch his tooth. He counted the lights on the mountain. The musicians sawed at their instruments furiously and on the dance floor the dancers moved faster and faster, picking up their feet and slamming them back down, spinning like flames.

Serena came into the ballroom. She was wearing the stretchy black dress and a pair of gaudy purple tights. She had washed her hair, and applied makeup to the bruise on her forehead. Her face was white and delicate as ivory, under a dusting of powder. She was wearing the silly red lipstick. *The better to kiss you, my dear,* someone said.

He stood up and went to her chair. "You look very beautiful," he said.

She let him seat her and said bluntly, "You look like shit. Does your tooth hurt? Will you be able to eat anything?"

"I don't know," he said. "But I'd like some wine."

She sat down next to Jasper, put her cool hand upon his forehead. "Poor kid," she said. "You're burning up."

Mr. Donner left the dance floor. He borrowed a chair from the table set for seven, and sat down next to them. He was breathing hard. Jasper thought he could almost see the breath leave his mouth, like tiny licks of wet flame. "Is your room adequate?" he said.

"Our room is fine," Serena said. She stretched her hands out across the tablecloth, towards Jasper. "What a nice hot fire!"

All the better to cook you, my dear, Jasper thought, and touched his tooth again. He said, "Where did all these people come from?"

"This is the first course," Mr. Donner said. Waiters put down bowls of thin pink broth and poured red wine into Serena and Jasper's glasses.

"Some of us have come from very far away," Mr. Donner said. "We meet every year. We meet to celebrate the triumph of the human spirit in situations of great adversity. We are all travelers, survivors of adventures, calamitous expeditions, of tragedies. We are widows and orphans, the survivors of marriages and shipwrecks. This is the 143rd Survivor's Ball."

"That's nice," Jasper said.

Serena squirmed in her seat. "You look so familiar," she said to Mr. Donner. "Have we met?"

"One meets so many people," Mr. Donner said. He took a sip of wine. "We're expecting one more party. They're a little late."

"Is that why you keep the windows open?" Serena asked.

"We're hoping that they'll hear the band playing," Mr. Donner said. "Music raises the spirits considerably, I find. We hope that they'll find their way back down the trail without further incident."

"You're talking about the lost hikers, right?" Serena said.

"There were twenty-three hikers," Jasper said. "They've only set seven places."

Mr. Donner shrugged. "Do try your soup, Mr. Todd."

Jasper took a small sip of the soup. It was warm and salty and as he swallowed, it burned. "I'm starving," Serena said. She showed them her empty bowl. "Jasper's tooth broke, but he's afraid to go see a dentist."

"It's fine," Jasper said. "I'll wait until we get back to Auckland." He had a very clear picture of a dentist in Auckland, who would be a kind man with a well-kept moustache. A gentle man with small knowledgeable hands, who believed in using gas. Or maybe the tooth would grow back.

The second course was a fatty cut of brown meat. There was a little dish of green jelly and carrots cooked with brown sugar. Steam rose up to Jasper's nose, thick and sweet. He diced up a carrot and ate it with his spoon. "I'm not really that hungry," he said.

"After dinner," Mr. Donner said, "we sit and tell stories in front of the fire. I do hope you like stories."

"Ghost stories!" Serena said. "It's just like Girl Scout Camp. I used to love the campfires."

Jasper's wineglass was full again. He didn't remember drinking the last glass. *The better to drink you, my dear,* his tooth said. He still had a sense of wrongness, an instinct that the proper thing to do would be to leave or perhaps just go up to bed. But that would mean the tunnel again, or the small coffin-like room with its sad, sagging bed. He took another sip of wine to fortify himself. The band was playing a new song. The song sounded familiar. It might have been "Autumn Leaves." It might have been a hymn.

"Have the two of you been traveling together long?" Mr. Donner asked.

"Oh no," Serena said. "We met three days ago in a bar in Queenstown. We're traveling around the world in opposite directions. I fly to Hawaii next Tuesday and then I'm supposed to go home again. This is just Jasper's second stop."

"Maybe I'll come back home with you," Jasper said.

"Don't be silly," she said, but under the table her foot moved up his calf, nudged in between his legs in a friendly way. "I'm trying to keep as far away from home as possible, for as long as possible. Not that I have a home any longer. It burned down."

"How sad," Mr. Donner said, smiling.

"Not really," Serena said primly. "I'm the one who burned it down, but I don't like to talk about that."

Jasper looked across the table at the girl he had met in a bar. She didn't look like a girl who would burn down her house. He wasn't really sure what girls who burned down houses looked like. What was the name of the lipstick color? That had been the silly thing, something like Berry Me, or Red Death, or maybe Red Delicious. Maybe Firetruck.

"See?" Serena said. "Do you still want to go home with me?" Under the table, her hand ran up and down his leg, pinching lightly. "Jasper isn't the sort who travels purposefully," she said to Mr. Donner. "He isn't the sort who's purposeful, or smart, or careful about the kinds of women in bars he picks up in bars, for that matter. You've got to be careful," she said, turning to Jasper for a moment, "about picking up girls in bars, good grief, what if I'd turned out to be weird, or something? But he isn't careful. He's lucky instead. For example, he won his trip by filling out a form in a travel agency."

"You are a fortunate young man," Mr. Donner said.

There was just a small smear of mint jelly on Serena's plate. "When he told me in the bar how he'd won, I thought it was just a great pick-up line," she said. "The tie-breaking question was *Why do you want to go around the world?* And he wrote, *Because you can't go through it.* Isn't that ridiculous?"

"It's true," Jasper said. He was careful to enunciate. "Sad but true."

Serena smiled at him. "I shouldn't complain, though. It's great traveling with Jasper. He gave me a plastic dinosaur. A stegosaurus. Thanks, Jasper," she said.

"Don't mention it," said Jasper. He wanted to say something, to explain that travel was important to him, that someday, he knew, if he traveled long enough he would eventually come to a wonderful—a magical—place. His toothache was almost gone, just the smallest twinge very far away. Practically in another country. Some place that he had been stuck in for a while. He looked past Serena, to the French window. The torches were now at the base of the trail. They swung back and forth, lighting up the great trunk of a kauri tree, a growth of ferns on the lawn before the hotel.

"Look," said Mr. Donner, "here they come. Just in time for dessert."

The whole room rose from their chairs, applauding. Five men and two women came into the room. They stopped just past the threshold as if uncertain of their welcome. They looked longingly at the fireplaces, at the empty plates piled up on dirty tables, but they did not move. Instead the crowd swept towards them.

"Excuse me," Serena said. She got up and went with the others. Jasper watched her recede: the black hair fallen down around her shoulders again, a tail tucked into her painted mouth, the long legs in the purple tights. Waiters were going back and forth between the tables extinguishing candles. Jasper watched as they pinched the small flames between their fingers. Soon the only light would be the red light of the fireplaces; the bulbs of the chandeliers were faint as starlight, guttering to blackness.

At the opposite end of the room, near the windows, he could no longer see Serena or the hikers. The crowd was clotted and indistinct in the dim light. It moved slowly across the dance floor, pouring through the window like the massy shadow of the black mountain. Sitting by the dance floor was a single cellist. He had put his instrument down, and was cramming balls of sheet music into his mouth. He chewed them slowly, his hands pulling the white pages out of the air around him as if they were alive. The wind blew out the chandeliers, but Jasper could still see the musician, his mouth and eyes wet and horrible. "Where are the other hikers?"

Mr. Donner was biting savagely at his thumb, frowning down at the table. "Sometimes people do unthinkable things, in order to come home safely," he said. "Impossible things, wonderful things. And afterwards, do you think they go home? No. You find it's much, much better to keep on traveling. Hard to stop, really."

The French doors had shut—the hikers were cut off from the trail and the mountain, should they wish to go back. The fire behind Jasper was flickering low, casting out more shadow than warmth, and yet the room seemed to grow hotter and hotter.

His tooth no longer hurt. The wine and the warmth were pleasant. "I can tell you're a good man, Mr. Donner. Otherwise my tooth would warn me. I've never had a toothache like this before. I've never been to a place like this before. I've never been to a party like this before. But your name, it's familiar. My tooth says your name is familiar."

The crowd was moving back across the dance floor, towards them, towards the table set with seven places, but he couldn't see Serena. She had been completely swallowed up. The cellist had finished his music, and like a magician, he lifted the bow of his instrument, lowered it into his wide unhappy mouth.

"Perhaps you recognize it," said the bearded man. "But on the other hand, what's a name, hmm? After a while names are just souvenirs. Places you've been. Let me introduce you to some of my friends." He waved towards the approaching crowd. "Mrs. Gomorrah over there, Mr. Belly of the Whale, Ms. Titanic, Little Miss Through the Looking-Glass, Mr. and Mrs. Really Bad Marriage, Mr. Over The Falls in a Wooden Barrel."

Off in the distance Jasper could hear a wolf howling. Which was strange. What had Serena said? It was all marsupials here. The plaintive noise reverberated in his tooth.

The bearded man was practically gnashing his teeth, smiling ferociously. "I have seen snow and I have been hungry, and I have seen nothing in my travels that is so bad as not living. I propose a toast, Mr. Todd."

They both raised their glasses. "To travel," one said.

"To life," said the other.

> —*Some are leaving this fall for Texas, and more are going in the spring to California and Oregon. For my part I have no desire to go anywhere. I am far enough west now and do believe some people might go west until they have been around the world and never find a place to stop.*
>
> Elvira Power Hynes, March 1852

SHOE AND MARRIAGE

1. The glass slipper.

He never found the girl, but he still goes out, looking for her. His wife—the woman he married—she has the most beautiful smile. But her feet are too big.

This girl looks at him, but she doesn't smile. She's wearing too much makeup. Blue eyeliner put on like house paint, lipstick, mascara, sexy glitter dusted all over her face and bare shoulders. If he touched her, it would come off on his fingers, fine and gritty and sad. He doesn't touch her. The other women in the house, they've probably told her things. Maybe she recognizes him. These women are paid to be discreet, but once, afterwards, a woman asked him for his autograph. He tried to think of something appropriate to write. She didn't have a piece of paper, so instead he wrote on the back of a takeout menu. He wrote, *I am a happy man. I love my wife very much.* He underlined *happy*.

They stand awkwardly in this girl's tiny room. The room is too small and the bed is too big. They stand as far from the bed as possible, crowded up against the wall. On the wall are posters of celebrities, pictures that this girl has cut out from newspapers and fashion magazines. The people in these pictures are glossy like horses. They look expensive. He sees his wife with her beautiful smile, looking down at them from the wall. If he were to look carefully he would probably find himself on the wall as well, looking comfortable and already too much at home here. He doesn't look at the wall. He looks at this girl's feet.

He was never a very good dancer. What he loved were the women in their long wide skirts. When they danced, the heavy taffeta and silk hitched up and belled out and then you saw their petticoats. More silk, more taffeta—as if underneath that's all they were, silk and taffeta. Their shoes left thin gritty smears along the marble floor.

He never saw what kind of shoes they were wearing. Only hers. Perhaps they were all wearing slippers made of glass. Perhaps glass slippers were fashionable at the time. Her feet must have been so small. And she was a tall girl, too. She leaned against his arms, and he hovered over her for a minute. He could smell her hair. It was stacked up on top of her head, all pinned up in some sort of wavy knot, just there beneath his nose. It tickled his nose. It smelled warm. He was so happy. He must have had the silliest smile on his face. Her dress went all the way down to the floor. There were diamonds on the hem, which was silk. The dress made a silky slithery scratchy noise against the floor, like tiny tails and claws. It sounded like mice.

So these are the two things he still wonders about. What's under those skirts? Those other people dancing—were they as happy as he was?

In the garden, the clock struck twelve and she went—when she went, where did she go? He never found that girl. He finds other girls.

(These girls) this girl (they don't wear) she isn't wearing enough clothes. Tangerine-colored see-through shirt; short skirt ripped all the way up the thigh; flesh—fat breasts squashed together in a black brassiere, goose-pimpled arms, long stalky legs balanced on these two tiny feet—he finds the body extremely distracting. "First of all," he says to her, "let's have a look in your closet."

In these closets there is always the right sort of dress. This dress is not the sort of dress one expects to find in a closet in this sort of house. It is prom dress-y—flouncy, lacy, long and demure. It's pink. This girl, he thinks, ran away from home on her tiny feet, with a backpack on her back, with these things in it: posters of her favorite rock stars, her prom dress. And the stuffed tiger with real glass eyes that he sees now, on top of the red velveteen bedspread. "What's your name?"

The girl folds her arms across her breasts defensively. She has realized that they are not the point after all. Her arms are freckled and also, he sees, bruised, as if someone has been holding her but not carefully enough. "Emily," she says. "Emily Apple."

"Emily," he says, "why don't you put on this dress?"

When he was a little boy it was always one of two things. He was petted and pampered and made much of, or he was ignored and left to his own devices. When he was alone what he liked best was to sit under things. He liked to hide in plain sight, to be in the middle of all the people. He sat under the piano in the music room. At banquets he slid down his enormous chair and sat under the table with his father's dogs. They licked at his face and arms with long thoughtful tongues. He hid in the fireplaces in the great hall, behind the wrought iron screens. In the summer there were sparrows up in the chimneys, also lizards, spiderwebs, broken sooty bits of shell, feathers and bones caught in the grates. The ladies-in-waiting stood dozing in the thin dusty sunlight of his mother's rooms, and he crept under their heavy skirts and sat at their spangled feet, quiet as a mouse.

He helps Emily Apple slide the beautiful pink dress over her head.

He buttons the row of buttons up her narrow back. He lifts her hair up, heaps it up and sticks pins all through the sticky teased mass. She sits perfectly still on the bed, the glass eyes of the tiger looking out at her from the folds of her skirt. He brings water in a basin and washes her face. He powders her face. He finds a locket in a heap of bangles and safety pins. Inside is a photograph of a young girl, maybe Emily Apple, or maybe not. The little girl stares at him. *What kind of a girl do you think I am?* He fastens the locket around Emily Apple's long neck. Her face is very naked, very beautiful. Her freckles stand out like spatters of soot on a white sheet. She looks as if she is going to a funeral or to a wedding. They find a pair of gloves and pull them up over her freckled arms. Her fingers stick out where mice have eaten the tips of the gloves, but the dress comes all the way down to the floor. They both feel more comfortable now.

Sometimes it surprises him, all these runaway girls—all these women—with their sad faces and their tiny feet. How long has this house been here? When he was looking for that girl, he went to a lot of houses. He knocked on the front doors. He announced who he was. These were eligible girls from good homes. They had maids. He asked the maids if they would try on the shoes, too. At night he dreamed about women's feet. But this house, he never came here.

He has been married for nine years. Perhaps this is the sort of house that only married men can find.

That girl, where did she go? He's still looking for her. He doesn't expect to find her, but he finds other girls. He loves his wife, but her feet are too big. It wasn't what he expected—his life, it isn't at all what he expected. His wife isn't the one that he was looking for. She was a surprise—he burst out laughing, the glass slipper hanging off her toes. She laughed and soot fell out of her hair. He loves her and she loves him, but that girl, he only danced with her one time before the clock struck midnight, and then she left her shoe behind. He was supposed to find it. He was supposed to find her. He never found her, but these girls—this girl, Emily Apple—the other girls in their tiny rooms: the woman downstairs knew exactly the sort of girl he was looking for. In one of these closets, he thinks, maybe there is (perhaps there is) a glass slipper, the match for the one in his pocket.

Some nights when he comes home, he's carrying the orphaned shoe in his coat pocket. It fits just fine. That's how small, how impossibly small it is. His wife smiles at him. She never asks where he's been. She sits in the kitchen beside the fire, with her feet tucked up under her, and he lays his head down in her lap. If only her feet weren't so big. When he was first looking for that girl, he got to lift up a lot of skirts. Only just so high. Really, not high enough. He knelt down and he tried the shoe on every single foot. But it never fit right and he always went away again with the shoe in his pocket.

His wife wasn't one of the eligible girls. She was a kitchen maid. When he saw her, she had her head stuck up the kitchen chimney. She was beating the broom up the chimney, shaking out the soot. Head to foot, she was covered in soot, black as a beetle. When she sneezed, the soot rose up in a cloud. She tried to curtsey when she saw him, and soot fell off her like a black cloak.

Everyone had crowded into the kitchen behind him: his footmen, the lady of the house, her daughters, the other maids. One of the footmen read the proclamation, and the sooty girl sneezed again. The eligible young ladies looked sulky and the maids looked haughty, as if they knew what was going to happen. They didn't like it one bit, but they weren't one bit surprised. The kitchen girl dusted off a kitchen stool and she sat her sooty self down on it, sooty arms akimbo. The long prehensile toes of her bare black feet gripped the stone floor as he knelt down beside her. Her foot was warm and gritty in his hand and her long toes wriggled as if he was tickling her. He hung the glass slipper off her toes. Soot came off on his fingers. There was soot in the long folds of her skirt. He stayed there for a minute, kneeling in the warm ashes at her feet.

"What size shoe do you wear?" he said. Her feet were so big.

"What kind of girl do you think I am?" she said. She sounded as if she were scolding him. When he looked up her face was so beautiful.

This girl sits perfectly still on the bed. There is just room enough for him to kneel down beside the bed. He lifts up her skirt, just high enough. He cups her tiny foot in his hand. How could anyone's foot be so small? It fits into the palm of his hand like a kitten or an egg. He wishes he were that small, like a shoe. He wishes he were a small, perfect shoe, that he could be matched to her foot and hidden under her skirt forever. He takes out the slipper and he slides it onto her foot. They both look down at her foot, beautiful in the glass slipper, and the girl sighs. "It fits just fine," she says. When he doesn't say anything, she says, "What do we do now?"

"What kind of girl do you think I am?" that sooty girl (his wife) said.

He says to the girl on the bed, "Take the shoe off. So we can put it on again."

2. Miss Kansas on Judgment Day.

We are sitting on our honeymoon bed in the honeymoon suite. We are in a state of honeymoon, in our honey month. These words are so sweet: *honey, moon*. This bed is so big, we could live on it. We have been happily marooned—honey marooned—on this bed for days. I have a pair of socks on and you've put your underwear on backwards. I mean, it's my underwear, which you've put on backwards. This is perfectly natural. Everything I have is yours now. My underwear is your underwear. We have made vows to this effect. Our underwear looks so cute on you.

I lean towards you. Marriage has affected the laws of gravity. We will now revolve around each other. You will exert gravity on me, and I will exert gravity on you. We are one another's moons. You are holding onto my feet with both hands, as if otherwise you might fall right off the bed. I think I might float up and hit the ceiling, splat, if you let go. Please don't let go.

How did we meet? When did we marry? Where are we, and how did we get here? One day, we think, we will have children. They will ask us these questions. We will make things up. We will tell them about this hotel. Our room overlooks the ocean. We have a balcony, although we have not made it that far, so far.

Where are we and how did we get here? We are so far away from home. This bed might as well be a foreign country. We are both a little bit homesick, although we have not confessed this to each other. We remember cutting the cake. We poured punch for each other, we linked our arms and drank out of each others' glasses. What was in that punch?

We are the only honeymooners in this hotel. Everyone else is a beauty pageant contestant or a beauty pageant contestant's chaperone. We have seen the chaperones in the halls, women armed with cans of hairspray and little eggs containing emergency pantyhose, looking harassed but utterly competent. Through the walls, we have heard the beauty pageant contestants talking in their sleep. We have held water glasses up to the walls in order to hear what they were saying.

As honeymooners, we are good luck tokens. As if our happiness, our good fortune, might rub off, contestants ask us for a light: they brush up against us in the halls, pull strands of hair off our clothing. Whenever we leave our bed, our room—not often—two or three are sure to be lurking just outside our door. But today—tonight—we have the hotel to ourselves.

The television is on, or maybe we are dreaming. Now that we are married, we will have the same dreams. We are watching (dreaming) the beauty pageant.

On television, Miss Florida is walking across the stage. She's blond and we know from eavesdropping in the hotel bar that this will count against her. Brunettes win more often. Three brunettes, Miss Hawaii, Miss Arkansas, Miss Pennsylvania, trail after her. They take big slow steps and roll their hips expertly. The colored stage lights bounce off their shiny sweetheart dresses. In television interviews, we learned that Miss Arkansas is dyslexic, or maybe it was Miss Arizona. We have hopes of Miss Arkansas, who has long straight brown hair that falls all the way down her back.

You say that if we hadn't just gotten married, you would want to marry Miss Arkansas. Even if she can't spell. She can sit on her hair. A lover could climb that hair like a gym rope. It's fairy-tale hair, Rapunzel hair. We saw her practicing for the pageant in the hotel ballroom with two wild pigs, her hair braided into two lassoes. We heard her say in her interview that she hasn't cut her hair since she was twelve years old. We can tell that she's an old-fashioned girl. Please don't let go of my feet.

We have to admit that we are impressed by Miss Pennsylvania's dress. In her interview, we found out that she makes all of her own clothes. This dress has over forty thousand tiny sequins handstitched onto it. It took a year and a day to stitch on all those sequins, which are supposed to look from a distance like that painting by Seurat. Sunday Afternoon on the Boardwalk. It really is a work of art. Her mother and her father helped Miss Pennsylvania sort the sequins by color. She has three younger brothers, football players, and they all helped, too. We imagine the pinprick sequins glittering in the large hands of her brothers. Her brothers are in the audience tonight, looking extremely proud of their sister, Miss Pennsylvania.

We are proud of Miss Pennsylvania as well, but we are fickle. Miss Kansas comes out onto the stage, and we fall in love with her feet. Don't let go of my feet. We would both marry Miss Kansas. You squeeze my foot so tight when she comes out on stage in her blue checked dress, the blue ribbon in her hair. She's wearing blue ankle socks and ruby red shoes. She practically skips across the stage. She doesn't look to the right, and she doesn't look to the left. She looks as if she is going somewhere. When Miss Kansas leaves the stage we instantly wish that she would come back again.

I wish I had a pair of shoes like that, you say. I say your feet are too big. But if I had a pair like that, I would let you wear them. Now that we are married, our feet will be the same size.

We are proud of Miss Pennsylvania, we love Miss Kansas, and we are afraid of Miss New Jersey. Miss New Jersey's red hair has been teased straight up into two horns. She has long red fingernails and she is wearing a candy red dress that comes up to her nipples. You can see that she isn't wearing pantyhose. Miss New Jersey hasn't even shaved her legs. What was her chaperone thinking? (We have heard rumors in the hall that Miss New Jersey ate her chaperone. Certainly no one has seen the chaperone in a few days.) When she smiles, you can see all her pointy teeth.

Miss New Jersey's complexion is greenish. She has small pointy breasts and a big ass and she twitches it from side to side. She has a tail. She twitches her ass, she lashes her tail; we both gasp. Her tail is prehensile. She scratches her big ass with it. It is indecent and we are simultaneously dismayed and aroused. The whole audience is aghast. One judge faints and one of the other judges douses him with a pitcher of ice water. Miss New Jersey purses her lips, blows a raspberry right at the television screen, and exits stage left.

Well, well, we say, shaken. We huddle together on the enormous bed. Please don't let go, please hold onto my feet.

Some of the other contestants: Miss Idaho wants to work with children. Miss Colorado raises sheep. She can shear a sheep in just under a minute. The dress she is wearing is of wool she cut and carded and knit herself. The pattern is her own. This wool dress is so fine, so thin, that it seems to us that Miss Colorado is not actually wearing anything at all. In fact, Miss Colorado is actually a man. We can see Miss Colorado's penis. But possibly this is just a trick of the light.

Miss Nevada has been abducted by aliens on numerous occasions. The stage spotlights appear to make her extremely nervous, and occasionally she addresses her interviewer as 9th Star Master. Miss Alabama has built her own nuclear device. She has a list of demands. Miss South Carolina wants to pursue a career in Hollywood. Miss North Carolina can kiss her own elbow. We try to kiss our own elbows, but it's a lot harder than it looks on television. Please hold me tight, I think I'm falling.

Miss Virginia and Miss Michigan are Siamese twins. Miss Maryland wants to be in Broadway musicals. Miss Montana is an arsonist. She is in love with fire. Miss Texas is a professional hit woman. She performs exorcisms on the side. She says that she is keeping her eye on Miss New Jersey.

Miss Kansas wants to be a weather girl.

Miss Rhode Island has big hair, all tendrilly looking and slicky-sleek. The top part of her jiggles as she wheels herself on stage in an extremely battered-looking wheelchair. She just has the two arms, but she seems to have too many legs. Also too many teeth. We have seen her practicing water ballet in the hotel swimming pool. (Later, during the talent show, she will perform in a tank made of specially treated glass.) We have to admit Miss Rhode Island has talent but we have trouble saying her name. Too many sibilants. Also, at breakfast her breath smells of raw fish and at night the hoarse mutterings of spells, incantations, the names of the elder gods heard through the wall have caused us to lose sleep.

Miss Rhode Island's bathing costume is designed to show off her many shapely legs, which she waves and writhes at the judges enticingly. We decide that we will never, never live in Rhode Island. Perhaps we will never leave this hotel: perhaps we will just live here.

We ogle some of the contestants in their bathing suits. We try not to look at others. We have made a sort of tent out of the bedspread and we feel perfectly safe inside our tent-bedspread. As long as you are holding onto me. Don't let go.

There are five judges. One of them, a former Miss America herself, is wearing a tiara, all her hair tucked away under a snood. She is very regal but her mouth is not kind. In her hand is a mirror, which she consults now and then in the scoring, reapplying her lipstick vigorously. Now and then she whispers, *I'll get you, my pretty!*

One of the other judges is an old drunk. We saw him down on the boardwalk outside the hotel lobby, wearing a sandwich board and preaching to the waves. He was getting his feet wet. His sandwich board says *the end of the world is nigh*. Beneath this someone has written in lipstick *lions and tigers and bears, oh migh!*

Two of the judges are holding hands under the table.

The last judge is notoriously publicity-shy, although great and powerful. A semi-transparent green curtain has been erected around his chair. We speculate that he is naked, or asleep, or possibly not there at all.

The talent show begins. There are all the usual sorts of performances, tap-dancing and mime, snake handling. Miss West Virginia speaks in tongues. Somehow we understand what she is saying. She is saying that the world will end soon, that we will have six children and all of them will have good teeth, that we will always be as happy as we are at this very moment as long as we don't let go. Don't let go. Miss Texas then comes out on stage and showily exorcises Miss West Virginia. The audience applauds uncertainly.

Miss Nebraska comes out on stage and does a few card tricks. Then she saws Miss Michigan and Miss Virginia in half.

Miss Montana builds her own pyre out of cinnamon and other household spices. She constructs a diving platform out of toothpicks and sugar cubes, held together with hairspray. She stands upon it for a moment, splendid and unafraid. Then she spreads her wings and jumps. Firemen stand on either side of the stage, ready to put her out. She emerges from the fire, new and pink and shining, even more beautiful than before. The firemen carry her out on their broad capable shoulders.

The million-gallon tank is filled before our eyes during a musical interlude. We make out, frisky as teenagers. This way we are feeling, we will always feel this way. We will always be holding each other in just this way. When we look at the television again, Miss Oregon is walking on water. We feel sure that this is done with mirrors.

Miss Rhode Island performs her water ballet, a tribute to Esther

Williams, only with more legs. She can hold her breath for a really long time. The first row of the audience has been issued raincoats and umbrellas. Miss Rhode Island douses them like candles. During the climax of her performance there is a brief unexplained rain of frogs. Miss Texas appears on stage again.

I loved you the first time I saw you. Scarecrow, my dear scarecrow, I loved you best of all. Who would have predicted that we would end up here in this hotel? It feels like the beginning of the world. This time, we tell each other, things are going to go exactly as planned. We have avoided the apple in the complimentary fruit basket. When the snake curled around the showerhead spoke to me, I called room service and Miss Ohio, the snake handler, came and took it away. When you are holding me, I don't feel homesick at all.

Miss Alaska raises the dead. This will later prove to have serious repercussions, but the judges have made a decision and Miss Texas is not allowed on the stage again. It is felt that she has been too pushy, too eager to make a spectacle of herself. She has lost points with the judges and with the audience.

You ask me to put on my wedding dress. You make me a crown out of the champagne foil and that little paper thing that goes around the toilet seat. We sit on the edge of the huge bed, my feet in your lap, your feet dangling dangerously. If only we had a pair of magic slippers. You have your tuxedo jacket on, and my underwear. Your underwear. We should have packed more underwear. What if we never get home again? You have one arm wrapped around my neck so tight I can hardly breathe. I can smell myself on your fingers.

Where will we go from here? How will we find our way home again? We should have carried stones in our pockets. Perhaps we will live here forever, in the honey month, on the honeymoon bed. We will live like kings and queens and eat room service every night and grow old together.

On television, stagehands have replaced the water tank with a trampoline. We wouldn't mind having a trampoline like that. Miss Kansas appears, her hair in two pigtails, her red shoes making our hearts ache. She isn't wearing a stitch of clothing otherwise. She doesn't need to wear anything else. She places her two hands on the frame of the trampoline and swings herself straight up so that she is standing upside down on the frame, her two braids pointing down, her shoes pointing straight up. She clicks her heels together smartly and flips onto the trampoline. As she soars through the air, plump breasts and buttocks bouncing, her arms wheeling in the air, she is starting to sing. Her strong homely voice pushes her through the air, her strong legs kicking at the tough skin of the trampoline as if she never intends to land.

We know we recognize this song.

We bounce on the edge of the bed experimentally. Tears run down our faces. The judges are weeping openly. That song sounds so familiar. Did they play it at our wedding? Miss Kansas rolls through the air, tucks her knees under her arms and drops like a stone, she springs up again and doesn't come back down, the air buoying her up the same way that you are holding me—naked as a jaybird, she hangs balanced in the air, the terrible, noisy, bonecracking air: we hold on tight to each other. The wind is rising. If you were to let go—don't let go—

3. The dictator's wife .

The dictator's wife lives in the shoe museum. During visiting hours she lies in bed downstairs with the rest of the exhibits. When you come in, you can't see her but you can hear her. She is talking about her husband. "He loved to eat strawberries. I don't care to eat strawberries. They taste like dead people to me. I'd rather drink soup made from a stone. We ate off the most beautiful plates every night. I don't know who they belonged to. I just kept track of the shoes."

The museum is a maze of cases. Visitors wander through narrow aisles, elbows tucked in to bodies, so they don't brush against the glass displays. They drift towards the center of the exhibit room, towards the voice of the old lady, until they come upon a bed. Glass boxes stacked up in tall rows hedge in the bed on all sides. In the boxes are pairs of shoes. In the bed is the dictator's wife, covers pulled up to her chin. Visitors stop and stare at the dictator's wife.

She stares back, old and fragile and crumbly. It is disconcerting, to be stared at by this old woman. In proper museums, you go to stare at the exhibits. They do not stare back at you. The dictator's wife is wrinkly like one of those dogs. She's wearing a black wig that's too small for her head. Her false teeth are in a souvenir glass beside the bed. She puts her teeth in.

The dictator's wife will stare at visitors' shoes until the visitors look down too, wondering if a shoelace has come untied.

Another old lady—but not quite as old—lets visitors in. On Tuesdays she dusts cases with an old silk dress. "Admission free today," she said. "Stay as long as you like."

"My shoes," the dictator's wife says to a visitor who has stopped to stare at her. She says this the way some people say, *My children.* She's got an accent, or maybe her teeth don't fit so well. "People don't think about shoes as much as they should. What happens to your shoes when you die? When you're dead, what do you need with shoes? Where are you planning to go?"

The dictator's wife says, "Every time my husband had someone killed, I went to that person's family and asked for a pair of their shoes. Sometimes there wasn't anyone to ask. My husband was a very suspicious man."

Now and then her right hand disappears up under her wig as if she's looking for something up there. "A family sits down to breakfast. The wife might say something about the weather. Someone might happen to walk by and hear the wife say something about the weather. Then soldiers would come along, and the soldiers would take them, husband, wife, children, away. They would be given shovels. They would dig an enormous hole, there would be other people digging other holes. Then the soldiers would line them up, fathers, mothers, children, and shoot them.

"In this country you think talking about the weather is safe but it isn't. Neither is breakfast. I gave soldiers bribes. They brought me the shoes of the people they shot. Eventually there were so many pits full of dead people in our country that you couldn't lay out a vegetable garden without digging someone up. It was a small country but dead people take up a lot of space. I had special closets made for all the shoes.

"Sometimes I dream about those dead people. They never say anything. They just stand there barefoot and look at me."

Under the covers, the dictator's wife looks like an arrangement of cups and bones, knives and sticks. The visitor can't tell if she's wearing shoes or not. Visitors don't like to think of the dictator's wife's shoes, shiny and black as coffins, hiding under the sheets. The visitor might not want to think of the dictator's wife's cold bare feet either. And that bed—who knows what's under it? Dead people, lined up in pairs like bedroom slippers.

The dictator's wife says, "When I married him I was fifteen."

The dictator's wife says:

I was considered to be the most beautiful girl in the country (remember, it was not a big country). My pictures were in all the papers. My parents wanted me to marry an older man who had a large estate. This man had bad teeth but his eyes were kind. I thought he would make a good husband, so I said yes. My dress was so beautiful. Nuns made the lace. The train was twelve feet long and I had two dozen girls from good families to hold it in the air behind me as we walked up the aisle. The dressmaker said that I looked like a movie star or a saint.

On my wedding day, the dictator saw me riding in my father's car. He followed me to the church and he offered me a choice.

The dictator said that he had fallen in love with me. He said that I could marry him instead or else he would have my fiancé shot.

The dictator had not been in power for very long. There had been rumors. No one believed them. My fiancé said that the dictator should go outside with him and they would talk like men, or else they could fight. But the dictator nodded to one of his soldiers and they dragged my fiancé outside and they shot him.

Then the dictator said that I could marry him or he would shoot my father. My father was an influential man. I think he believed that the dictator wouldn't dare shoot him. But they took him outside and they shot him just outside the church door, although I was begging them not to.

Then my mother said that he would have to shoot her as well because she didn't plan on living any longer. She was shaking. The dictator looked very disappointed. She was not being reasonable. She looked at me as they led her out, but she didn't say anything. One shoe fell off. They didn't stop to let her pick it up.

I had twin brothers, a year older than me. When the soldiers took my mother, my brothers ran after them. The soldiers shot them as they ran through the door. I thought that next the dictator would have me taken outside, but my sister Effie began to sob. All the bridesmaids were crying as well. Effie said that she didn't want to die and that she didn't want me to die either. She was very young. So I said I would marry the dictator.

The soldiers escorted us outside. At the door, the dictator bent over. He picked up my mother's shoe and gave it to me, as if it were a love token. A souvenir.

The next day Effie and I buried my parents and my brothers and my fiancé. We washed their bodies and we dressed them. We put them in good sturdy coffins and buried them, but we buried them barefoot. I took my parents' shoes and my fiancé's shoes to the dictator's house for my trousseau, but I gave Effie to an aunt to look after.

Underneath the messy wig, the face of the dictator's wife looks like the face of an evil old man and—just for a minute—the visitor may think that it isn't the dictator's wife at all, lying there in the old woman's bed, but the dictator himself, disguised in an old dirty wig.

"I was too beautiful," the dictator's wife says. "I killed a lot of men. The dictator killed anyone—men, women—who stared at me too long. He killed women because he heard someone say that they were more beautiful than his wife. He killed my hairdresser because I told my hairdresser to cut off all my hair. I didn't want people to stare at me. I thought if I had no hair, no one would stare at me because I was beautiful."

The dictator's wife says, "My hair never grew back. I wore dead women's hair, made into wigs by dead wigmakers. I had closets full of dead people's shoes. I went and sat in my closets sometimes. I tried on shoes."

She says, "I used to think all the time about killing him. But it was difficult. There were children who sat at the table with us and tasted his food. Every night before I went to bed, his soldiers searched me. He slept in a bulletproof vest. He had a charm made for him by witches. I was young. I was afraid of him.

"I never slept alone with him—I thought for a long time that that was how a marriage was, a man and his wife in a room with a bodyguard to watch what they did. When the dictator fell asleep, the bodyguard stayed awake. He stood beside the bed to watch me. It used to make me feel safe. I didn't really want to be in a room alone with the dictator.

"I don't know why he killed people. He had bad dreams. A fortune-teller used to come to the dictator's house to explain his dreams to him. They would be alone for hours. Then I would go in, to tell her my dreams. He would stand just outside the room listening to my dreams. I could smell him standing there.

"I never dreamed about the dictator. I had the most wonderful dreams. I was married. My husband was kind and handsome. We lived in a little house. We fought about little things. What we would name our children. Whose turn it was to make dinner. Whether I was as beautiful as a movie star.

"Once we had an argument and I threw the kettle at him. I missed. I burned my hand. After that, whenever I was dreaming, I had a scar on my hand. A burn. In dreams my husband used to kiss it."

The dictator's wife says, "The fortune-teller never said anything when I told her my dreams. But she got skinnier and skinnier. I think it was a bad diet, the dictator's dreams and his wife's dreams, like eating stones.

"I dreamed I got fat from having children. Every night my dream was like the most wonderful story that I was telling to myself. I would fall asleep in the same bed as the dictator. The guard would be looking down at us, and all night I would dream about my house and my husband and my children.

"Here's the weird thing," the dictator's wife says. "In my dream, all our children were shoes. I only ever gave birth to shoes."

The visitor may agree that this is strange. In dreams the visitor's children are always younger than they really are. You can pick them up in one hand, all of them, like pebbles. In the rain, or in bathwater, they become transparent, only their outlines faintly visible.

"My life was weird," the dictator's wife says. "Why wouldn't my dreams be? But I loved those children. They were good children. They cried sometimes at night, just like real babies. Sometimes they cried so hard I woke up. I would wake up and not know where I was, until I looked up and saw the dictator's bodyguard looking back down at me. Then I could go back to sleep."

She says, "One night, the dictator had a dream. I don't know what. He tossed and turned all night. When he woke up, he had the fortune-teller brought to him. It was early in the morning. The sun wasn't up yet. I went and hid in my closets. He told the fortune-teller something. I don't know what. Then his soldiers came and got her and I could hear them dragging her away, down the stairs, out into the garden. They shot her, and in a little while I went out to the garden and pulled off her shoes. I was happy for her."

"I never asked him why he killed her or why he killed anybody. When we were married, I never asked him a question. I was like the fortune-teller. I never said anything unless he asked me a question. I never looked at his face. I used to stare at his shoes instead. I think he thought I was staring at his shoes because they weren't clean, or shiny enough. He would have them polished until I could see my face in them. He wore a size eight and a half. I tried his shoes on once but

186

they pinched the sides of my feet. I have peasant's feet. His shoes were narrow as coffins."

Tears slide down the dictator's wife's face and she licks at them. She says, "I had a daughter. Did I tell you that? The night before she was born, the dictator had another dream. He woke up with a shout and grabbed my arm. He told me his dream. He said that he had dreamed that our child would grow up and that she would kill him."

She doesn't say anything for a while. Visitors may grow uncomfortable, look away at the rows of shoes in glass boxes. The bed and the dictator's wife are reflected in each pane of glass.

The dictator's wife says, "When my daughter was born, they put her in a box. They threw the box in the harbor and the box sank. I never gave her a name. She never wore any shoes. She was bald just like me."

The dictator's wife is silent again. In the silence, the glass boxes seem to buzz faintly. There is a smell as if someone is standing nearby. All the people under the bed are listening. Far away, the other old woman is humming as she dusts the cases. At this point, the visitor asks, hesitantly, "So how did she grow up and kill the dictator?"

The dictator's wife says, "She was dead so she couldn't. One day the dictator was picking strawberries in his garden. He stepped on a piece of metal. It went right though his shoe. The dictator's foot got infected. He went to his bed, and he died there six days later."

The dictator's wife's voice gets scratchy and small. She yawns. "Nobody knew what to do. Some people thought I should be executed. Other people thought that I was a heroine. They wanted to elect me to office. I didn't want to be dead yet and I didn't want to stay there, so I packed up the shoes. I packed up every single shoe. I went to my aunt and she packed up Effie's things. Effie had gotten so tall! She was walking around outside without a hat on, as if sunlight wouldn't hurt her. We didn't recognize each other. We got on a ship and went as far away as we could. That was here. I had ninety-four steamer trunks and there wasn't anything in them but shoes."

The dictator's wife stops talking. She stares greedily at the visitor, as if the visitor is delicious. She looks as if she would like to eat the visitor up. She looks as if she would like to eat the visitor up in one bite, spit out the visitor's shoes like peach stones. The visitor can hear Effie coming down the aisle, but the dictator's wife doesn't say another word. She just lies there on the bed with her teeth out again, in the glass beside the bed.

Effie motions for the visitor to follow her. Each case has a name printed on a tiny card. You can't see over the top of the stacked cases, but you can see through them. Light has collected in the boxes and the glass is warm.

Effie says, "Here. These shoes belonged to a famous opera singer."

The opera singer's shoes have tall green heels. They have ivory buttons up the side. The visitor looks down at Effie's feet. She is wearing wooden sandals—Dr. Scholl's—with thick red leather buckles. Her toenails are red. They match the red buckles. When she sees the visitor looking, she bends over. She turns a small key in the side of the shoe. Red wheels pop out of the bottom of the Dr. Scholls. She turns the key in the other shoe, and then she straightens up. Now she's quite tall.

She rubs a glass case with the dusty dress one more time, and then raps it sharply. It rings like a bell. "Museum's closed now," she says to the visitor. "There's a three o'clock matinee with a happy ending. I want to see it." She skates off down the narrow glass aisle, balanced precariously on her splendid shoes.

4. Happy ending.

The man and the woman are holding hands. They are getting married soon. If you looked under the table, you'd see that they aren't wearing any shoes. Their shoes are up on the table instead. The fortune-teller says, "It's just luck that you found each other, you know. Most people aren't so lucky." She is staring at the shoes—a pair of old black boots, a pair of canvas tennis shoes—as if she has never seen such a splendid, such an amazing pair of shoes. No one has ever presented her with such a pair of shoes. That's what the look on her face says.

"You're going to get a lot of nice wedding presents," she says. "I don't want to spoil any surprises, but you'll get two coffee makers. You should probably keep them both. You might break one."

"What else?" says the man.

"You want to know if you'll have kids, right? Yeah, you'll have kids, a couple of them. Smart kids. Smart grandkids too. Redheads. Do you garden?"

The man and woman look at each other. They shrug.

"Well, I see a garden," the fortune-teller says. "Yes, a garden, definitely. You'll grow roses. Roses and tomatoes. Moses supposes his toeses are roses. But Moses supposes erroneously. Do you know that song? Squashes. Is that right?"

"Cole Porter. Squash," the man says. "Squash is the plural of squash."

"Okay," the fortune-teller says. "Squash, plural not singular, and tomatoes and roses. That's when you get older. What else do you want to know?"

"We get old together?" the woman says.

"Well, looks like," the fortune-teller says, "um, it looks good to me. Yeah. You get old together. White hair and everything. You grow things in the garden, your grandkids come over, you have friends, they come over too. It's a party every night." She turns the boot over and studies the heel. "Huh."

"What?" the woman says.

"How you met. That's sweet. Look here." The fortune-teller points to the worn-down tread. "It was a blind date. See what I mean about luck?"

"You can see that in her shoe?" the man says.

"Yeah," the fortune-teller says. "Plain as anything. Just like the garden and the grandkids. Blind date, first kiss, hunh! The next date, she invited you over for dinner. She washed the sheets first. Do you want me to go on?"

"Where will we live?" the woman says. "Do we fight about money? Does he still snore when he gets old? His sense of humor—does he still tell the same dumb jokes?"

"Look," the fortune-teller says, "You'll have a good life. You don't want all the details, do you? Go home, make wedding plans, get married. You should probably get married inside. I think it might rain. I'm not good at weather. You'll be happy, I promise. I'm good at the happy stuff. It's what I see best. You want to know about snoring, or breast cancer, or mortgages, go see the woman next door who reads tea leaves."

She says, "You'll get old together. You'll be comfortable together. I promise. Trust me. I can see you, then, the two of you, you'll be sitting in your garden. There's dirt under your fingernails. You're drinking lemonade. I can't tell if it's homemade or not, but it's perfect. Not too sweet. You're remembering I told you this. Remember I told you this. How lucky you were, to find each other! You'll be comfortable together, like an old pair of shoes."

Most of My Friends Are Two-Thirds Water

"Okay, Joe. As I was saying, our Martian women are
gonna be blond, because, see, just because."
—RAY BRADBURY, "The Concrete Mixer"

A few years ago, Jack dropped the C from his name and became
Jak. He called me up at breakfast one morning to tell me this.
He said he was frying bacon for breakfast and that all his
roommates were away. He said that he was walking around stark
naked. He could have been telling the truth, I don't know. I could
hear something spitting and hissing in the background that could
have been bacon, or maybe it was just static on the line.

Jak keeps a journal in which he records the dreams he has about
making love to his ex-girlfriend Nikki, who looks like Sandy Duncan.
Nikki is now married to someone else. In the most recent dream, Jak
says, Nikki had a wooden leg. Sandy Duncan has a glass eye in real
life. Jak calls me up to tell me this dream.

He calls to say that he is in love with the woman who does the
Braun coffee-maker commercial, the one with the short blond hair,

191

like Nikki, and eyes that are dreamy and a little too far apart. He can't tell from the commercial if she has a wooden leg, but he watches TV every night, in the hopes of seeing her again.

If I were blond, I could fall in love with Jak.

Jak calls me with the first line of a story. Most of my friends are two-thirds water, he says, and I say that this doesn't surprise me. He says, no, that this is the first line. There's a Philip K. Dick novel, I tell him, that has a first line like that, but not exactly and I can't remember the name of the novel. I am listening to him while I clean out my father's refrigerator. The name of the Philip K. Dick novel is *Confessions of a Crap Artist*, I tell Jak. What novel, he says.

He says that he followed a woman home from the subway, accidentally. He says that he was sitting across from her on the Number 1 uptown and he smiled at her. This is a bad thing to do in New York when there isn't anyone else in the subway car, traveling uptown past 116th Street, when it's one o'clock in the morning, even when you're Asian and not much taller than she is, even when *she* made eye contact first, which is what Jak says she did. Anyway he smiled and she looked away. She got off at the next stop, 125th, and so did he. 125th is his stop. She looked back and when she saw him, her face changed and she began to walk faster.

Was she blond, I ask, casually. I don't remember, Jak says. They came up onto Broadway, Jak just a little behind her, and then she looked back at him and crossed over to the east side. He stayed on the west side so she wouldn't think he was following her. She walked fast. He dawdled. She was about a block ahead when he saw her cross at La Salle, towards him, towards Claremont and Riverside, where Jak lives on the fifth floor of a rundown brownstone. I used to live in this building before I left school. Now I live in my father's garage. The woman on Broadway looked back and saw that Jak was still following her. She walked faster. He says he walked even more slowly.

By the time he came to the corner market on Riverside, the one that stays open all night long, he couldn't see her. So he bought a pint of ice cream and some toilet paper. She was in front of him at the counter, paying for a carton of skim milk and a box of dish detergent. When she saw him, he thought she was going to say something to the cashier but instead she picked up her change and hurried out of the store.

Jak says that the lights on Claremont are always a little dim and fizzy, and sounds are muffled, as if the street is under water. In the summer, the air is heavier and darker at night, like water on your skin. I say that I remember that. He says that up ahead of him, the woman was flickering under the street light like a light bulb. What do you mean, like a light bulb? I ask. I can hear him shrug over the phone. She flickered, he says. I mean like a light bulb. He says that she would turn back to look at him, and then look away again. Her face was pale. It flickered.

By this point, he says, he wasn't embarrassed. He wasn't worried anymore. He felt almost as if they knew each other. It might have been a game they were playing. He says that he wasn't surprised when she stopped in front of his building and let herself in. She slammed the security door behind her and stood for a moment, glaring at him through the glass. She looked exactly the way Nikki looked, he says, when Nikki was still going out with him, when she was angry at him for being late or for misunderstanding something. The woman behind the glass pressed her lips together and glared at Jak.

He says when he took his key out of his pocket, she turned and ran up the stairs. She went up the first flight of stairs and then he couldn't see her anymore. He went inside and took the elevator up to the fifth floor. On the fifth floor, when he was getting out, he says that the woman who looked like Nikki was slamming shut the door of the apartment directly across from his apartment. He heard the chain slide across the latch.

She lives across from you, I say. He says that he thinks she just moved in. Nothing like meeting new neighbors, I say. In the back of the refrigerator, behind wrinkled carrots and jars of pickled onions and horseradish, I find a bottle of butterscotch sauce. I didn't buy this, I tell Jak over the phone. Who bought this? My father's diabetic. I know your father's diabetic, he says.

I've known Jak for seven years. Nikki has been married for three months now. He was in Ankara on an archeological dig when they broke up, only he didn't know they'd broken up until he got back to New York. She called and told him that she was engaged. She invited him to the wedding and then disinvited him a few weeks later. I was invited to the wedding, too, but instead I went to New York and spent the weekend with Jak. We didn't sleep together.

Saturday night, which was when Nikki was supposed to be getting married, we watched an episode of *Baywatch* in which the actor David Hasselhoff almost marries the beautiful blond lifeguard, but in the end doesn't, because he has to go save some tourists whose fishing boat has caught fire. Then we watched *The Princess Bride*. We drank a lot of Scotch and I threw up in Jak's sink while he stood outside the bathroom door and sang a song he had written about Nikki getting married. When I wouldn't come out of the bathroom, he said good night through the door.

I cleaned up the sink and brushed my teeth and went to sleep on a lumpy foldout futon. I dreamed that I was in Nikki's bridal party. Everyone was blond in my dream, the bridegroom, the best man, the mother of the bride, the flower girl, everyone looked like Sandy Duncan except for me. In the morning I got up and drove my father's car back to Virginia, and my father's garage, and Jak went to work at VideoArt, where he has a part-time job which involves technical videos about beauty school, and the Gulf War, and things like that. He mostly edits, but I once saw his hands on a late night commercial, dialing the number for a video calendar featuring exotic beauties. Women, not flowers. I almost ordered the calendar.

I haven't spoken to Nikki since before Jak went to Turkey and she got engaged.

When I first moved into my father's garage, I got a job at the textile mill where my father has worked for the last twenty years. I answered phones. I listened to men tell jokes about blondes. I took home free packages of men's underwear. My father and I pretended we didn't know each other. After a while, I had all the men's underwear that I needed. I knew all the jokes by heart. I told my father that I was going to take a sabbatical from my sabbatical, just for a while. I was going to write a book. I think that he was relieved.

Jak calls me up to ask me how my father is doing. My father loves Jak. They write letters to each other a couple of times a year, in which my father tells Jak how I am doing, and whom I am dating. These tend to be very short letters. Jak sends articles back to my father about religion, insects, foreign countries where he has been digging things up.

My father and Jak aren't very much alike, at least I don't think so, but they *like* each other. Jak is the son that my father never had, the son-in-law he will never have.

I ask Jak if he has run into his new neighbor, the blond one, again, and there is a brief silence. He says, yeah, he has. She knocked on his door a few days later, to borrow a cup of sugar. That's original, I say. He says that she didn't seem to recognize him and so he didn't bring it up. He says that he has noticed that there seem to be an unusually high percentage of blond women in his apartment building.

Let's run away to Las Vegas, I say, on impulse. He asks why Las Vegas. We could get married, I say, and the next day we could get divorced. I've always wanted an ex-husband, I tell him. It would make my father very happy. He makes a counter-proposal: we could go to New Orleans and not get married. I point out that we've already done that. I say that maybe we should try something new, but in the end we decide that he should come to Charlottesville in May. I am going to give a reading.

My father would like Jak to marry me, but not necessarily in Las Vegas.

The time that we went to New Orleans, we stayed awake all night in the lobby of a hostel, playing Hearts with a girl from Finland. Every time that Jak took a heart, no matter what was in his hand, no matter whether or not someone else had already taken a point, he'd try to shoot the moon. We could have done it, I think, we could have fallen in love in New Orleans, but not in front of the girl from Finland, who was blond.

A year later, Jak found an ad for tickets to Paris, ninety-nine dollars round trip. This was while we were still in school. We went for Valentine's Day because that was one of the conditions of the promotional fare. Nikki was spending a semester in Scotland. She was studying mad cow disease. They were sort of not seeing each other while she was away and in any case she was away and so I went with Jak to Paris for Valentine's Day. Isn't it romantic, I said, we're going to be in Paris on Valentine's Day. Maybe we'll meet someone, Jak said.

I lied. We didn't go to Paris for Valentine's Day, although Jak really did find the ad in the paper, and the tickets were really only ninety-nine dollars round trip. We didn't go and he never asked me, and anyway Nikki came home later that month and they got back together again. We did go to New Orleans, though. I don't think I've made that up.

I realize there is a problem with Las Vegas, which is that there are a lot of blond women there.

You are probably wondering why I am living in my father's garage. My father is probably wondering why I am living in his garage. It worries his neighbors.

Jak calls to tell me that he is quitting his job at VideoArt. He has gotten some grant money, which will not only cover the rest of the school year, but will also allow him to spend another summer in Turkey, digging things up. I tell him that I'm happy for him. He says that a weird thing happened when he went to pick up his last paycheck. He got into an elevator with seven blond women who all looked like Sandy Duncan. They stopped talking when he got on and the elevator was so quiet he could hear them all breathing. He says that they were all breathing in perfect unison. He says that all of their bosoms were rising and falling in unison like they had been running, like some sort of synchronized Olympic breast event. He says that they smelled wonderful—that the whole elevator smelled wonderful—like a box of Lemon Fresh Joy soap detergent. He got off on the thirtieth floor and they all stayed on the elevator, although he was telepathically communicating with them that they should all get off with him, that all seven of them should spend the day with him, they could all go to the Central Park Zoo, it would be wonderful.

But not a single one got off, although he thought they looked wistful when he did. He stood in the hall and the elevator door closed and he watched the numbers and the elevator finally stopped on the

197

forty-fifth floor, the top floor. After he picked up his paycheck, he went up to the forty-fifth floor and this is the strange thing, he says.

He says that when the elevator doors opened and he got out, the forty-fifth floor was completely deserted. There was plastic up everywhere and drills and cans of paint and bits of molding lying on the floor, like the whole top floor was being renovated. A piece of the ceiling had been removed and he could see the girders and the sky through the girders. All the office doors were open and so he walked around, but he says he didn't see anyone, anyone at all. So where did the women go, he says. Maybe they were construction workers, I say. They didn't smell like construction workers, he says.

If I say that some of my friends are two-thirds water, then you will realize that some of my friends aren't, that some of them are probably more and some are probably less than two-thirds, that maybe some of them are two-thirds something besides water, maybe some of them are two-thirds Lemon Fresh Joy. When I say that some women are blondes, you will realize that I am probably not. I am probably not in love with Jak.

I have been living in my father's garage for a year and a half. My bed is surrounded by boxes of Christmas tree ornaments (his) and boxes of college textbooks (mine). We are pretending that I am writing a novel. I don't pay rent. The novel will be dedicated to him. So far, I've finished the dedication page and the first three chapters. Really, what I do is sleep late, until he goes to work, and then I walk three miles downtown to the dollar movie theater that used to be a porn theater, the used bookstore where I stand and read trashy romance novels in the aisle. Sometimes I go to the coffeehouse where, in a few months, I am supposed to give a reading. The owner is a friend of my father's and gives me coffee. I sit in the window and write letters. I go home,

I fix dinner for my father, and then sometimes I write. Sometimes I watch TV. Sometimes I go out again. I go to bars and play pool with men that I couldn't possibly bring home to my father. Sometimes I bring them back to his garage instead. I lure them home with promises of free underwear.

Jak calls me at three in the morning. He says that he has a terrific idea for a sci-fi story. I say that I don't want to hear a sci-fi idea at three in the morning. Then he says that it isn't really a story idea, that it's true. It happened to him and he has to tell someone about it, so I say okay, tell me about it.

I lie in bed listening to Jak. There is a man lying beside me in bed that I met in a bar a few hours ago. He has a stud in his penis. This is kind of a disappointment, not that he has a stud in his penis, but the stud itself. It's very small. It's not like an earring. I had pictured something more baroque—a great big gaudy clip-on like the ones that grandmothers wear—when he told me about it in the bar. I made the man in my bed take the stud out when we had sex, but he put it in again afterwards because otherwise the hole will close up. It was just three weeks ago when he got his penis pierced and having sex at all was probably not a good idea for either of us, although I don't even have pierced ears. I noticed him in the bar immediately. He was sitting gingerly, his legs far apart. When he got up to buy me a beer, he walked as if walking was something that he had just learned.

I can't remember his name. He is sleeping with his mouth open, his hands curled around his penis, protecting it. The sheets are twisted down around his ankles. I can't remember his name but I think it started with a C.

Hold on a minute, I say to Jak. I untangle the phone cord as far as I can, until I am on the driveway outside my father's garage, closing the door gently behind me. My father never wakes up when the phone rings in the middle of the night. He *says* he never wakes up. The man in my bed, whose name probably begins with a C, is either still asleep or pretending to be. Outside the asphalt is rough and damp under me. I'm naked, I tell Jak, it's too hot to wear anything to sleep in. No you're not, Jak says. I'm wearing blue and white striped pajamas bottoms but I lie again and tell him that I am truly, actually not wearing clothes. Prove it, he says. I ask how I'm supposed to prove over the phone that I'm naked. Take my word for it, I just am. Then so am I, he says.

So what's your great idea for a sci-fi story, I ask. Blond women are actually aliens, he says. All of them, I ask. Most of them, Jak says. He says that all the ones that look like Sandy Duncan are definitely aliens. I tell him that I'm not sure that this is such a great story idea. He says that it's not a story idea, that it's true. He has proof. He tells me about the woman who lives in the apartment across from him, the woman who looks like Nikki, who looks like Sandy Duncan. The woman that he accidentally followed home from the subway.

According to Jak, this woman invited him to come over for a drink because a while ago he had lent her a cup of sugar. I say that I remember the cup of sugar. According to Jak they sat on her couch, which was deep and plush and smelled like Lemon Fresh Joy, and they drank most of a bottle of Scotch. They talked about graduate school—he says she said she was a second-year student at the business school, she had a little bit of an accent, he says. She said she was from Luxembourg—and then she kissed him. So he kissed her back for a while and then he stuck his hand down under the elastic of her skirt. He says the first thing he noticed was that she wasn't wearing any underwear. He says the second thing he noticed was that she was smooth down there like a Barbie doll. She didn't have a vagina.

I interrupt at this point and ask him what exactly he means when he says this. Jak says he means exactly what he said, which is that she didn't have a vagina. He says that her skin was unusually warm, hot actually. She reached down and gently pushed his hand away. He says that at this point he was a little bit drunk and a little bit confused, but still not quite ready to give up hope. He says that it had been so long since the last time he slept with a woman, he thought maybe he'd forgotten exactly what was where.

He says that the blond woman, whose name is either Cordelia or Annamarie (he's forgotten which), then unzipped his pants, pushed down his boxers, and took his penis in her mouth. I tell him that I'm happy for him, but I'm more interested in the thing he said about how she didn't have a vagina.

He says that he's pretty sure that they reproduce by parthenogenesis. Who reproduce by parthenogenesis, I ask. Aliens, he says, blond women. That's why there are so many of them. That's why they all look alike. Don't they go to the bathroom, I ask. He says he hasn't figured out that part yet. He says that he's pretty sure that Nikki is now an alien, although she used to be a human, back when they were going out. Are you sure, I say. She had a vagina, he says.

I ask him why Nikki got married then, if she's an alien. Camouflage, he says. I say that I hope her fiancé, her husband, I mean, doesn't mind. Jak says that New York is full of blond women who resemble Sandy Duncan and most of them are undoubtedly aliens, that this is some sort of invasion. After he came in Chloe or Annamarie's mouth—probably neither name is her real name, he says—he says that she said she hoped they could see each other again and let him out of her apartment. So what do the aliens want with you, I ask. I don't know, Jak says and hangs up.

I try to call him back but he's left the phone off the hook. So I go back inside and wake up the man in my bed and ask him if he's ever made love to a blonde and if so did he notice anything unusual about her vagina. He asks me if this is one of those jokes and I say that I don't know. We try to have sex, but it isn't working, so instead

I open up a box of my father's Christmas tree decorations. I take out tinsel and strings of light and ornamental glass fruit. I hang the fruit off his fingers and toes and tell him not to move. I drape the tinsel and lights around his arms and legs and plug him in. He complains some but I tell him to be quiet or my father will wake up. I tell him how beautiful he looks, all lit up like a Christmas tree or a flying saucer. I put his penis in my mouth and pretend that I am Courtney (or Annamarie, or whatever her name is), that I am blond, that I am an alien. The man whose name begins with a C doesn't seem to notice.

I am falling asleep when the man says to me, I think I love you. What time is it, I say. I think you better leave, before my father wakes up. He says, but it's not even five o'clock yet. My father wakes up early, I tell him.

He takes off the tinsel and the Christmas lights and the ornamental fruit. He gets dressed and we shake hands and I let him out through the side door of the garage.

Some jokes about blondes. Why did the M&M factory fire the blonde? Because she kept throwing away the Ws. Why did the blonde stare at the bottle of orange juice? Because it said concentrate. A blonde and a brunette work in the same office, and one day the brunette gets a bouquet of roses. Oh great, she says, I guess this means I'm going to spend the weekend flat on my back, with my legs up in the air. Why, says the blonde, don't you have a vase?

I never find out the name of the man in my bed, the one with the stud in his penis. Probably this is for the best. My reading is coming up and I have to concentrate on that. All week I leave messages on Jak's machine but he doesn't call me back. On the day that I am supposed to go to the airport to pick him up, the day before I am supposed to give a reading, although I haven't written anything new for over a year, Jak finally calls me.

He says he's sorry but he's not going to be able to come to Virginia after all. I ask him why not. He said that he got the Carey bus at Grand Central, and that a blond woman sat next to him. Let me guess, I say, she didn't have a vagina. He says he has no idea if she had a vagina or not, that she just sat next to him, reading a trashy romance by Catherine Cookson. I say that I've never read Catherine Cookson, but I'm lying. I read a novel by her once. It occurs to me that the act of reading Catherine Cookson might conclusively prove that the woman either had a vagina or that she didn't, that the blond woman who sat beside Jak might have been an alien, or else incontrovertibly human, but I'm not sure which. Really, I could make a case either way.

Jak says that the real problem was when the bus pulled into the terminal at LaGuardia and he went to the check-in gate. The woman behind the counter was blond, and so was every single woman behind him in line, he tells me, when he turned around. He says that he realized that what he had was a one-way ticket to Sandy Duncan Land, that if he didn't turn around and go straight back to Manhattan, that he was going to end up on some planet populated by blond women with Barbie-smooth crotches. He says that Manhattan may be suffering from some sort of alien infestation, but he's coming to terms with that. He says he can live with an apartment full of rats, in a building full of women with no vaginas. He says that for the time being, it's safest.

He says that when he got home, the woman in the apartment on the fifth floor was looking through the keyhole. How do you know, I say. He says that he could smell her standing next to the door. The whole hallway was warm with the way she was staring, that the whole hallway smelled like Lemon Fresh Joy. He says that he's sorry that he can't come to Virginia for my reading, but that's the way it is. He says that when he goes to Ankara this summer, he might not be coming back. There aren't so many blond women out there, he says.

When I give the reading, my father is there, and the owner of the coffeehouse, and so are about three other people. I read a story I wrote a few years ago about a boy who learns how to fly. It doesn't make him happy. Afterwards my father tells me that I sure have a strange imagination. This is what he always says. His friend tells me that I have a nice clear reading voice, that I enunciate very well. I tell her that I've been working on my enunciation. She says that she likes my hair this color.

I think about calling Jak and telling him that I am thinking of dyeing my hair. I think about telling him that this might not even be necessary, that when I wake up in the mornings, I am finding blond hairs on my pillow. If I called him and told him this, I might be making it up; I might be telling the truth. Before I call him, I am waiting to see what happens next. I am sitting here on my father's living-room couch, which smells like Lemon Fresh Joy, watching a commercial in which someone's hands are dialing the number for a video calendar of exotic beauties. I am eating butterscotch out of the jar. I am waiting for the phone to ring.

LOUISE'S GHOST

Two women and a small child meet in a restaurant. The
restaurant is nice—there are windows everywhere. The
women have been here before. It's all that light that makes
the food taste so good. The small child—a girl dressed all in green,
hairy green sweater, green T-shirt, green corduroys and dirty sneakers
with green-black laces—sniffs. She's a small child but she has a big
nose. She might be smelling the food that people are eating. She
might be smelling the warm light that lies on top of everything.

None of her greens match except of course they are all green.

"Louise," one woman says to the other.

"Louise," the other woman says.

They kiss.

The maitre d' comes up to them. He says to the first woman,
"Louise, how nice to see you. And look at Anna! You're so big. Last
time I saw you, you were so small. This small." He holds his index
finger and his thumb together as if pinching salt. He looks at the
other woman.

Louise says, "This is my friend, Louise. My best friend. Since Girl Scout camp. Louise."

The maitre d' smiles. "Yes, Louise. Of course. How could I forget?"

Louise sits across from Louise. Anna sits between them. She has a notebook full of green paper, and a green crayon. She's drawing something, only it's difficult to see what, exactly. Maybe it's a house.

Louise says, "Sorry about you know who. Teacher's day. The sitter canceled at the last minute. And I had such a lot to tell you, too! About you know, number eight. Oh boy, I think I'm in love. Well, not in love."

She is sitting opposite a window, and all that rich soft light falls on her. She looks creamy with happiness, as if she's carved out of butter. The light loves Louise, the other Louise thinks. Of course it loves Louise. Who doesn't?

This is one thing about Louise. She doesn't like to sleep alone. She says that her bed is too big. There's too much space. She needs someone to roll up against, or she just rolls around all night. Some mornings she wakes up on the floor. Mostly she wakes up with other people.

When Anna was younger, she slept in the same bed as Louise. But now she has her own room, her own bed. Her walls are painted green. Her sheets are green. Green sheets of paper with green drawings are hung up on the wall. There's a green teddy bear on the green bed and a green duck. She has a green light in a green shade. Louise has been in that room. She helped Louise paint it. She wore sunglasses while she painted. This passion for greenness, Louise thinks, this longing for everything to be a variation on a theme, it might be hereditary.

This is the second thing about Louise. Louise likes cellists. For about four years, she has been sleeping with a cellist. Not the same cellist. Different cellists. Not all at once, of course. Consecutive cellists. Number eight is Louise's newest cellist. Numbers one through seven were cellists as well, although Anna's father was not. That was before the cellists. BC. In any case, according to Louise, cellists generally have low sperm counts.

Louise meets Louise for lunch every week. They go to nice restaurants. Louise knows all the maitre d's. Louise tells Louise about the cellists. Cellists are mysterious. Louise hasn't figured them out yet. It's something about the way they sit, with their legs open and their arms curled around, all hunched over their cellos. She says they look solid but inviting. Like a door. It opens and you walk in.

Doors are sexy. Wood is sexy, and bows strung with real hair. Also cellos don't have spit valves. Louise says that spit valves aren't sexy.

Louise is in public relations. She's a fundraiser for the symphony—she's good at what she does. It's hard to say no to Louise. She takes rich people out to dinner. She knows what kinds of wine they like to drink. She plans charity auctions and masquerades. She brings sponsors to the symphony to sit on stage and watch rehearsals. She takes the cellists home afterwards.

Louise looks a little bit like a cello herself. She's brown and curvy and tall. She has a long neck and her shiny hair stays pinned up during the day. Louise thinks that the cellists must take it down at night—Louise's hair—slowly, happily, gently.

At camp Louise used to brush Louise's hair.

Louise isn't perfect. Louise would never claim that her friend was perfect. Louise is a bit bow-legged and she has tiny little feet. She wears long, tight silky skirts. Never pants, never anything floral. She has a way of turning her head to look at you, very slowly. It doesn't matter that she's bowlegged.

The cellists want to sleep with Louise because she wants them to. The cellists don't fall in love with her, because Louise doesn't want them to fall in love with her. Louise always gets what she wants.

Louise doesn't know what she wants. Louise doesn't want to want things.

Louise and Louise have been friends since Girl Scout camp. How old were they? Too young to be away from home for so long. They were so small that some of their teeth weren't there yet. They were so young they wet the bed out of homesickness. Loneliness. Louise slept in the bunk bed above Louise. Girl Scout camp smelled like pee. Summer camp is how Louise knows Louise is bowlegged. At summer camp they wore each other's clothes.

Here is something else about Louise, a secret. Louise is the only one who knows. Not even the cellists know. Not even Anna.

Louise is tone deaf. Louise likes to watch Louise at concerts. She has this way of looking at the musicians. Her eyes get wide and she doesn't blink. There's this smile on her face as if she's being introduced to someone whose name she didn't quite catch. Louise thinks that's really why Louise ends up sleeping with them, with the cellists. It's because she doesn't know what else they're good for. Louise hates for things to go to waste.

A woman comes to their table to take their order. Louise orders the grilled chicken and a house salad and Louise orders salmon with lemon butter. The woman asks Anna what she would like. Anna looks at her mother.

Louise says, "She'll eat anything as long as it's green. Broccoli is good. Peas, lima beans, iceberg lettuce. Lime sherbet. Bread rolls. Mashed potatoes."

The woman looks down at Anna. "I'll see what we can do," she says.

Anna says, "Potatoes aren't green."

Louise says, "Wait and see."

Louise says, "If I had a kid—"

Louise says, "But you don't have a kid." She doesn't say this meanly. Louise is never mean, although sometimes she is not kind.

Louise and Anna glare at each other. They've never liked each other. They are polite in front of Louise. It is humiliating, Louise thinks, to hate someone so much younger. The child of a friend. I should feel sorry for her instead. She doesn't have a father. And soon enough, she'll grow up. Breasts. Zits. Boys. She'll see old pictures of herself and be embarrassed. She's short and she dresses like a Keebler Elf. She can't even read yet!

Louise says, "In any case, it's easier than the last thing. When she only ate dog food."

Anna says, "When I was a dog—"

Louise says, hating herself. "You were never a dog."

Anna says, "How do you know?"

Louise says, "I was there when you were born. When your mother was pregnant. I've known you since you were this big." She pinches her fingers together, the way the maitre d' pinched his, only harder.

Anna says, "It was before that. When I was a dog."

Louise says, "Stop fighting, you two. Louise, when Anna was a dog, that was when you were away. In Paris. Remember?"

"Right," Louise says. "When Anna was a dog, I was in Paris."

Louise is a travel agent. She organizes package tours for senior citizens. Trips for old women. To Las Vegas, Rome, Belize, cruises to the Caribbean. She travels frequently herself and stays in three-star hotels. She tries to imagine herself as an old woman. What she would want.

Most of these women's husbands are in care or dead or living with younger women. The old women sleep two to a room. They like hotels with buffet lunches and saunas, clean pillows that smell good, chocolates on the pillows, firm mattresses. Louise can see herself wanting these things. Sometimes Louise imagines being old, waking up in the mornings, in unfamiliar countries, strange weather, foreign beds. Louise asleep in the bed beside her.

Last night Louise woke up. It was three in the morning. There was a man lying on the floor beside the bed. He was naked. He lay on his back, staring up at the ceiling, his eyes open, his mouth open, nothing coming out. He was bald. He had no eyelashes, no hair on his arms or legs. He was large, not fat but solid. Yes, he was solid. It was hard to tell how old he was. It was dark, but Louise doesn't think he was circumcised. "What are you doing here?" she said loudly.

The man wasn't there anymore. She turned on the lights. She looked under the bed. She found him in her bathroom, above the bathtub, flattened up against the ceiling, staring down, his hands and feet pressed along the ceiling, his penis drooping down, apparently the only part of him that obeyed the laws of gravity. He seemed smaller now. Deflated. She wasn't frightened. She was angry.

"What are you doing?" she said. He didn't answer. Fine, she thought. She went to the kitchen to get a broom. When she came back, he was gone. She looked under the bed again, but he was really gone this time. She looked in every room, checked to make sure that the front door was locked. It was.

Her arms creeped. She was freezing. She filled up her hot water bottle and got in bed. She left the light on and fell asleep sitting up. When she woke up in the morning, it might have been a dream, except she was holding the broom.

The woman brings their food. Anna gets a little dish of peas, brussel sprouts, and collard greens. Mashed potatoes and bread. The plate is green. Louise takes a vial of green food coloring out of her purse. She adds three drops to the mashed potatoes. "Stir it," she tells Anna.

Anna stirs the mashed potatoes until they are a waxy green. Louise mixes more green food coloring into a pat of butter and spreads it on the dinner roll.

"When I was a dog," Anna says, "I lived in a house with a swimming pool. And there was a tree in the living room. It grew right through the ceiling. I slept in the tree. But I wasn't allowed to swim in the pool. I was too hairy."

"I have a ghost," Louise says. She wasn't sure that she was going to say this. But if Anna can reminisce about her former life as a dog, then surely she, Louise, is allowed to mention her ghost. "I think it's a ghost. It was in my bedroom."

Anna says, "When I was a dog I bit ghosts."

Louise says, "Anna, be quiet for a minute. Eat your green food before it gets cold. Louise, what do you mean? I thought you had ladybugs."

"That was a while ago," Louise says. Last month she woke up because people were whispering in the corners of her room. Dead leaves were crawling on her face. The walls of her bedroom were alive. They heaved and dripped red. "What?" she said, and a ladybug walked into her mouth, bitter like soap. The floor crackled when she walked on it, like red cellophane. She opened up her windows. She swept ladybugs out with her broom. She vacuumed them up. More flew in the windows, down the chimney. She moved out for three days. When she came back, the ladybugs were gone—mostly gone—she still finds them tucked into her shoes, in the folds of her underwear, in her cereal bowls and her wine glasses and between the pages of her books.

Before that it was moths. Before the moths, an opossum. It shat on her bed and hissed at her when she cornered it in the pantry. She called an animal shelter and a man wearing a denim jacket and heavy gloves came and shot it with a tranquilizer dart. The opossum sneezed and shut its eyes. The man picked it up by the tail. He posed like that for a moment. Maybe she was supposed to take a picture. Man with possum. She sniffed. He wasn't married. All she smelled was possum.

"How did it get in here?" Louise said.

"How long have you been living here?" the man asked. Boxes of Louise's dishes and books were still stacked up against the walls of the rooms downstairs. She still hadn't put the legs on her mother's dining room table. It lay flat on its back on the floor, amputated.

"Two months," Louise said.

"Well, he's probably been living here longer than that," the man from the shelter said. He cradled the possum like a baby. "In the walls or the attic. Maybe in the chimney. Santa claws. Huh." He laughed at his own joke. "Get it?"

"Get that thing out of my house," Louise said.

"Your house!" the man said. He held out the opossum to her, as if she might want to reconsider. "You know what he thought? He thought this was his house."

"It's my house now," Louise said.

Louise says, "A ghost? Louise, it is someone you know? Is your mother okay?"

"My mother?" Louise says. "It wasn't my mother. It was a naked man. I'd never seen him before in my life."

"How naked?" Anna says. "A little naked or a lot?"

"None of your beeswax," Louise says.

"Was it green?" Anna says.

"Maybe it was someone that you went out with in high school," Louise says. "An old lover. Maybe they just killed themselves, or were in a horrible car accident. Was he covered in blood? Did he say anything? Maybe he wants to warn you about something."

"He didn't say anything," Louise says, "And then he vanished.

First he got smaller and then he vanished."

Louise shivers and then so does Louise. For the first time she feels frightened. The ghost of a naked man was levitating in her bathtub. He could be anywhere. Maybe while she was sleeping, he was floating above her bed. Right above her nose, watching her sleep. She'll have to sleep with the broom from now on.

"Maybe he won't come back," Louise says, and Louise nods. What if he does? Who can she call? The rude man with the heavy gloves?

The woman comes to their table again. "Any dessert?" she wants to know. "Coffee?"

"If you had a ghost," Louise says, "How would you get rid of it?"

Louise kicks Louise under the table.

The woman thinks for a minute. "I'd go see a psychiatrist," she says. "Get some kind of prescription. Coffee?"

But Anna has to go to her tumble class. She's learning how to stand on her head. How to fall down and not be hurt. Louise gets the woman to put the leftover mashed green potatoes in a container, and she wraps up the dinner rolls in a napkin and bundles them into her purse along with a few packets of sugar.

They walk out of the restaurant together, Louise first. Behind her, Anna whispers something to Louise. "Louise?" Louise says.

"What?" Louise says, turning back.

"You need to walk behind me," Anna says. "You can't be first."

"Come back and talk to me," Louise says, patting the air. "Say thank you, Anna."

Anna doesn't say anything. She walks before them, slowly so that they have to walk slowly as well.

"So what should I do?" Louise says.

"About the ghost? I don't know. Is he cute? Maybe he'll creep in bed with you. Maybe he's your demon lover."

"Oh please," Louise says. "Yuck."

Louise says, "Sorry. You should call your mother."

"When I had the problem with the ladybugs," Louise says, "she said they would go away if I sang them that nursery rhyme. Ladybug, ladybug, fly away home."

"Well," Louise says, "they did go away, didn't they?"

"Not until I went away first," Louise says.

"Maybe it's someone who used to live in the house before you moved in. Maybe he's buried under the floor of your bedroom or in the wall or something."

"Just like the possum," Louise says. "Maybe it's Santa Claus."

Louise's mother lives in a retirement community two states away. Louise cleaned out her mother's basement and garage, put her mother's furniture in storage, sold her mother's house. Her mother wanted this. She gave Louise the money from the sale of the house so that Louise could buy her own house. But she won't come visit Louise in her new house. She won't let Louise send her on a package vacation. Sometimes she pretends not to recognize Louise when Louise calls. Or maybe she really doesn't recognize her. Maybe this is why Louise's clients travel. Settle down in one place and you get lazy. You don't bother to remember things like taking baths, or your daughter's name.

When you travel, everything's always new. If you don't speak the language, it isn't a big deal. Nobody expects you to understand everything they say. You can wear the same clothes every day and the other travelers will be impressed with your careful packing. When you wake up and you're not sure where you are. There's a perfectly good reason for that.

"Hello, Mom," Louise says when her mother picks up the phone.

"Who is this?" her mother says.

"Louise," Louise says.

"Oh yes," her mother says. "Louise, how nice to speak to you."

There is an awkward pause and then her mother says, "If you're calling because it's your birthday, I'm sorry. I forgot."

"It isn't my birthday," Louise says. "Mom, remember the ladybugs?"

"Oh yes," her mother says. "You sent pictures. They were lovely."

"I have a ghost," Louise says, "and I was hoping that you would know how to get rid of it."

"A ghost!" her mother says. "It isn't your father, is it?"

"No!" Louise says. "This ghost doesn't have any clothes on, Mom. It's naked and I saw it for a minute and then it disappeared and then I saw it again in my bathtub. Well, sort of."

"Are you sure it's a ghost?" her mother says.

"Yes, positive." Louise says.

"And it isn't your father?"

"No, it's not Dad. It doesn't look like anyone I've ever seen before."

Her mother says, "Lucy—you don't know her—Mrs. Peterson's husband died two nights ago. Is it a short fat man with an ugly moustache? Dark-complected?"

"It isn't Mr. Peterson," Louise says.

"Have you asked what it wants?"

"Mom, I don't care what it wants," Louise says. "I just want it to go away."

"Well," her mother says. "Try hot water and salt. Scrub all the floors. You should polish them with lemon oil afterwards so they don't get streaky. Wash the windows too. Wash all the bed linens and beat all the rugs. And put the sheets back on the bed inside out. And turn all your clothes on the hangers inside out. Clean the bathroom."

"Inside out," Louise says.

"Inside out," her mother says. "Confuses them."

"I think it's pretty confused already. About clothes, anyway. Are you sure this works?"

"Positive," her mother says. "We're always having supernatural infestations around here. Sometimes it gets hard to tell who's alive and who's dead. If cleaning the house doesn't work, try hanging garlic up on strings. Ghosts hate garlic. Or they like it. It's either one or the other, love it, hate it. So what else is happening? When are you coming to visit?"

"I had lunch today with Louise," Louise says.

"Aren't you too old to have an imaginary friend?" her mother says.

"Mom, you know Louise. Remember? Girl Scouts? College? She has the little girl, Anna? Louise?"

"Of course I remember Louise," her mother says. "My own daughter. You're a very rude person." She hangs up.

Salt, Louise thinks. Salt and hot water. She should write these things down. Maybe she could send her mother a tape recorder. She sits down on the kitchen floor and cries. That's one kind of salt water. Then she scrubs floors, beats rugs, washes her sheets and her blankets. She washes her clothes and hangs them back up, inside out. While she works, the ghost lies half under the bed, feet and genitalia pointed at her accusingly. She scrubs around it. Him. It.

She is being squeamish, Louise thinks. Afraid to touch it. And that makes her angry, so she picks up her broom. Pokes at the fleshy thighs, and the ghost hisses under the bed like an angry cat. She jumps back and then it isn't there anymore. But she sleeps on the living room sofa. She keeps all the lights on in all the rooms of the house.

"Well?" Louise says.

"It isn't gone," Louise says. She's just come home from work. "I just don't know *where* it is. Maybe it's up in the attic. It might be standing behind me, for all I know, while I'm talking to you on the phone and every time I turn around, it vanishes. Jumps back in the mirror or wherever it is that it goes. You may hear me scream. By the

Louise's Ghost

time you get here, it will be too late."

"Sweetie," Louise says. "I'm sure it can't hurt you."

"It hissed at me," Louise says.

"Did it just hiss, or did you do something first?" Louise says. "Kettles hiss. It just means the water's boiling."

"What about snakes?" Louise says. "I'm thinking it's more like a snake than a pot of tea."

"You could ask a priest to exorcise it. If you were Catholic. Or you could go to the library. They might have a book. Exorcism for dummies. Can you come to the symphony tonight? I have extra tickets."

"You've always got extra tickets," Louise says.

"Yes, but it will be good for you," Louise says. "Besides I haven't seen you for two days."

"Can't do it tonight," Louise says. "What about tomorrow night?"

"Well, okay," Louise says. "Have you tried reading the Bible to it?"

"What part of the Bible would I read?"

"How about the begetting part? That's official sounding," Louise says.

"What if it thinks I'm flirting? The guy at the gas station today said I should spit on the floor when I see it and say, 'In the name of God, what do you want?'"

"Have you tried that?"

"I don't know about spitting on the floor," Louise says. "I just cleaned it. What if it wants something gross, like my eyes? What if it wants me to kill someone?"

"Well," Louise says, "that would depend on who it wanted you to kill."

Louise goes to dinner with her married lover. After dinner, they will go to a motel and fuck. Then he'll take a shower and go home, and she'll spend the night at the motel. This is a *Louise*-style economy. It

217

makes Louise feel slightly more virtuous. The ghost will have the house to himself.

Louise doesn't talk to Louise about her lover. He belongs to her, and to his wife, of course. There isn't enough left over to share. She met him at work. Before him she had another lover, another married man. She would like to believe that this is a charming quirk, like being bowlegged or sleeping with cellists. But perhaps it's a character defect instead, like being tone deaf or refusing to eat food that isn't green.

Here is what Louise would tell Louise, if she told her. I'm just borrowing him—I don't want him to leave his wife. I'm glad he's married. Let someone else take care of him. It's the way he smells—the way married men smell. I can smell when a happily married man comes into a room, and they can smell me too, I think. So can the wives—that's why he has to take a shower when he leaves me.

But Louise doesn't tell Louise about her lovers. She doesn't want to sound as if she's competing with the cellists.

"What are you thinking about?" her lover says. The wine has made his teeth red.

It's the guiltiness that cracks them wide open. The guilt makes them taste so sweet, Louise thinks. "Do you believe in ghosts?" she says.

Her lover laughs. "Of course not."

If he were her husband, they would sleep in the same bed every night. And if she woke up and saw the ghost, she would wake up her husband. They would both see the ghost. They would share responsibility. It would be a piece of their marriage, part of the things they don't have (can't have) now, like breakfast or ski vacations or fights about toothpaste. Or maybe he would blame her. If she tells him now that she saw a naked man in her bedroom, he might say that it's her fault.

"Neither do I," Louise says. "But if you did believe in ghosts.

Because you saw one. What would you do? How would you get rid of it?"

Her lover thinks for a minute. "I wouldn't get rid of it," he says. "I'd charge admission. I'd become famous. I'd be on *Oprah*. They would make a movie. Everyone wants to see a ghost."

"But what if there's a problem," Louise says. "Such as. What if the ghost is naked?"

Her lover says, "Well, that would be a problem. Unless you were the ghost. Then I would want you to be naked all the time."

But Louise can't fall asleep in the motel room. Her lover has gone home to his home which isn't haunted, to his wife who doesn't know about Louise. Louise is as unreal to her as a ghost. Louise lies awake and thinks about her ghost. The dark is not dark, she thinks, and there is something in the motel room with her. Something her lover has left behind. Something touches her face. There's something bitter in her mouth. In the room next door someone is walking up and down. A baby is crying somewhere, or a cat.

She gets dressed and drives home. She needs to know if the ghost is still there or if her mother's recipe worked. She wishes she'd tried to take a picture.

She looks all over the house. She takes her clothes off the hangers in the closet and hangs them back right-side out. The ghost isn't anywhere. She can't find him. She even sticks her face up the chimney.

She finds the ghost curled up in her underwear drawer. He lies face down, hands open and loose. He's naked and downy all over like a baby monkey.

Louise spits on the floor, feeling relieved. "In God's name," she says, "What do you want?"

The ghost doesn't say anything. He lies there, small and hairy and forlorn, face down in her underwear. Maybe he doesn't know what he wants any more than she does. "Clothes?" Louise says. "Do you want me to get you some clothes? It would be easier if you stayed the same size."

The ghost doesn't say anything. "Well," Louise says. "You think about it. Let me know." She closes the drawer.

Anna is in her green bed. The green light is on. Louise and the babysitter sit in the living room while Louise and Anna talk. "When I was a dog," Anna says, "I ate roses and raw meat and borscht. I wore silk dresses."

"When you were a dog," Louise hears Louise say, "you had big silky ears and four big feet and a long silky tail and you wore a collar made out of silk and a silk dress with a hole cut in it for your tail."

"A green dress," Anna says. "I could see in the dark."

"Good night, my green girl," Louise says, "good night, good night."

Louise comes into the living room. "Doesn't Louise look beautiful," she says, leaning against Louise's chair and looking in the mirror. "The two of us. Louise and Louise and Louise and Louise. All four of us."

"Mirror, mirror on the wall," the babysitter says, "who is the fairest Louise of all?" Patrick the babysitter doesn't let Louise pay him. He takes symphony tickets instead. He plays classical guitar and composes music himself. Louise and Louise would like to hear his compositions, but he's too shy to play for them. He brings his guitar sometimes, to play for Anna. He's teaching her the simple chords.

"How is your ghost?" Louise says. "Louise has a ghost," she tells Patrick.

"Smaller," Louise says. "Hairier." Louise doesn't really like Patrick. He's in love with Louise for one thing. It embarrasses Louise, the hopeless way he looks at Louise. He probably writes love songs for her. He's friendly with Anna. As if that will get him anywhere.

"You tried garlic?" Louise says. "Spitting? Holy water? The library?"

"Yes," Louise says, lying.

"How about country music?" Patrick says. "Johnny Cash, Patsy Cline, Hank Williams?"

"Country music?" Louise says. "Is that like holy water?"

"I read something about it," Patrick says. "In *New Scientist*, or *Guitar* magazine, or maybe it was *Martha Stewart Living*. It was something about the pitch, the frequencies. Yodeling is supposed to be effective. Makes sense when you think about it."

"I was thinking about summer camp," Louise says to Louise. "Remember how the counselors used to tell us ghost stories?"

"Yeah," Louise says. "They did that thing with the flashlight. You made me go to the bathroom with you in the middle of the night. You were afraid to go by yourself."

"I wasn't afraid," Louise says. "You were afraid."

At the symphony, Louise watches the cellists and Louise watches Louise. The cellists watch the conductor and every now and then they look past him, over at Louise. Louise can feel them staring at Louise. Music goes everywhere, like light and, like light, music loves Louise. Louise doesn't know how she knows this—she can just feel the music, wrapping itself around Louise, insinuating itself into her beautiful ears, between her lips, collecting in her hair and in the little scoop between her legs. And what good does it do Louise, Louise thinks? The cellists might as well be playing jackhammers and spoons.

Well, maybe that isn't entirely true. Louise may be tone deaf, but she's explained to Louise that it doesn't mean she doesn't like music. She feels it in her bones and back behind her jaw. It scratches itches.

It's like a crossword puzzle. Louise is trying to figure it out, and right next to her, Louise is trying to figure out Louise.

The music stops and starts and stops again. Louise and Louise clap at the intermission and then the lights come up and Louise says, "I've been thinking a lot. About something. I want another baby."

"What do you mean?" Louise says, stunned. "You mean like Anna?"

"I don't know," Louise says. "Just another one. You should have a baby too. We could go to Lamaze classes together. You could name yours Louise after me and I could name mine Louise after you. Wouldn't that be funny?"

"Anna would be jealous," Louise says.

"I think it would make me happy," Louise says. "I was so happy when Anna was a baby. Everything just tasted good, even the air. I even liked being pregnant."

Louise says, "Aren't you happy now?"

Louise says, "Of course I'm happy. But don't you know what I mean? Being happy like that?"

"Kind of," Louise says. "Like when we were kids. You mean like Girl Scout camp."

"Yeah," Louise says. "Like that. You would have to get rid of your ghost first. I don't think ghosts are very hygienic. I could introduce you to a very nice man. A cellist. Maybe not the highest sperm count, but very nice."

"Which number is he?" Louise says.

"I don't want to prejudice you," Louise says. "You haven't met him. I'm not sure you should think of him as a number. I'll point him out. Oh, and number eight, too. You have to meet my beautiful boy, number eight. We have to go out to lunch so I can tell you about him. He's smitten. I've smited him."

Louise goes to the bathroom and Louise stays in her seat. She thinks of her ghost. Why can't she have a ghost and a baby? Why is she always supposed to give up something? Why can't other people share?

Why does Louise want to have another baby anyway? What if this new baby hates Louise as much as Anna does? What if it used to be a dog? What if her own baby hates Louise?

When the musicians are back on stage, Louise leans over and whispers to Louise, "There he is. The one with big hands, over on the right."

It isn't clear to Louise which cellist Louise means. They all have big hands. And which cellist is she supposed to be looking for? The nice cellist she shouldn't be thinking of as a number? Number eight? She takes a closer look. All of the cellists are handsome from where Louise is sitting. How fragile they look, she thinks, in their serious black clothes, letting the music run down their strings like that and pour through their open fingers. It's careless of them. You have to hold onto things.

There are six cellists on stage. Perhaps Louise has slept with all of them. Louise thinks, if I went to bed with them, with any of them, I would recognize the way they tasted, the things they liked and the ways they liked them. I would know which number they were. But they wouldn't know me.

The ghost is bigger again. He's prickly all over. He bristles with hair. The hair is reddish brown and sharp looking. Louise doesn't think it would be a good idea to touch the ghost now. All night he moves back and forth in front of her bed, sliding on his belly like a snake. His fingers dig into the floorboards and he pushes himself forward with his toes. His mouth stays open as if he's eating air.

Louise goes to the kitchen. She opens a can of beans, a can of pears, hearts of palm. She puts the different things on a plate and places the plate in front of the ghost. He moves around it. Maybe he's like Anna—picky. Louise doesn't know what he wants. Louise refuses to sleep in the living room again. It's her bedroom after all. She lies awake and listens to the ghost press himself against her clean floor, moving backwards and forwards before the foot of the bed all night long.

In the morning the ghost is in the closet, upside down against the wall. Enough, she thinks, and she goes to the mall and buys a stack of CDs. Patsy Cline, Emmylou Harris, Hank Williams, Johnny Cash, Lyle Lovett. She asks the clerk if he can recommend anything with yodeling on it, but he's young and not very helpful.

"Never mind," she says. "I'll just take these."

While he's running her credit card, she says, "Wait. Have you ever seen a ghost?"

"None of your business, lady," he says. "But if I had, I'd make it show me where it buried its treasure. And then I'd dig up the treasure and I'd be rich and then I wouldn't be selling you this stupid country shit. Unless the treasure had a curse on it."

"What if there wasn't any treasure?" Louise says.

"Then I'd stick the ghost in a bottle and sell it to a museum," the kid says. "A real live ghost. That's got to be worth something. I'd buy a hog and ride it to California. I'd go make my own music, and there wouldn't be any fucking yodeling."

The ghost seems to like Patsy Cline. It isn't that he says anything. But he doesn't disappear. He comes out of the closet. He lies on the floor so that Louise has to walk around him. He's thicker now, more solid. Maybe he was a Patsy Cline fan when he was alive. The hair stands up all over his body, and it moves gently, as if a breeze is blowing through it.

They both like Johnny Cash. Louise is pleased—they have something in common now.

"I'm onto Jackson," Louise sings. "You big talken man."

The phone rings in the middle of the night. Louise sits straight up in bed. "What?" she says. "Did you say something?" Is she in a hotel room? She orients herself quickly. The ghost is under the bed again, one hand sticking out as if flagging down a bedroom taxi. Louise picks up the phone.

"Number eight just told me the strangest thing," Louise says. "Did you try the country music?"

"Yes," Louise says. "But it didn't work. I think he liked it."

"That's a relief," Louise says. "What are you doing on Friday?"

"Working," Louise says. "And then I don't know. I was going to rent a video or something. Want to come over and see the ghost?"

"I'd like to bring over a few people," Louise says. "After rehearsal. The cellists want to see the ghost, too. They want to play for it, actually. It's kind of complicated. Maybe you could fix dinner. Spaghetti's fine. Maybe some salad, some garlic bread. I'll bring wine."

"How many cellists?" Louise says.

"Eight," Louise says. "And Patrick's busy. I might have to bring Anna. It could be educational. Is the ghost still naked?"

"Yes," Louise says. "But it's okay. He got furry. You can tell her he's a dog. So what's going to happen?"

"That depends on the ghost," Louise says. "If he likes the cellists, he might leave with one of them. You know, go into one of the cellos. Apparently it's very good for the music. And it's good for the ghost too. Sort of like those little fish that live on the big fishes. Remoras. Number eight is explaining it to me. He said that haunted instruments aren't just instruments. It's like they have a soul. The musician doesn't play the instrument any more. He or she plays the ghost."

"I don't know if he'd fit," Louise says. "He's largish. At least part of the time."

Louise says, "Apparently cellos are a lot bigger on the inside than they look on the outside. Besides, it's not like you're using him for anything."

"I guess not," Louise says.

"If word gets out, you'll have musicians knocking on your door day and night, night and day," Louise says. "Trying to steal him. Don't tell anyone."

Gloria and Mary come to see Louise at work. They leave with a group in a week for Greece. They're going to all the islands. They've been working with Louise to organize the hotels, the tours, the passports, and the buses. They're fond of Louise. They tell her about their sons, show her pictures. They think she should get married and have a baby.

Louise says, "Have either of you ever seen a ghost?"

Gloria shakes her head. Mary says, "Oh honey, all the time when I was growing up. It runs in families sometimes, ghosts and stuff like that. Not as much now, of course. My eyesight isn't so good now."

"What do you do with them?" Louise says.

"Not much," Mary says. "You can't eat them and you can't talk to most of them and they aren't worth much."

"I played with a Ouija board once," Gloria says. "With some other girls. We asked it who we would marry, and it told us some names. I forget. I don't recall that it was accurate. Then we got scared. We asked it who we were talking to, and it spelled out Z-E-U-S. Then it was just a bunch of letters. Gibberish."

"What about music?" Louise says.

"I like music," Gloria says. "It makes me cry sometimes when I hear a pretty song. I saw Frank Sinatra sing once. He wasn't so special."

"It will bother a ghost," Mary says. "Some kinds of music will stir it up. Some kinds of music will lay a ghost. We used to catch ghosts in my brother's fiddle. Like fishing, or catching fireflies in a jar. But my mother always said to leave them be."

"I have a ghost," Louise confesses.

"Would you ask it something?" Gloria says. "Ask it what it's like being dead. I like to know about a place before I get there. I don't mind going someplace new, but I like to know what it's going to be like. I like to have some idea."

Louise asks the ghost but he doesn't say anything. Maybe he can't remember what it was like to be alive. Maybe he's forgotten the language. He just lies on the bedroom floor, flat on his back, legs open, looking up at her like she's something special. Or maybe he's thinking of England.

Louise makes spaghetti. Louise is on the phone talking to caterers. "So you don't think we have enough champagne," she says. "I know it's a gala, but I don't want them falling over. Just happy. Happy signs checks. Falling over doesn't do me any good. How much more do you think we need?"

Anna sits on the kitchen floor and watches Louise cutting up tomatoes. "You'll have to make me something green," she says.

"Why don't you just eat your crayon," Louise says. "Your mother isn't going to have time to make you green food when she has another baby. You'll have to eat plain food like everybody else, or else eat grass like cows do."

"I'll make my own green food," Anna says.

"You're going to have a little brother or a little sister," Louise says. "You'll have to behave. You'll have to be responsible. You'll have to share your room and your toys—not just the regular ones, the green ones, too."

"I'm not going to have a sister," Anna says. "I'm going to have a dog."

"You know how it works, right?" Louise says, pushing the drippy tomatoes into the saucepan. "A man and a woman fall in love and they kiss and then the woman has a baby. First she gets fat and then she goes to the hospital. She comes home with a baby."

"You're lying," Anna says. "The man and the woman go to the pound. They pick out a dog. They bring the dog home and they feed it baby food. And then one day all the dog's hair falls out and it's pink. And it learns how to talk, and it has to wear clothes. And they give it a new name, not a dog name. They give it a baby name and it has to give the dog name back."

"Whatever," Louise says. "I'm going to have a baby, too. And it will have the same name as your mother and the same name as me. Louise. Louise will be the name of your mother's baby, too. The only person named Anna will be you."

"My dog name was Louise," Anna says. "But you're not allowed to call me that."

Louise comes in the kitchen. "So much for the caterers," she says. "So where is it?"

"Where's what?" Louise says.

"The you know what," Louise says, "you know."

"I haven't seen it today," Louise says. "Maybe this won't work. Maybe it would rather live here." All day long she's had the radio turned on, tuned to the country station. Maybe the ghost will take the hint and hide out somewhere until everyone leaves.

The cellists arrive. Seven men and a woman. Louise doesn't bother to remember their names. The woman is tall and thin. She has long arms and a long nose. She eats three plates of spaghetti. The cellists talk to each other. They don't talk about the ghost. They talk about music. They complain about acoustics. They tell Louise that her spaghetti is delicious. Louise just smiles. She stares at the woman cellist, sees Louise watching her. Louise shrugs, nods. She holds up five fingers.

Louise and the cellists seem comfortable. They tease each other. They tell stories. Do they know? Do they talk about Louise? Do they brag? Compare notes? How could they know Louise better than Louise knows her? Suddenly Louise feels as if this isn't her house after all. It belongs to Louise and the cellists. It's their ghost, not hers. They live here. After dinner they'll stay and she'll leave.

Number five is the one who likes foreign films, Louise remembers. The one with the goldfish. Louise said number five had a great sense of humor.

Louise gets up and goes to the kitchen to get more wine, leaving Louise alone with the cellists. The one sitting next to Louise says, "You have the prettiest eyes. Have I seen you in the audience sometimes?"

"It's possible," Louise says.

"Louise talks about you all the time," the cellist says. He's young, maybe twenty-four or twenty-five. Louise wonders if he's the one with the big hands. He has pretty eyes, too. She tells him that.

"Louise doesn't know everything about me," she says, flirting.

Anna is hiding under the table. She growls and pretends to bite the cellists. The cellists know Anna. They're used to her. They probably think she's cute. They pass her bits of broccoli, lettuce.

The living room is full of cellos in black cases the cellists brought in, like sarcophaguses on little wheels. Sarcophabuses. Dead baby carriages. After dinner the cellists take their chairs into the living room. They take out their cellos and tune them. Anna insinuates herself between cellos, hanging on the backs of chairs. The house is full of sound.

Louise and Louise sit on chairs in the hall and look in. They can't talk. It's too loud. Louise reaches into her purse, pulls out a packet of earplugs. She gives two to Anna, two to Louise, keeps two for herself. Louise puts her earplugs in. Now the cellists sound as if they are underground, down in some underground lake, or in a cave. Louise fidgets.

The cellists play for almost an hour. When they take a break Louise feels tender, as if the cellists have been throwing things at her. Tiny lumps of sound. She almost expects to see bruises on her arms.

The cellists go outside to smoke cigarettes. Louise takes Louise aside. "You should tell me now if there isn't a ghost," she says. "I'll tell them to go home. I promise I won't be angry."

"There is a ghost," Louise says. "Really." But she doesn't try to sound too convincing. What she doesn't tell Louise is that she's stuck a Walkman in her closet. She's got the Patsy Cline CD on repeat with the volume turned way down.

Louise says, "So he was talking to you during dinner. What do you think?"

"Who?" Louise says. "Him? He was pretty nice."

Louise sighs. "Yeah. I think he's pretty nice, too."

The cellists come back inside. The young cellist with the glasses and the big hands looks over at both of them and smiles a big blissed smile. Maybe it wasn't cigarettes that they were smoking.

Anna has fallen asleep inside a cello case, like a fat green pea in a coffin.

Louise tries to imagine the cellists without their clothes. She tries to picture them naked and fucking Louise. No, fucking *Louise*, fucking her instead. Which one is number four? The one with the beard? Number four, she remembers, likes Louise to sit on top and bounce up and down. She does all the work while he waves his hand. He conducts her. Louise thinks it's funny.

Louise pictures all of the cellists, naked and in the same bed. She's in the bed. The one with the beard first. Lie on your back, she tells him. Close your eyes. Don't move. I'm in charge. I'm conducting this affair. The one with the skinny legs and the poochy stomach. The young one with curly black hair, bent over his cello as if he might fall in. Who was flirting with her. Do this, she tells a cellist. Do this, she tells another one. She can't figure out what to do with the woman. Number five. She can't even figure out how to take off number five's clothes. Number five sits on the edge of the bed, hands tucked under her buttocks. She's still in her bra and underwear.

Louise thinks about the underwear for a minute. It has little flowers on it. Periwinkles. Number five waits for Louise to tell her what to do. But Louise is having a hard enough time figuring out where everyone else goes. A mouth has fastened itself on her breast. Someone is tugging at her hair. She is holding onto someone's penis with both hands, someone else's penis is rubbing against her cunt. There are penises everywhere. Wait your turn, Louise thinks. Be patient.

Number five has pulled a cello out of her underwear. She's playing a sad little tune on it. It's distracting. It's not sexy at all. Another cellist stands up on the bed, jumps up and down. Soon they're all doing it. The bed creaks and groans, and the woman plays faster and faster on her fiddle. Stop it, Louise thinks, you'll wake the ghost.

"Shit!" Louise says—she's yanked Louise's earplug out, drops it in Louise's lap. "There he is under your chair. Look. Louise, you really do have a ghost."

The cellists don't look. Butter wouldn't melt in their mouths. They are fucking their cellos with their fingers, stroking music out, promising the ghost yodels and Patsy Cline and funeral marches and whole cities of music and music to eat and music to drink and music to put on and wear like clothes. It isn't music Louise has ever heard before. It sounds like a lullaby, and then it sounds like a pack of wolves, and then it sounds like a slaughterhouse, and then it sounds like a motel room and a married man saying I love you and the shower is running at the same time. It makes her teeth ache and her heart rattle.

It sounds like the color green. Anna wakes up. She's sitting in the cello case, hands over her ears.

This is too loud, Louise thinks. The neighbors will complain. She bends over and sees the ghost, small and unobjectionable as a lapdog, lying under her chair. Oh, my poor baby, she thinks. Don't be fooled. Don't fall for the song. They don't mean it.

But something is happening to the ghost. He shivers and twists and gapes. He comes out from under the chair. He leaves all his fur behind, under the chair in a neat little pile. He drags himself along the floor with his strong beautiful hands, scissoring with his legs along the floor like a swimmer. He's planning to change, to leave her and go away. Louise pulls out her other earplug. She's going to give them to the ghost. "Stay here," she says out loud, "stay here with me and the real Patsy Cline. Don't go." She can't hear herself speak. The cellos roar like lions in cages and licks of fire. Louise opens her mouth to say it louder, but the ghost is going. Fine, okay, go comb your hair. See if I care.

Louise and Louise and Anna watch as the ghost climbs into a cello. He pulls himself up, shakes the air off like drops of water. He gets smaller. He gets fainter. He melts into the cello like spilled milk. All the other cellists pause. The cellist who has caught Louise's ghost plays a scale. "Well," he says. It doesn't sound any different to Louise but all the other cellists sigh.

It's the bearded cellist who's caught the ghost. He holds onto his cello as if it might grow legs and run away if he let go. He looks like he's discovered America. He plays something else. Something old-fashioned, Louise thinks, a pretty old-fashioned tune, and she wants to cry. She puts her earplugs back in again. The cellist looks up at Louise as he plays and he smiles. You owe me, she thinks.

But it's the youngest cellist, the one who thinks Louise has pretty eyes, who stays. Louise isn't sure how this happens. She isn't sure that she has the right cellist. She isn't sure that the ghost went into the right cello. But the cellists pack up their cellos and they thank her and they drive away, leaving the dishes piled in the sink for Louise to wash.

The youngest cellist is still sitting in her living room. "I thought I had it," he says. "I thought for sure I could play that ghost."

"I'm leaving," Louise says. But she doesn't leave.

"Good night," Louise says.

"Do you want a ride?" Louise says to the cellist.

He says, "I thought I might hang around. See if there's another ghost in here. If that's okay with Louise."

Louise shrugs. "Good night," she says to Louise.

"Well," Louise says, "good night." She picks up Anna, who has fallen asleep on the couch. Anna was not impressed with the ghost. He wasn't a dog and he wasn't green.

"Good night," the cellist says, and the door slams shut behind Louise and Anna.

Louise inhales. He's not married, it isn't that smell. But it reminds her of something.

"What's your name?" she says, but before he can answer her, she puts her earplugs back in again. They fuck in the closet and then in the bathtub and then he lies down on the bedroom floor and Louise sits on top of him. To exorcise the ghost, she thinks. Hotter in a chilly sprout.

The cellist's mouth moves when he comes. It looks like he's saying, "Louise, Louise," but she gives him the benefit of the doubt. He might be saying her name.

She nods encouragingly. "That's right," she says. "Louise."

The cellist falls asleep on the floor. Louise throws a blanket over

233

him. She watches him breathe. It's been a while since she's watched a man sleep. She takes a shower and she does the dishes. She puts the chairs in the living room away. She gets an envelope and she picks up a handful of the ghost's hair. She puts it in the envelope and she sweeps the rest away. She takes her earplugs out but she doesn't throw them away.

In the morning, the cellist makes her pancakes. He sits down at the table and she stands up. She walks over and sniffs his neck. She recognizes that smell now. He smells like Louise. Burnt sugar and orange juice and talcum powder. She realizes that she's made a horrible mistake.

Louise is furious. Louise didn't know Louise knew how to be angry. Louise hangs up when Louise calls. Louise drives over to Louise's house and no one comes to the door. But Louise can see Anna looking out the window.

Louise writes a letter to Louise. "I'm so sorry," she writes. "I should have known. Why didn't you tell me? He doesn't love me. He was just drunk. Maybe he got confused. Please, please forgive me. You don't have to forgive me immediately. Tell me what I should do."

At the bottom she writes, "P.S. I'm not pregnant."

Three weeks later, Louise is walking a group of symphony patrons across the stage. They've all just eaten lunch. They drank wine. She is pointing out architectural details, rows of expensive spotlights. She is standing with her back to the theater. She is talking, she points up, she takes a step back into air. She falls off the stage.

A man—a lawyer—calls Louise at work. At first she thinks it must be her mother who has fallen. The lawyer explains. Louise is the one who is dead. She broke her neck.

While Louise is busy understanding this, the lawyer, Mr. Bostick, says something else. Louise is Anna's guardian now.

"Wait, wait," Louise says. "What do you mean? Louise is in the hospital? I have to take care of Anna for a while?"

No, Mr. Bostick says. Louise is dead.

"In the event of her death, Louise wanted you to adopt her daughter Anna Geary. I had assumed that my client Louise Geary had discussed this with you. She has no living family. Louise told me that you were her family."

"But I slept with her cellist," Louise said. "I didn't mean to. I didn't realize which number he was. I didn't know his name. I still don't. Louise is so angry with me."

But Louise isn't angry with Louise anymore. Or maybe now she will always be angry with Louise.

Louise picks Anna up at school. Anna is sitting on a chair in the school office. She doesn't look up when Louise opens the door. Louise goes and stands in front of her. She looks down at Anna and thinks, this is all that's left of Louise. This is all I've got now. A little girl who only likes things that are green, who used to be a dog. "Come on, Anna," Louise says. "You're going to come live with me."

Louise and Anna live together for a week. Louise avoids her married lover at work. She doesn't know how to explain things. First a ghost and now a little girl. That's the end of the motel rooms.

Louise and Anna go to Louise's funeral and throw dirt at Louise's coffin. Anna throws her dirt hard, like she's aiming for something. Louise holds on to her handful too tightly. When she lets go, there's dirt under her fingernails. She sticks a finger in her mouth.

All the cellists are there. They look amputated without their cellos, smaller, childlike. Anna, in her funereal green, looks older than they do. She holds Louise's hand grudgingly. Louise has promised that Anna can have a dog. No more motels for sure. She'll have to buy a bigger house, Louise thinks, with a yard. She'll sell her house and Louise's house and put the money in trust for Anna. She did this for her mother—this is what you have to do for family.

While the minister is still speaking, number eight lies down on the ground beside the grave. The cellists on either side each take an arm and pull him back up again. Louise sees that his nose is running. He doesn't look at her, and he doesn't wipe his nose, either. When the two cellists walk him away, there's grave dirt on the seat of his pants.

Patrick is there. His eyes are red. He waves his fingers at Anna, but he stays where he is. Loss is contagious—he's keeping a safe distance.

The woman cellist, number five, comes up to Louise after the funeral. She embraces Louise, Anna. She tells them that a special memorial concert has been arranged. Funds will be raised. One of the smaller concert halls will be named the Louise Geary Memorial Hall. Louise agrees that Louise would have been pleased. She and Anna leave before the other cellists can tell them how sorry they are, how much they will miss Louise.

In the evening Louise calls her mother and tells her that Louise is dead.

"Oh sweetie," her mother says. "I'm so sorry. She was such a pretty girl. I always liked to hear her laugh."

"She was angry with me," Louise says. "Her daughter Anna is staying with me now."

"What about Anna's father?" her mother says. "Did you get rid of that ghost? I'm not sure it's a good idea having a ghost in the same house as a small girl."

"The ghost is gone," Louise says.

There is a click on the line. "Someone's listening in," her mother says. "Don't say anything—they might be recording us. Call me back from a different phone."

Anna has come into the room. She stands behind Louise. She says,

"I want to go live with my father."

"It's time to go to sleep," Louise says. She wants to take off her funeral clothes and go to bed. "We can talk about this in the morning."

Anna brushes her teeth and puts on her green pajamas. She does not want Louise to read to her. She does not want a glass of water. Louise says, "When I was a dog . . ."

Anna says, "You were never a dog—" and pulls the blanket, which is not green, up over her head and will not say anything else.

Mr. Bostick knows who Anna's father is. "He doesn't know about Anna," he tells Louise. "His name is George Candle and he lives in Oregon. He's married and has two kids. He has his own company—something to do with organic produce, I think, or maybe it was construction."

"I think it would be better for Anna if she were to live with a real parent," Louise says. "Easier. Someone who knows something about kids. I'm not cut out for this."

Mr. Bostick agrees to contact Anna's father. "He may not even admit he knew Louise," he says. "He may not be okay about this."

"Tell him she's a fantastic kid," Louise says. "Tell him she looks just like Louise."

In the end George Candle comes and collects Anna. Louise arranges his airline tickets and his hotel room. She books two return tickets out to Portland for Anna and her father and makes sure Anna has a window seat. "You'll like Oregon," she tells Anna. "It's green."

"You think you're smarter than me," Anna says. "You think you know all about me. When I was a dog, I was ten times smarter than you. I knew who my friends were because of how they smelled. I know things you don't."

But she doesn't say what they are. Louise doesn't ask.

George Candle cries when he meets his daughter. He's almost as hairy as the ghost. Louise can smell his marriage. She wonders what Anna smells.

"I loved your mother very much," George Candle says to Anna. "She was a very special person. She had a beautiful soul."

They go to see Louise's grave. The grass on her grave is greener than the other grass. You can see where it's been tipped in, like a bookplate. Louise briefly fantasizes her own funeral, her own grave, her own married lover standing beside her grave. She knows he would go straight home after the funeral to take a shower. If he went to the funeral.

The house without Anna is emptier than Louise is used to. Louise didn't expect to miss Anna. Now she has no best friend, no ghost, no adopted former dog. Her lover is home with his wife, sulking, and now George Candle is flying home to his wife. What will she think of Anna? Maybe Anna will miss Louise just a little.

That night Louise dreams of Louise endlessly falling off the stage. She falls and falls and falls. As Louise falls she slowly comes apart. Little bits of her fly away. She is made up of ladybugs.

Anna comes and sits on Louise's bed. She is a lot furrier than she was when she lived with Louise. "You're not a dog," Louise says.

Anna grins her possum teeth at Louise. She's holding a piece of okra. "The supernatural world has certain characteristics," Anna says. "You can recognize it by its color, which is green, and by its texture, which is hirsute. Those are its outside qualities. Inside the supernatural world things get sticky but you never get inside things, Louise. Did you know that George Candle is a werewolf? Look out for hairy men, Louise. Or do I mean married men? The other aspects of the green world include music and smell."

Anna pulls her pants down and squats. She pees on the bed, a long acrid stream that makes Louise's eyes water.

Louise wakes up sobbing. "Louise," Louise whispers. "Please

come and lie on my floor. Please come haunt me. I'll play Patsy Cline
for you and comb your hair. Please don't go away."

She keeps a vigil for three nights. She plays Patsy Cline. She sits
by the phone because maybe Louise could call. Louise has never not
called, not for so long. If Louise doesn't forgive her, then she can
come and be an angry ghost. She can make dishes break or make
blood come out of the faucets. She can give Louise bad dreams.
Louise will be grateful for broken things and blood and bad dreams.
All of Louise's clothes are up on their hangers, hung right-side out.
Louise puts little dishes of flowers out, plates with candles and candy.
She calls her mother to ask how to make a ghost appear but her
mother refuses to tell her. The line may be tapped. Louise will have
to come down, she says, and she'll explain in person.

Louise wears the same dress she wore to the funeral. She sits up in
the balcony. There are enormous pictures of Louise up on the stage.
Influential people go up on the stage and tell funny stories about
Louise. Members of the orchestra speak about Louise. Her charm,
her beauty, her love of music. Louise looks through her opera glasses
at the cellists. There is the young one, number eight, who caused all
the trouble. There is the bearded cellist who caught the ghost. She
stares through her glasses at his cello. Her ghost runs up and down
the neck of his cello, frisky. It coils around the strings, hangs upside-
down from a peg.

She examines number five's face for a long time. Why you, Louise
thinks. If she wanted to sleep with a woman, why did she sleep with
you? Did you tell her funny jokes? Did you go shopping together for
clothes? When you saw her naked, did you see that she was bowlegged? Did you think that she was beautiful?

The cellist next to number five is holding his cello very carefully.
He runs his fingers down the strings as if they were tangled and he

were combing them. Louise stares through her opera glasses. There is something in his cello. Something small and bleached is looking back at her through the strings. Louise looks at Louise and then she slips back through the f hole, like a fish.

They are in the woods. The fire is low. It's night. All the little girls are in their sleeping bags. They've brushed their teeth and spit, they've washed their faces with water from the kettle, they've zipped up the zippers of their sleeping bags.

A counselor named Charlie is saying, "I am the ghost with the one black eye, I am the ghost with the one black eye."

Charlie holds her flashlight under her chin. Her eyes are two black holes in her face. Her mouth yawns open, the light shining through her teeth. Her shadow eats up the trunk of the tree she sits under.

During the daytime Charlie teaches horseback riding. She isn't much older than Louise or Louise. She's pretty and she lets them ride the horses bareback sometimes. But that's daytime Charlie. Nighttime Charlie is the one sitting next to the fire. Nighttime Charlie is the one who tells stories.

"Are you afraid?" Louise says.

"No," Louise says.

They hold hands. They don't look at each other. They keep their eyes on Charlie.

Louise says, "Are you afraid?"

"No," Louise says. "Not as long as you're here."

THE GIRL DETECTIVE

*The girl detective looked at her reflection in the mirror. This
was a different girl. This was a girl who would chew gum.*
—DORA KNEZ, *in conversation*

The girl detective's mother is missing.

The girl detective's mother has been missing for a long time.

The underworld.

Think of the underworld as the back of your closet, behind all those
racks of clothes that you don't wear anymore. Things are always getting
pushed back there and forgotten about. The underworld is full of
things that you've forgotten about. Some of them, if only you could
remember, you might want to take them back. Trips to the underworld
are always very nostalgic. It's darker in there. The seasons don't match.
Mostly people end up there by accident, or else because in the end
there was nowhere else to go. Only heroes and girl detectives go to the
underworld on purpose.

There are three kinds of food.

One is the food that your mother makes for you. One is the kind of food that you eat in restaurants. One is the kind of food that you eat in dreams. There's one other kind of food, but you can only get that in the underworld, and it's not really food. It's more like dancing.

The girl detective eats dreams.

The girl detective won't eat her dinner. Her father, the housekeeper—they've tried everything they can think of. Her father takes her out to eat—Chinese restaurants, once even a truckstop two states away for chicken-fried steak. The girl detective used to love chicken-fried steak. Her father has gained ten pounds, but the girl detective will only have a glass of water, not even a slice of lemon. I saw them once at that new restaurant downtown, and the girl detective was folding her napkin while her father ate. I went over to their table after they'd left. She'd folded her napkin into a swan. I put it into my pocket, along with her dinner roll and a packet of sugar. I thought these things might be clues.

The housekeeper cooks all the food that the girl detective used to love. Green beans, macaroni and cheese, parsnips, stewed pears—the girl detective used to eat all her vegetables. The girl detective used to love vegetables. She always cleaned her plate. If only her mother were still here, the housekeeper will say, and sigh. The girl detective's father sighs. Aren't you the littlest bit hungry? they ask her. Wouldn't you like a bite to eat? But the girl detective still goes to bed hungry.

There is some debate about whether the girl detective needs to eat food at all. Is it possible that she is eating in secret? Is she anorexic? Bulimic? Is she protesting something? What could we cook that would tempt her?

I am doing my best to answer these very questions. I am detecting the girl detective. I sit in a tree across the street from her window, and this is what I see. The girl detective goes to bed hungry, but she eats our dreams while we are asleep. She has eaten my dreams. She has eaten your dreams, one after the other, as if they were grapes or oysters. The girl detective is getting fat on other people's dreams.

The case of the tap-dancing bankrobbers.

Just a few days ago, I saw this on the news. You remember, that bank downtown. Maybe you were in line for a teller, waiting to make a deposit. Perhaps you saw them come in. They had long, long legs, and they were wearing sequins. Feathers. Not much else. They wore tiny black dominos, hair pinned up in tall loopy curls, and their mouths were wide and red. Their eyes glittered.

You were being interviewed on the news. "We all thought that someone in the bank must be having a birthday," you said. "They had on these skimpy outfits. There was music playing."

They spun. They pranced. They kicked. They were carrying purses, and they took tiny black guns out of their purses. Sit down on the floor, one of them told you. You sat on the floor. Sitting on the floor, it was possible to look up their short, flounced skirts. You could see their underwear. It was satin, and embroidered with the days of the week. There were twelve bank robbers: Monday, Tuesday, Wednesday, Thursday, Friday, Saturday, Sunday, and then Mayday, Payday, Yesterday, Someday, and Birthday. The one who had spoken to you was Birthday. She seemed to be the leader. She went over to a teller, and pointed the little gun at him. They spoke earnestly. They went away, through a door over to the side. All the other bank robbers went with them, except for Wednesday and Thursday, who were keeping an eye on you. They shuffled a little on the marble floor as they waited. They did a couple of pliés. They kept their guns pointed at the security guard, who had been asleep on a chair by the door. He stayed asleep.

In about a minute, the other bank robbers came back through the door again, with the teller. They looked satisfied. The teller looked confused, and he went and sat on the floor next to you. The bank robbers left. Witnesses say they got in a red van with something written in gold on the side and drove away. The driver was an older woman. She looked stern.

Police are on the lookout for this woman, for this van. When they arrived, what did they find inside the vault? Nothing was missing. In fact, things appeared to have been left behind. Several tons of mismatched socks, several hundred pairs of prescription glasses, retainers, a ball python six feet long, curled decoratively around the bronze vault dial. Also a woman claiming to be Amelia Earhart. When police questioned this woman, she claimed to remember very little. She remembers a place, police suspect that she was held hostage there by the bank robbers. It was dark, she said, and people were dancing. The food was pretty good. Police have the woman in protective custody, where she has reportedly received serious proposals from lonely men and major publishing houses.

In the past two months the tap-dancing robbers have kept busy. Who are these masked women? Speculation is rife. All dance performances, modern, classical, even student rehearsals, are well-attended. Banks have become popular places to go on dates or on weekdays, during lunch. Some people bring roses to throw. The girl detective is reportedly working on the case.

Secret origins of the girl detective.

Some people say that she doesn't exist. Someone once suggested that

I was the girl detective, but I've never known whether or not they were serious. At least I don't think that I am the girl detective. If I were the girl detective, I would surely know.

Things happen.

When the girl detective leaves her father's house one morning, a man is lurking outside. I've been watching him for a while now from my tree. I'm a little stiff, but happy to be here. He's a fat man with pouched, beautiful eyes. He sighs heavily a few times. He takes the girl detective by the arm. Can I tell you a story, he says.

All right, says the girl detective politely. She takes her arm back, sits down on the front steps. The man sits down beside her and lights a smelly cigar.

The girl detective saves the world.

The girl detective has saved the world on at least three separate occasions. Not that she is bragging.

The girl detective doesn't care for fiction.

The girl detective doesn't actually read much. She doesn't have the time. Her father used to read fairy tales to her when she was little. She didn't like them. For example, the twelve dancing princesses. If their father really wants to stop them, why doesn't he just forbid the royal shoemaker to make them any more dancing shoes? Why do they have to go underground to dance? Don't they have a ballroom? Do they like dancing or are they secretly relieved when they get caught? Who taught them to dance?

The girl detective has thought a lot about the twelve dancing princesses. She and the princesses have a few things in common. For instance, shoe leather. Possibly underwear. Also, no mother. This is another thing about fiction, fairy tales in particular. The mother is usually missing. The girl detective imagines, all of a sudden, all of these mothers. They're all in the same place. They're far away, some place she can't find them. It infuriates her. What are they up to, all of these mothers?

The fat man's story.

This man has twelve daughters, says the fat man. All of them lookers. Nice gams. He's a rich man but he doesn't have a wife. He has to take care of the girls all by himself. He does the best he can. The oldest one is still living at home when the youngest one graduates from high school. This makes their father happy. How can he take care of them if they move away from home?

But strange things start to happen. The girls all sleep in the same bedroom, which is fine, no problem, because they all get along great. But then the girls start to sleep all day. He can't wake them up. It's as if they've been drugged. He brings in specialists. The specialists all shake their heads.

At night the girls wake up. They're perky. Affectionate. They apply makeup. They whisper and giggle. They eat dinner with their father, and everyone pretends that everything's normal. At bedtime they go to their room and lock the door, and in the morning when their father knocks on the door to wake them up, gently at first, tapping, then harder, begging them to open the door, beside each bed is a worn-out pair of dancing shoes.

Here's the thing. He's never even bought them dancing lessons. They all took horseback riding, tennis, those classes where you learn to make dollhouse furniture out of cigarette boxes and doilies.

So he hires a detective. Me, says the fat man—you wouldn't think it, but I used to be young and handsome and quick on my feet. I used to be a pretty good dancer myself.

The man puffs on his cigar. Are you getting all this? the girl detective calls to me, where I'm sitting up in the tree. I nod. Why don't you take a hike, she says.

Why we love the girl detective.

We love the girl detective because she reminds us of the children we wish we had. She is courteous, but also brave. She loathes injustice; she is passionate, but also well-groomed. She keeps her room neat, but not too neat. She feeds her goldfish. She will get good grades, keep her curfew when it doesn't interfere with fighting crime. She'll come home from an Ivy League college on weekends to do her laundry.

She reminds us of the girl we hope to marry one day. If we ask her, she will take care of us, cook us nutritious meals, find our car keys when we've misplaced them. The girl detective is good at finding things. She will balance the checkbook, plan vacations, and occasionally meet us at the door when we come home from work, wearing nothing but a blue ribbon in her hair. She will fill our eyes. We will bury our faces in her dark, light, silky, curled, frizzed, teased, short, shining, long, shining hair. Tangerine, clove, russet, coal-colored, oxblood, buttercup, clay-colored, tallow, titian, lampblack, sooty, scented hair. The color of her hair will always inflame us.

She reminds us of our mothers.

Dance with Beautiful Girls.

The father hides me in the closet one night, and I wait until the girls, they all come to bed. It's a big closet. And it smells nice, like girl sweat and cloves and mothballs. I hold onto the sleeve of someone's dress to balance while I'm looking through the keyhole. Don't think I don't go through all the pockets. But all I find is a marble and a deck of cards with the Queen of Spades missing, a napkin folded into a swan maybe, a box of matches from a Chinese restaurant.

I look through the keyhole, maybe I'm hoping to see one or two of them take off their clothes, but instead they lock the bedroom door and move one of the beds, knock on the floor and guess what? There's a secret passageway. Down they go, one after the other. They look so demure, like they're going to Sunday School.

I wait a bit and then I follow them. The passageway is plaster and bricks first, and then it's dirt with packed walls. The walls open up and we could be walking along, all of us holding hands if we wanted to. It's pretty dark, but each girl has a flashlight. I follow the twelve pairs of feet in twelve new pairs of kid leather dancing shoes, each in its own little puddle of light. I stretch my hands up and I stand on my toes, but I can't feel the roof of the tunnel anymore. There's a breeze, raising the hair on my neck.

Up till then I think I know this city pretty well, but we go down and down, me after the last girl, the youngest, and when at last the passageway levels out, we're in a forest. There's this moss on the trunk of the trees, which glows. It looks like paradise by the light of the moss. The ground is soft like velvet, and the air tastes good. I think I must be dreaming, but I reach up and break off a branch.

The youngest girl hears the branch snap and she turns around, but I've ducked behind a tree. So she goes on and we go on.

Then we come to a river. Down by the bank there are twelve young men, Oriental, gangsters by the look of 'em, black hair slicked back, smooth-faced in the dim light, and I can see they're all wearing guns under their nice dinner jackets. I stay back in the trees. I think maybe it's the white slave trade, but the girls go peaceful, and they're smiling and laughing with their escorts, so I stay back in the trees and think for a bit. Each man rows one of the girls across the river in a little canoe. Me, I wait a while and then I get in a canoe and start rowing myself across, quiet as I can. The water is black and there's a bit of a current, as if it knows where it's going. I don't quite trust this water. I get close to the last boat with the youngest girl in it and water from my oar splashes up and gets her face wet, I guess, because she says to the man, someone's out there.

Alligator, maybe, he says, and I swear he looks just like the waiter who brought me orange chicken in that new restaurant downtown. I'm so close, I swear they must see me, but they don't seem to. Or maybe they're just being polite.

We all get out on the other side and there's a nightclub all lit up with paper lanterns on the veranda. Men and women are standing out on the veranda, and there's a band playing inside. It's the kind of music that makes you start tapping your feet. It gets inside me and starts knocking inside my head. By now I think the girls must have seen me, but they don't look at me. They seem to be ignoring me. "Well, here they are," this one woman says. "Hello, girls." She's tall, and so beautiful she looks like a movie star, but she's stern-looking too, like she probably plays villains. She's wearing one of them tight silky dresses with dragons on it, but she's not Oriental.

"Now let's get started," she says. Over the door of the nightclub is a sign. DANCE WITH BEAUTIFUL GIRLS. They go in. I wait a bit and go in, too.

I dance with the oldest and I dance with the youngest and of course they pretend that they don't know me, but they think I dance pretty fine. We shimmy and we grind, we bump and we do the Charleston. This girl she opens up her legs for me but she's got her hands down in an X, and then her knees are back together and her arms fly open like she's going to grab me, and then her hands are crossing over and back on her knees again. I lift her up in the air by her armpits and her skirt flies up. She's standing on the air like it was solid as the dance floor, and when I put her back down, she moves on the floor like it was air. She just floats. Her feet are tapping the whole time and sparks are flying up from her shoes and my shoes and everybody's shoes. I dance with a lot of girls and they're all beautiful, just like the sign says, even the ones who aren't. And when the band starts to sound tired, I sneak out the door and back across the river, back through the forest, back up the secret passageway into the girls' bedroom.

I get back in the closet and wipe my face on someone's dress. The sweat is dripping off me. Pretty soon the girls come home too, limping a little bit, but smiling. They sit down on their beds and they take off their shoes. Sure enough, their shoes are worn right through. Mine aren't much better.

That's when I step out of the closet and while they're all screaming, lamenting, shrieking, scolding, yelling, cursing, I unlock the bedroom door and let their father in. He's been waiting there all night. He's hangdog. There are circles under his eyes. Did you follow them? he says.

I did, I say.

Did you stick to them? he says. He won't look at them.

I did, I say. I give him the branch. A little bit later, when I get to know the oldest girl, we get married. We go out dancing almost every night, but I never see that club again.

There are two kinds of names.

The girl detective has learned to distrust certain people. People who don't blink enough, for example. People who don't fidget. People who dance too well. People who are too fat or too thin. People who cry and don't need to blow their noses afterwards. People with certain kinds of names are prone to wild and extravagant behavior. Sometimes they turn to a life of crime. If only their parents had been more thoughtful. These people have names like Bernadette, Sylvester, Arabella, Apocolopus, Thaddeus, Gertrude, Gomez, Xavier, Xerxes. Flora. They wear sinister lipsticks, plot world destruction, ride to the hounds, take up archery instead of bowling. They steal inheritances, wear false teeth, hide wills, shoplift, plot murders, take off their clothes and dance on tables in crowded bars just after everyone has gotten off work.

On the other hand, it doesn't do to trust people named George or Maxine, or Sandra, or Bradley. People with names like this are obviously hiding something. Men who limp. Who have crooked, or too many teeth. People who don't floss. People who are stingy or who leave overgenerous tips. People who don't wash their hands after going to the bathroom. People who want things too badly. The world is a dangerous place, full of people who don't trust each other. This is why I am staying up in this tree. I wouldn't come down even if she asked me to.

The girl detective is looking for her mother.

The girl detective has been looking for her mother for a long time. She doesn't expect her mother to be easy to find. After all, her mother is also a master of disguises. If we fail to know the girl detective when she comes to find us, how will the girl detective know her mother?

She sees her sometimes in other people's dreams. Look at the way this woman is dreaming about goldfish, her mother says. And the girl detective tastes the goldfish and something is revealed to her. Maybe a broken heart, maybe something about money, or a holiday that the woman is about to take. Maybe the woman is about to win the lottery.

Sometimes the girl detective thinks she is missing her mother's point. Maybe the thing she is supposed to be learning is not about vacations or broken hearts or lotteries or missing wills or any of these things. Maybe her mother is trying to tell the girl detective how to get to where she is. In the meantime, the girl detective collects the clues from other people's dreams and we ask her to find our missing pets, to tell us if our spouses are being honest with us, to tell us who are really our friends, and to keep an eye on the world while we are sleeping.

About three o'clock this morning, the girl detective pushed up her window and looked at me. She looked like she hadn't been getting much sleep either. "Are you still up in that tree?"

Why we fear the girl detective.

She reminds us of our mothers. She eats our dreams. She knows what we have been up to, what we are longing for. She knows what we are capable of, and what we are not capable of. She is looking for something. We are afraid that she is looking for us. We are afraid that she is not looking for us. Who will find us, if the girl detective does not?

The girl detective asks a few questions.

"I think I've heard this story before," the girl detective says to the fat man.

"It's an old story."

The man stares at her sadly and she stares back. "So why are you telling me?"

252

"Don't know," he says. "My wife disappeared a few months ago. I mean, she passed on, she died. I can't find her is what I mean. But I thought that maybe if someone could find that club again, she might be there. But I'm old and her father's house burned down thirty years ago. I can't even find that Chinese restaurant anymore."

"Even if I found the club," the girl detective says, "if she's dead, she probably won't be there. And if she is there, she may not want to come back."

"I guess I know that too, girlie," he says. "But to talk about her, how I met her. Stuff like that helps. Besides, you don't know. She might be there. You never know about these things."

He gives her a photograph of his wife.

"What was your wife's name?" the girl detective says.

"I've been trying to remember that myself," he says.

Some things that have recently turned up in bank vaults.

Lost pets. The crew and passengers of the Mary Celeste. More socks. Several boxes of Christmas tree ornaments. A play by Shakespeare, about star-crossed lovers. It doesn't end well. Wedding rings. Some albino alligators. Several tons of seventh-grade homework. Ballistic missiles. A glass slipper. Some African explorers. A whole party of Himalayan mountain climbers. Children, whose faces I knew from milk cartons. The rest of that poem by Coleridge. Also fortune cookies.

Further secret origins of the girl detective.

Some people say that she was the child of missionaries, raised by wolves, that she is the Princess Anastasia, last of the Romanovs. Some people say that she is actually a man. Some people say that she came here from another planet and that some day, when she finds what she is looking for, she'll go home. Some people are hoping that she will take us with her.

If you ask them what she is looking for, they shrug and say, "Ask the girl detective."

Some people say that she is two thousand years old.

Some people say that she is not one girl but many—that is, she's actually a secret society of Girl Scouts. Or possibly a sub-branch of the FBI.

Whom does the girl detective love?

Remember that boy, Fred, or Nat? Something like that. He was in love with the girl detective, even though she was smarter than him, even though he never got to rescue her even once from the bad guys, or when he did, she was really just letting him, to be kind. He was a nice boy with a good sense of humor, but he used to have this recurring dream in which he was a golden retriever. The girl detective knew this, of course, the way she knows all our dreams. How could she settle down with a boy who dreamed that he was a retriever?

Everyone has seen the headlines. "Girl Detective Spurns Head of State." "I Caught My Husband in Bed with the Girl Detective." "Married Twenty Years, Husband and Father of Four, Revealed to Be the Girl Detective."

I myself was the girl detective's lover for three happy months. We met every Thursday night in a friend's summer cottage beside a small lake. She introduced herself as Pomegranate Buhm. I was besotted with her, her long legs so pale they looked like two slices of moonlight. I loved her size 11 feet, her black hair that always smelled like grapefruit. When we made love, she stuck her chewing gum on the headboard. Her underwear was embroidered with the days of the week.

We always met on Thursday, as I have said, but according to her underwear, we also met on Saturdays, on Wednesdays, on Mondays, Tuesdays, and once, memorably, on a Friday. That Friday, or rather that Thursday, she had a tattoo of a grandfather clock beneath her right breast. I licked it, surreptitiously, but it didn't come off. The previous Thursday (Monday according to the underwear) it had been under her left breast. I think I began to suspect then, although I said nothing and neither did she.

The next Thursday the tattoo was back, tucked discreetly under the left breast, but it was too late. It ended as I slept, dreaming about the waitress at Frank's Inland Seafood, the one with Monday nights off, with the gap between her teeth and the freckles on her ass. I was dreaming that she and I were in a boat on the middle of the lake. There was a hole in the bottom of the boat. I was putting something in it—to keep the water out—when I became aware that there was another woman watching us, an older woman, tall with a stern expression. She was standing on the water as if it were a dance floor. "Did you think she wouldn't find out?" she said. The waitress pushed me away, pulling her underwear back up. The boat wobbled. This waitress's underwear had a word embroidered on it:

Payday.

I woke up and the girl detective was sitting beside me on the bed, stark naked and dripping wet. The shower was still running. She had a strange expression on her face, as if she'd just eaten a large meal and it was disagreeing with her.

"I can explain everything," I said. She shrugged and stood up. She walked out of the room stark naked and the next time I saw her, it was two years later and she was disguised as an Office Lady in a law firm in downtown Tokyo, tapping out Morse code on the desk with one long petal-pink fingernail. It was something about expense accounts, or possibly a dirty limerick. She winked at me

255

and I fell in love all over again.

But I never saw the waitress again.

What the girl detective eats for dinner.

The girl detective lies down on her bed and closes her eyes. Possibly the girl detective has taken the fat man's case. Possibly she is just tired. Or curious.

All over the city, all over the world, people are asleep. Sitting up in my tree, I am getting tired just thinking about them. They are dreaming about their children, they are dreaming about their mothers, they are dreaming about their lovers. They dream that they can fly. They dream that the world is round like a dinner plate. Some of them fall off the world in their dreams. Some of them dream about food. The girl detective walks through these dreams. She picks an apple off a tree in someone's dream. Someone else is dreaming about the house they lived in as a child. The girl detective breaks off a bit of their house. It pools in her mouth like honey.

The woman down the street is dreaming about her third husband, the one who ran off with his secretary. That's what she thinks. He went for takeout one night five years ago and never came back. It was a long time ago. His secretary said she didn't know a thing about it, but the woman could tell the other woman was lying. Or maybe he ran away and joined the circus.

There is a man who lives in her basement, although the woman doesn't know it. He's got a television down there, and a small refrigerator, and a couch that he sleeps on. He's been living there for the past two years, very quietly. He comes up for air at night. The woman wouldn't recognize this man if she bumped into him on the street. They were married about twenty years and then he went to pick up the lo mein and the wontons and the shrimp fried rice, and it's taken him a while to get back home. He still had his set of keys. She hasn't been down in the basement in years. It's hard for her to get down the stairs.

The man is dreaming too. He's working up his courage to go upstairs and walk out the front door. In his dream he walks out to the street and then turns around. He'll walk right back up to the front door, ring the bell. Maybe they'll get married again someday. Maybe she never divorced him. He's dreaming about their honeymoon. They'll go out for dinner. Or they'll go down in the basement, down through the trapdoor into the underworld. He'll show her the sights. He'll take her dancing.

The girl detective takes a bite of the underworld.

Chinese restaurants.

I used to eat out a lot. I had a favorite restaurant, which had really good garlic shrimp, and I liked the pancakes, too; the scallion pancakes. But you have to be careful. I knew someone, their fortune said, "Your life right now is like a rollercoaster. But don't worry, it will soon be over." Now what is that supposed to mean?

Then it happened to me. The first fortune was ominous. "No one will ever love you the way that you love them." I thought about it. Maybe it was true. I came back to the restaurant a week later and I ordered the shrimp and I ate it and when I opened the fortune cookie I read, "Your friends are not who you think they are."

I became uneasy. I thought I would stay away for a few weeks. I ate Thai food instead. Italian. But the thing is, I still wasn't safe. No restaurants are safe—except maybe truckstops, or automats. Waiters, waitresses—they pretend to be kind. They bring us what we ask for. They ask us if there is anything else we want. They are solicitous of our health. They remember our names when we come back again. They are as kind to us as if they were our own mothers, and we are familiar with them. Sometimes we pinch their fannies.

I don't like to cook for myself. I live alone, and there doesn't seem to be much point to it. Sometimes I dream about food—for instance, a cake, it was made of whipped cream. It was the size of a living room. Just as I was about to take a bite, a dancing girl kicked out of it. Then another dancing girl. A whole troop of dancing girls, in fact, all covered in whipped cream. They were delicious.

I like to eat food made by other people. It feels like a relationship. But you can't trust other people. Especially not waiters. They aren't our friends, you see. They aren't our mothers. They don't give us the food that we long for—not the food that we dream about—although they could. If they wanted to.

We ask them for recommendations about the menu, but they know so much more than that—if only they should choose to tell us. They do not choose to tell us. Their kindnesses are arbitrary, and not to be counted as lasting. We sit here in this world, and the food that they bring us isn't of this world, not entirely. They are not like us. They serve a great mystery.

I returned to the Chinese restaurant like a condemned man. I ate my last meal. A party of women in big hats and small dresses sat at the table next to me. They ordered their food and then departed for the bathroom. Did they ever come back? I never saw them come back.

The waiter brought me the check and a fortune cookie. I uncurled my fortune and read my fate. "You will die at the hands of a stranger." As I went away, the waiter smiled at me. His smile was inscrutable.

I sit here in my tree, eating takeout food, hauled up on a bit of string. I put my binoculars down to eat. Who knows what my fortune will say?

What color is the girl detective's hair?

Some people say that the girl detective is a natural blonde. Others say that she's a redhead, how could the girl detective be anything else? Her father just smiles and says she looks just like her mother. I myself am not even sure that the girl detective remembers the original color of her hair. She is a master of disguises. I feel I should make it clear that no one has ever seen the girl detective in the same room as the aged housekeeper. She and her father have often been seen dining out together, but I repeat, the girl detective is a master of disguises. She is capable of anything.

Further secret origins of the girl detective.

Some people say that a small child in a grocery store bit her. It was one of those children who are constantly asking their parents why the sky is blue and are there really giant alligators—formerly the pets of other small children—living in the sewers of the city and if China is directly below us, could we drill a hole and go right through the center of the earth and if so would we come up upside-down and so on. This child, radioactive with curiosity, bit the girl detective, and in that instant the girl detective suddenly saw all of these answers, all at once. She was so overcome she had to lie down in the middle of the aisle with the breakfast cereal on one side and the canned tomatoes on the other, and the store manager came over and asked if she was all right? She wasn't all right, but she smiled and let him help her stand up again, and that night she went home and stitched the days of the week on her underwear, so that if she was ever run over by a car, at least it would be perfectly clear when the accident had occurred. She thought this would make her mother happy.

Why did the girl detective cross the road?

Because she thought she saw her mother.

Why did the girl detective's mother cross the road?

If only the girl detective knew!

The girl detective was very small when her mother left. No one ever speaks of her mother. It causes her father too much pain even to hear her name spoken. To see it written down. Possibly the girl detective was named after her mother and this is why we must not say her name.

No one has ever explained to the girl detective why her mother left, although it must have been to do something very important. Possibly she died. That would be important enough, almost forgivable.

In the girl detective's room there is a single photograph in a small gold frame of a woman, tall and with a very faint smile, rising up on her toes. Arms flung open. She is wearing a long skirt and a shirt with no sleeves, a pair of worn dancing shoes. She is holding a sheaf of wheat. She looks as if she is dancing. The girl detective suspects that this is her mother. She studies the photograph nightly. People dream about lost or stolen things, and this woman, her mother, is always in these dreams.

She remembers a woman walking in front of her. The girl detective was holding this woman's hand. The woman said something to her. It might have been something like, "Always look both ways," or "Always wash your hands after you use a public bathroom," or maybe "I love you," and then the woman stepped into the street. After that the girl detective isn't sure what happened. There was a van, red and gold, going fast around the corner. On the side was "Eat at Mom's Chinese Restaurant." "Or maybe "Eat at Moon's." Maybe it hit the woman.

Maybe it stopped and the woman got in. She said her mother's name then, and no one said anything back.

The girl detective goes out to eat.

I only leave my tree to go to the bathroom. It's sort of like camping. I have a roll of toilet paper and a little shovel. At night I tie myself to the branch with a rope. But I don't really sleep much. It's about seven o'clock in the evening when the girl detective leaves her house. "Where are you going," I say, just to make conversation.

She says that she's going to that new restaurant downtown, if it's any of my business. She asks if I want to come, but I have plans. I can tell that something's up. She's disguised as a young woman. Her eyes are keen and they flash a lot. "Can you bring me back an order of steamed dumplings?" I call after her, "Some white rice?"

She pretends she doesn't hear me. Of course I follow her. She takes a bus. I climb between trees. It's kind of fun. Occasionally there aren't any trees and I have to make do with telephone poles, or water towers. Generally I keep off the ground.

There's a nice little potted ficus at Mom's Chinese Restaurant. I sit in it and ponder the menu. I try not to catch the waiter's eye. He's a tall, stern-looking man. The girl detective is obviously trying to make up her mind between the rolling beef and the glowing squid. Listed under appetizers, there's scallion pancakes, egg rolls with shrimp, and wantons (which I have ordered many times. But they always turn out to be wontons instead), also dancing girls. The girl detective orders a glass of water, no lemon. Then she asks the waiter, "Where are you from?"

"China," he says.

"I mean, where do you live now," the girl detective says.

"China," he says. "I commute."

The girl detective tries again. "How long has this restaurant been here?"

"Sometimes, for quite a while," he says. "Don't forget to wash your hands before you eat."

The girl detective goes to the bathroom.

At the next table there are twelve women wearing dark glasses. They may have been sitting there for quite a while. They stand up, they file one by one into the women's bathroom. The girl detective sits for a minute. Then she follows them. After a minute I follow her. No one stops me. Why should they? I step carefully from table to table. I slouch behind the flower arrangements.

In the bathroom there aren't any trees, so I climb up on the electric dryer and sit with my knees up by my ears and my hands around my knees. I try to look inconspicuous. There is only one stall and absolutely no sign of the twelve women. Maybe they're all in the same stall, but I can see under the door and I don't see any feet. The girl detective is washing her hands. She washes her hands thoughtfully, for a long time. Then she comes over and dries them. "What next?" I ask her.

Her eyes flash keenly. She pushes open the door of the stall with her foot. It swings. Both of us can see that the stall is empty. Furthermore there isn't even a toilet in it. Instead there is a staircase going down. A draft is coming up. I almost think I can hear alligators, scratching and slithering around somewhere further down the stairs.

The girl detective goes to the underworld.

She has a flashlight of course. She stands at the top of the stairs and looks back at me. The light from the flashlight puddles around her feet. "Are you coming or not?" she says. What can I say? I fall in love with the girl detective all over again. I come down off the dryer. "I guess," I say. We start down the stairs.

The underworld is everything I've been telling you. It's really big. We don't see any alligators, but that doesn't mean that there aren't any. It's dark. It's a little bit cool and I'm glad that I'm wearing my cardigan. There are trees with moss on them. The moss glows. I take to the trees. I swing from branch to branch. I was always good at gym. Beneath me the girl detective strides forward purposefully, her large feet lit up like two boats. I am in love with the top of her head, with the tidy part straight down the middle. I feel tenderly towards this part. I secretly vow to preserve it. Not one hair on her head shall come to harm.

But then we come to a river. It's a wide river and probably deep. I sit in a tree at the edge of the river, and I can't make up my mind to climb down. Not even for the sake of the part in the hair of the girl detective. She looks up at me and shrugs. "Suit yourself," she says.

"I'll wait right here," I say. There are cute little canoes by the side of the river. Some people say that the girl detective can walk on water, but I see her climb in one of the canoes. This isn't the kind of river that you want to stick your toes in. It's too spick-and-span. You might leave footprints.

I watch her go across the river. I see her get out on the other side. There is a nightclub on the other side, with a veranda and a big sign over the veranda. DANCE WITH BEAUTIFUL GIRLS. There is a woman standing on the veranda. People are dancing. There is music playing. Up in my tree, my feet are tapping air. Someone says, "Mom?" Someone embraces someone else. Everyone is dancing. "Where have you been?" someone says. "Spring cleaning," someone says.

It is hard to see what is going on across the river. Chinese waiters in elegant tuxedos are dipping dancing princesses. There are a lot of sequins. They are dancing so fast, things get blurry. Things run together. I think I see alligators dancing. I see a fat old man dancing with the girl detective's mother. Maybe even the housekeeper is dancing. It's hard to tell if their feet are even touching the ground. There are sparks. Fireworks. The musicians are dancing, too, but they don't stop playing. I'm dancing up in my tree. The leaves shake and the branch groans, but the branch doesn't break.

We dance for hours. Maybe for days. It's hard to tell when it stays dark all the time. Then there is a line of dancers coming across the river. They skip across the backs of the white alligators, who snap at their heels. They are hand in hand, spinning and turning and falling back, and leaping forward. It's hard to see them, they're moving so fast. It's so dark down here. Is that a dancing princess, or a bank robber? Is that a fat old man, or an alligator, or a housekeeper? I wish I knew. Is that the girl detective or is it her mother? One looks back at the other and smiles. She doesn't say a thing, she just smiles.

I look, and in the mossy glow they all look like the girl detective. Or maybe the girl detective looks like all of them. They all look so happy. Passing in the opposite direction is a line of Chinese waiters. They swing the first line as they pass. They cut across and dosey-do. They clap hands. They clutch each other, across the breast and the back, and tango. But the girl detectives keep up towards the restaurant and the bathroom and the secret staircase. The waiters keep on towards the water, towards the nightclub. Down in that nightclub, there's a bathroom. In the bathroom, there's another staircase. The waiters are going home to bed.

I'm exhausted. I can't keep up with the girl detectives. "Wait!" I yell. "Hold it for just a second. I'm coming with you."

They all turn and look back at me. I'm dizzy with all of that looking. I fall out of my tree. I hit the ground. Really, that's all I remember.

When I woke up.

Someone had carried me back to my tree and tucked me in. I was snug as a bug. I was back in the tree across the street from the girl detective's window. This time the blind was down. I couldn't see a thing.

The end of the girl detective?

Some people say that she never came back from the underworld.

The return of the girl detective.

I had to go to the airport for some reason. It's a long story. It was an important case. This wasn't that long ago. I hadn't been down out of the tree for very long. I was missing the tree.

I thought I saw the girl detective in the bar in Terminal B. She was sitting in one of the back booths, disguised as a fat old man. There was a napkin in front of her, folded into a giraffe. She was crying but there was the napkin folded into a giraffe—she had nothing to wipe her nose on. I would have gone over and given her my handkerchief, but someone sat down next to her. It was a kid about twelve years old. She had red hair. She was wearing overalls. She just sat next to him, and she put down another napkin. She didn't say a word to him. The old man blew his nose on it and I realized that he wasn't the girl detective at all. He was just an old man. It was the kid in the overalls—what a great disguise! Then the waitress came over to take their order. I wasn't sure about the waitress. Maybe *she* was the girl detective. But she gave me such a look—I had to get up and leave.

Why I got down out of the tree.

She came over and stood under the tree. She looked a lot like my mother. Get down out of that tree this instant! she said. Don't you know it's time for dinner?

PUBLICATION HISTORY

These stories were previously published as follows:

Carnation, Lily, Lily, Rose, *Fence*, 1998
Water Off a Black Dog's Back, *Century*, 1995
The Specialist's Hat, *Event Horizon*, 1998
Flying Lessons, *Asimov's*, 1995
Travels with the Snow Queen, *Lady Churchill's Rosebud Wristlet*, winter 1996/7
Vanishing Act, *Realms of Fantasy*, 1996
Survivor's Ball, or, The Donner Party, *Lady Churchill's Rosebud Wristlet*, 1998
Shoe and Marriage, *4 Stories*, 2000
The Girl Detective, *Event Horizon*, 1999

ACKNOWLEDGEMENTS

I am extremely grateful to the following people. Some of them are relatives, some are friends, some are writers or editors. All of them have been incredibly kind and encouraging. Some of them have cooked meals for me, or taught me various card games, or pointed me towards necessary books, or read my stories when I needed readers. I was a member of various workshops while writing these stories: I owe a lot to the instructors and members of the MFA workshop at UNC-G, Clarion East, Sycamore Hill, the Cambridge Auxiliary Women's Workshop, CSFW, and Rio Hondo. Partial inspiration for "The Specialist's Hat" came from an exhibit at the Peabody Museum in Cambridge, MA. I borrowed part of a passage (stuck up beside an empty exhibit case) to begin the longest poem in that story. Also adapted, for that same story, is a passage about snake whiskey from a folklore exhibit in Raleigh, NC. I would like to thank my mother, Annabel J. Link, who read to me until her voice gave out; my father, Bill Link, who read me books when my mother was too hoarse; my sister, Holly; my brother, Ben; Sam, Babs, Bryan and Laurie Jones; my grandparents, Edwin and Lou Jones; my wicked stepmother, Linda. I am indebted to Joyce Nissim, Michele Harley, Barb Gilly, Lynne and Tom Casey, Fleur Penman, Ada Vassilovski, Pete Cramer, Jack Cheng, Margaret Muirhead, Cassandra Silvia, Vincent McCaffrey, the fabulous Avenue Victor Hugo Bookshop, Bill Desmond, Kaye Wyndham, Mimi Levin, Janis Fields, Lea and Anna (girl sleuths), Christopher Hammond, Jim Clarke, Fred Chappell, Lee Zacharias, Michael Parker, Raymond Kennedy, RAchele Taylor, Hadas Steiner, Melissa DeJong, John Golz, Lauren Stearns, Justine Larbalestier, Jenna A. Felice, Vanessa Felice, Veronica Shanoes, William Smith, Anna Genoese, Steve Pasechnick, Bryan Cholfin, Terra Cholfin, Ian McDowell, Anne Abrams, Mr. Jeremy Cavin, Ellen Datlow, Terri Windling, Delia Sherman, Ellen Kushner, Gwenda Bond, Neil Gaiman, Nalo Hopkinson, Dora Knez, James Patrick Kelly, Sarah Smith, John Kessel, Richard Butner, Walter Jon Williams, Greg Frost, Sean Stewart, Tim and Serena Powers, Jonathan Lethem, Shelley Jackson, and Karen Joy Fowler. (Especially Karen Joy Fowler.) I am so very grateful for the hard work and patience and generosity of Gavin J. Grant, who has given me, among other things, a pair of shoes, a glass eye (I broke it), CDs by Mayumi Kojima and Super Butter Dog, a kimono, and, on my thirtieth birthday, thirty books, wrapped up in paper.

Kelly Link's story "Travels with the Snow Queen" won the James Tiptree Jr. Award in 1997. Her story "The Specialist's Hat" won the World Fantasy Award in 1999. She received her BA from Columbia University and her MFA from the University of North Carolina at Greensboro. She once won a free trip around the world. She co-edits the zine *Lady Churchill's Rosebud Wristlet*. She currently lives in Brooklyn. This is her first collection.